For Keith,

With love,

Rick

Autumn, 2013

RICHARD HAWLEY

The Other World

STORIES

Copyright © 2013 by Richard Hawley

ISBN: 978-0-9882497-2-1
Library of Congress Control Number: 2013947539

Printed in the United States of America

Publisher: Short Story America Press
Design: Soundview Design Studio

All rights reserved. No part of this book may be transmitted in any form or by any means, electronic or mechanical, including photocopying, recording, or by any information storage or retrieval system, in part, in any form, without the permission of the publisher.

Requests for such permissions should be addressed to:

Short Story America
2121 Boundary Street, Suite 204
Beaufort, SC 29902
Visit us online at www.shortstoryamerica.com

In loving memory of

Kathleen and Robert Hawley

SELECTED BOOKS BY RICHARD HAWLEY

FICTION:

The Guru
Paul and Juliana
The Headmaster's Papers
The Headmaster's Wife

POETRY:

Twenty-One Visits With a Darkly Sun-Tanned Angel
The Headmaster's Poems
With Love to My Survivors
St. Julian

NON-FICTION:

Boys Will Be Men
Souls in Boxes
Kiski: The Story of a Boys' School
Hail, University!
Beyond The Icarus Factor
Papers from the Headmaster
Hard Lessons and Other Talks to the School
In Praise of the Teaching Life
The Big Issues in the Adolescent Journey
Drugs and Society
The Purposes of Pleasure
Seeing Things: A Chronicle of Surprises
Reaching Boys/Teaching Boys *with Michael Reichert*
For Whom the Boy Toils *with Michael Reichert*

CONTENTS

BORN INTO CHRISTMAS 1

UNDERGROUND 19

CLIMBING 39

FOR LOVE 53

THE END OF BASEBALL 69

TEN 81

THE OTTAWANNA WAY 105

THE REAL THING 119

JUNIOR HIGH 127

SEX AND MUSIC 137

LOSING ANNABEL 151

ONE OF THE POPULAR KIDS 163

ALL THE PRIZES 197

BORN INTO CHRISTMAS

I was born into Christmas. It's true, and I can tell you everything about it. I must have been about one. I was lying there, curled into the damp, sweet, lovely warmth of my own sleep when I opened my eyes to it. There was that milky winter light that lets you see the air, and the gray and pink swirls of the wallpaper were moving a little in the light, and through the dark wooden archway of the open door I could see the spangles and flashing jewels on the evergreen boughs in the living room. The plastic kitchen radio was playing Joy to the World, which I did not know as words then, but I knew it, and it grew in me, swelled up in me until, just as I knew she would, my mother's beautiful dark figure filled the doorway arch, and for a moment all I knew was the shape of her red mouth, which said, "Merry Christmas, Jonathan."

Then there was laughter, Mother's and mine, fused together, and I was lifted wonderfully, still wet and warm, up into her arms, and over her shoulder the tree with its sparkles and pine sweet smell was no longer striped by the slats of my crib, and I was carried from a happiness to a still greater happiness so fine and so full I did not believe I could bear it.

And that is the way Christmas has always been in my life — being picked up and carried into an aching beauty, a beauty that opens and opens. Christmas was the first thing I really knew, and since that time the other necessary and important things have gathered themselves to that first knowing. Of course the family gathered, in the morning my mother and father and sister, later in the day my grandparents Nana and Papa and their sons, my uncles. There were presents, mounds of brightly wrapped and bowed presents under the tree, then as guests arrived, box loads and bag loads of more presents. There were presents stacked on the lamp tables, heaped on the piano, and so many of them opened and unopened on the floor that we waded through wrappings and tissue and swizzles of ribbon in order to cross the room. From the midday arrival of guests until their departure late that night there would be a fire in the fireplace, a strong crackling blaze when first lit, then quieting to a radiant mound of lavender, blue and buttery gold. The scent of the burning hardwood met the blood-rich cooking smells of the slowly roasting turkey, the sage dressing, creamed onions, apple pies and pumpkin pies. As the dinner was readied, drinks were prepared, amber cocktails in martini glasses with delicate stems. Secure in the vee of each glass was the beckoning scarlet orb of a candied cherry. In time it was understood that these were to be saved for me; the ritual of handing them over became to me a kind of sacrament, token after token of pulpy cherry sweetness, of Christmas itself, held between tongue and palate for as long as I could stand it.

In the course of what must have been many years, Christmas came to include the outdoors. I always felt that the secret of the day, the secret of winter itself, was the lively tension between outdoors and in, between shallow breathed ventures out into the cold and the relief to be back inside. From my first winter swaddling at the hands of others, I was fascinated by the ritual of girding for the cold: knitted caps, long heavy coats the arms of which grew stiff in the freezing air, woolen scarves sealing the neck, mittens which within minutes of true cold reduced the fingered hand to a numbed club, high black rubber boots fastened tight with complicated metal clasps. To be outdoors in winter cold felt like stolen time. I was out where seemingly no one was supposed to be. The cold clarified everything. It seemed to want silence. The easiest thing became effortful in the cold, but marvelous for that. Then snow came into the picture, the whirl and blur of it in the air, thrilling the first time, thrilling always. Snow was specks and clumps of lively light against the gray of winter afternoons. Snow at night, silent snow, whitening the void felt to me holy.

I cannot tell you where I got this picture, although it is a fixture in my Christmas memory. The impression is so cold and fresh that I could be there now. It is deep winter, and I am stopped still in a sloping field of cedar trees. It is late afternoon, and the sun is about to set. The sky is clear, and as I look out toward the horizon, the glass-blue overhead gives way to vivid rose and peach and shimmering gold as it meets the sinking sun on the horizon line. I am fascinated by the look of the snow resting on the branches of the cedars, how the snow holds rosy afternoon light, and all of it is saying "afterward," as if beauty itself was explaining the end of beauty.

Somehow the snow on the branches in the declining afternoon and the cedar boughs sparkling with lights and ornaments beyond my crib on that first Christmas morning form a single picture, and it is all Christmas, and it is forever about to begin and yet has always been over.

* * *

A few years after my mother gathered me up and walked me under the archway into Christmas, I was taken to church one winter night and beheld Jesus in the manger. I recall that it was a Lutheran church. We were not Lutherans, and Lutheran meant nothing to me at the time. But my mother had said it was the Lutheran church, and that became important. The sanctuary was darkened for a Christmas service of some kind, and it smelled of the musty hymnals and of the slightly sweet, slightly sour smell of flowers standing out too long. A bright light from high over the apse beamed down on the manger where colorfully-robed shepherds knelt and little goats and lambs looked on. The light shone directly on the baby's face in his crib.

This was the holy child. I don't know if Mother told me or I heard it in the carols or if I just knew it. But everything that evening was about the holy child, how long the world had waited, and now here he was. Of course it was a holy child. Wasn't I?

Everything about that Lutheran service was serious, gentle, and strangely sad. The baby Jesus had always been coming.

And it came to pass in those days,

that there went out a decree

from Caesar Augustus that all

the world should be taxed…

It was important to kings, it was important to wise men. Angels and shepherds were waiting for it. The waiting was unbearable and very beautiful. It was like waiting for Christmas to come. Silent night, holy night. Then the announcement, the arrival—even more beautiful, but cheerful and loud. Hark the herald, joy to the world. It came upon a midnight clear in the sanctuary of the Lutheran church.

* * *

So that was the first of the Three Great Things, the coming of the holy child, and just as it was in my case, the coming involved Christmas. But there was the other story about my coming. In the course of my growing up I heard it again and again, and when I knew enough to ask, I would check the facts and details. The other story is not a very good one, far, far from beautiful and even farther from Christmas.

I was born during the war, World War II, near the end. Later I was confused in school about the war because I felt I had long known the enemies. I had lived with them, and they were good, kind people—my family. That is, my mother's parents, Nana and Papa, were English and German. They had fallen in love and gotten married after the previous war, World War I, in which my German grandfather who had become an American and was fighting for the Americans got shot in the leg and was shipped to England where my English grandmother met him, nursed him and fell in love with him. She followed him back to Chicago where they married and had my mother and my uncles. They were such kind, beautiful people, and they made such a beautiful house.

England was married to Germany in that house, and when my father got drafted into the Navy, he had to leave his job as a trumpet player in the dance band and board a battleship in the Pacific. My mother worked as a secretary in an office, but when she got pregnant with me and then very sick she had to quit work and move in with her parents. There wasn't much money then, she told me. The Navy pay wasn't very much, and so she could no longer afford her own place which, she told me when I was much older, made her feel like a girl again and not a woman, and this made her feel worthless and small. Then she got sick and almost died. The good doctors, people told her later, were all in the service, and she had a bad one who didn't understand what was wrong with her. We know what was wrong now, a condition called *edema*. Edema made my mother swell up to almost twice her size. Her legs and arms filled with fluid, and her joints—elbows, knees, ankles—felt as if they were about to burst open. My mother told me about sitting in a chair and watching in helpless tears as her legs filled with fluid and her ankles swelled enormously so that the flesh of her legs spilled out over the sides of her shoes. I cannot bear picturing my mother picturing this. She had been such a beautiful woman. The edema, doctors told her later, could have killed her. Moreover, there were simple medicines that could have helped, but Mother's doctor didn't know about them, and she suffered. Possibly, I had edema too, although no one has ever told me that. It cannot have been good, my mother so unhappy, feeling no longer a grown woman but a little girl back in her childhood room in her parents' house, her husband far away on a battle ship in the Pacific where, he wrote, the Japanese suicide planes dive-bombed the ship, the U.S.S. West Virginia, as often as they could. What could she do but sit there waiting for the swelling to subside, wondering if my father would ever come home, wondering if she would ever have her exquisite woman's body again?

Whether or not the edema was to blame, I was cut out of my mother by a Caesarean section, which further weakened her, and I came into the world early, undersized, and quite ill. I had pneumonia, of which I have no recollection, except in a kind of bodily awareness that has inclined me to bronchial troubles all my life.

I had to stay in the hospital two weeks after my mother was able to go home. I wish I could remember what that was like, or maybe I don't. I'm sure my mother came to see me, or somebody,

The Other World

probably Nana, did. They had to have started feeding me, formula in a bottle, not my mother's breast. It feels funny to have only a voided impression of all of that, to have no feeling or recollection of any kind until the Christmas story. By then my father was back from the war. I can't remember anything about that either. Sometimes I think I do, but it's just the memory of a photograph we have of my father, still in his navy uniform, the old fashioned dark blue wool kind with the white stripes around the open neck on the jersey and the square flap at the back. My father is standing in our back yard in that uniform, looking pleased and kind of jaunty. With one arm he is holding me to his chest in a blanket, and his other hand is gripping his trumpet under the valves, as if he has just played a riff. He doesn't look quite related to me in the picture. He looks like a boy.

As hard as my mother's life was while my father was away in the Pacific, she said it didn't get much better after he returned. My father had to get work and save some money before they could move out of my grandparents' house and live on their own again. My mother didn't like this at all, and one day my father made a big mistake that made him feel uncomfortable for years. It happened one morning when he came back into the house after doing an errand. He went upstairs to the bedroom to look for Mother. He said he had a sense of her in the room as he entered. She was leaning over the bed, making it up, and my father reached out and, he said, gave her bottom a good squeeze. But it wasn't my mother; it was Nana. She was startled and then quite angry. My father was so surprised and embarrassed he couldn't say anything. He tried to explain and to apologize, but Nana was too flustered to hear him, and she bolted from the room. Once, not too many years before he died, my father tried to tell the story as a funny story, but even then I could feel the misery in it. But I think that goosing of Nana accelerated my mother and father's departure plans and their eventual independence.

There are plenty of stories like that from that period in my waking up to the world—stories that I will never forget, stories that trouble me or that for some reason won't subside into oblivion, but they are not good, not holy and alive like the Christmas story. For a long stretch there I felt not only far from a holy child, I felt that the child I was and the things that kept happening to me were a teasing mockery of what I sensed should have been a much, much better world. There was only one miracle that I remember from that time. It involved the biggest turtle I have ever seen.

One cool gray spring morning my mother let me out into our small fenced-in back yard to play. There was not much to do in the yard. There was no swing or sand box, just a narrow concrete walkway to a back gate that opened up onto a narrow alley of cinders. I was shuffling along this walk toward the alley, where it was possible to get a glimpse sometimes of the trash man's blinkered horse or of a stray cat out on a rove or possibly rats, which were known to slither about the trash cans set out in the alley. About halfway down the walk I saw something amazing: the large, oily-looking black shell of a turtle. It was enormous, half as big as I was, its girth wider than the walkway. I didn't think turtle at first, because all I could see was the great heavy looking shell, but then its black scaly head came out a little and looked around, and I knew. I could not have seen a real turtle before, but I knew this was one, and my heart flew up, and I jumped back a little because I was afraid it might bite me. I wanted it to move, so I stamped my feet on the concrete, but all it did was draw in its head. I just stood there, bent at the waist, looking hard at the shell, I think for quite a while. I was certain this was an agent from the other world. Then it moved a little, and I was startled again. It occurred to me that Mother must see this. I felt it would amaze her to see it, amaze her that I had found it. Inside, Mother was doing dishes, and it took her a long time to make sense of what I was telling her and even longer before she would come outside into the yard to look. When we got to the spot, the turtle was gone. I ran to the back fence hoping to catch sight of it, but it was gone. I assured my mother it had been there, indicating its size with my arms. My mother smiled in an odd way, which let me know she didn't believe me. Where would a turtle live around here, she asked. We lived in a densely-packed neighborhood of wooden shingled houses, close to the elevated train, far from any open land or rivers or streams. A huge black turtle was as likely to show up in our yard as a puma or an ostrich. Mother went back into the house, and I remember standing for some time in the empty yard, thinking. The turtle, for some reason, had appeared, and I understood that I must bear the burden of this kind of knowledge alone.

Blackie, our duck, was not quite a miracle, but I will never forget him. I was four by then, my sister Annabel was six, and we had moved to a fresh, raw housing development on the prairie edge of Chicago's northwest side. My father worked for a big bank now in the city, and the bank staff was invited to a summer outing in a state park. There was a picnic, boat rides, and races and games and contests for the kids. There were contests for the grownups, too, and one of them, which fascinated me, was to ring a duck. The rings were wooden hoops about the circumference of a small pie. For a quarter you got three hoops and tried to toss them around the neck of one of the ducks huddled in a little pen about ten yards behind the throwing counter. I stood a long time watching, and nobody succeeded in landing a hoop around a duck's neck. The exercise was actually kind of upsetting. The tossed hoops grazed the ducks' heads and flanks and sent them scuttling and quacking into each other. My father appeared and bought three hoops. I was barely paying attention, and then there was a tremendous shriek of surprise and laughter, because my father's toss had fallen around the neck of a black duck. That meant we had won him; he was ours. Annabel was so surprised and happy she started to cry. She loved animals of all kinds. She cut out pictures of especially cute ones and taped them to the top of her dresser. The man selling the rings said the ducks' wings were "clipped" so that they couldn't fly away. My dad held the duck in the crook of his elbow and exchanged jokes and cracks with the people standing around, and then he handed the duck down to Annabel, who was so transported with pleasure she could not speak.

As we drove home in the car afterward, Annabel still clutching and petting the duck, my mother and father talked about what we would do with it. There was the terrifying suggestion in the air that we would have to "get rid" of it. I felt Annabel tense up at the words, her eyes welling with tears. From the back seat I shouted out, "We're keeping it! We're keeping it!" to make Annabel feel better. When we got home, my father went down into the basement and reworked a big cardboard box our washing machine had come in, and put the duck inside. Mother and Annabel brought down a little bowl of water and some cut-up vegetables for the duck, then left us alone with it. For a long time we just watched it, and Annabel decided to name it Blackie, as it was a black duck. I was now as mesmerized and in love with Blackie as Annabel was. This was partly because the force of her feeling was so overwhelming I felt drawn up into it. But there was something about the duck itself that was impossible to resist. It was just so beautiful, if that is the word, or cute. Something about it was more vivid and wonderful than we were. I could not stop looking at it. The perfectly rounded top of its shiny black head somehow matched the beautiful curve of its breast, and its bright black eyes flashed a fiery fleck of gold in the basement light.

It was not easy to pick Blackie up and hold him, because he would get excited and push away with surprising force with his little legs and duck feet. But every few minutes we could not bear not to pick him up again and hold him close, so we took turns grabbing him up out of the box until in one clumsy attempt he got away from us and disappeared between the furnace and the basement wall. Even my father with the aid of a broom handle could not dislodge Blackie from behind the furnace, so Annabel and I had to bathe and go to bed in agonizing uncertainty.

In the bright morning, my father was able to retrieve Blackie, and all was well again. Annabel decided to take Blackie's box outside, so that he could breathe the air and get some sun. We also were eager to show him to the Weisblatts, our neighbors. Not wanting to lose him again, Annabel took special care lifting Blackie out of the box, but as she held him quietly in her arms, something—a shout or a car door slamming—startled him and he erupted out of my sister's grasp and onto the sidewalk down which he scooted with phenomenal speed, trailed by me, my sister, and the shrieking Weisblatts. I remember a warm, smiling feeling in my heart because this was an adventure and Blackie's wings were "clipped," which meant he could not really escape

The Other World

us—but then he did. After a run of perhaps a quarter of a block, Blackie arose. Powerful and sure in flight, he ascended, up over the power lines, then the treetops and in a minute or two disappeared into the sunny blue sky. Blackie's escape was so sudden and so sure that it seemed to me, and I suspect Annabel too, natural and right. The loss was stunning, but something about Blackie had seemed from the outset too good to be true. Blackie, I decided, was a clue, but far from the whole story.

Of course I had no idea then how far away I was from anything like the whole story. It took a long time for me to realize that something in the world *doesn't want* us to see the whole story. Something wants to overwhelm us with the ordinary, usually bad stories that carry us away from, not into, the better world. Some kind of force—including plenty of people—won't let us see or even talk about the golden side of things, as if they cannot bear so much unspoiled possibility, such gladness. Sometimes for days and weeks on end I felt as if the holy child were being slapped out of me. These were the times when seemingly everybody, but especially my father, was telling me I couldn't do anything right. My father liked to joke about me, "Jonathan, you get dumber every day," but it was no joke to me. Some days I knew I was dumber, and I remember feeling that there was no end to how dumb I could get, and I began to think up ways to conceal from others how dumb I was, a dumbness at my very core of which I was so ashamed I could barely breathe.

When I say I thought the holy child was being slapped out of me, I don't mean slaps or punches right in the face. My slaps were what my father called "cracks in the head." Every now and then my father would look at me or at something I had done or just hear about something I had done and then give me a crack in the head. These cracks in the head were jarring, upward clouts against the back of my skull. If the annoyance was minor, if I just said something that irritated him, he might just crack me with the first two fingers of his right hand. But if he was really mad, I'd get the full force of his open palm against the back of my head. I hated getting cracks in the head. I never got used to them, and the worst were the ones that I did not see coming, which, because they came up from behind me, was a lot of the time. My father wasn't always angry with me, and when he was in a good mood, he liked to make jokes about cracking me in the head, so that I'd see the funny side of it, but I could not see it. When I got a sudden, full-handed crack in the head, I'd see a terrible white light and feel as if my existence had stopped altogether for a second. A crack in the head, even the two-finger, always surprised me and scared me. Cracks in the head also made me cry, which made me feel babyish and ashamed, not ashamed of whatever I had done, which sometimes I didn't really know, but that I had been cracked in the head and that I was crying. Once, after several years of being cracked in the head, I looked up at my father after a really rotten crack and even though I was crying and afraid, said to him, "What am I, a dog?" A jolt, white light—another terrific crack in the head.

I don't think my skull or my brain was ever in any danger from all the cracks in the head, but they had a terrible effect on me in another way. I started to lose confidence. I started to lose my connection to the bright world, the Christmas world, and to the clues and signs that had once made me so excited and happy. Even worse, I could not seem to forget being cracked in the head. I felt as if I were carrying them around with me. After the first one, I wondered if I might die.

Just before I got that crack, I thought I was doing a good thing. I had figured out how to move my chair around the kitchen to get up to things I was interested in, like the crackers and the cookies on the counter. I could pull the chair across the kitchen floor to the table and get up there too, to see what was going on. I was actually quite excited about this new range of operations. Between meals my chair was placed in a little nook between the side of the ice box and a counter near the back door of the kitchen. It wasn't a baby's high chair with a tray, but it was higher than a regular chair and it had a kind of step in front that enabled me to climb up onto it by myself. I liked the feeling of moving the chair around the floor. I think Mother liked it that at mealtimes I would drag it out of its nook across the linoleum to the table without even having to be asked.

One winter evening I was in the bright kitchen with my mother while she prepared dinner. She had just finished stirring up a huge white bowl of cake frosting and had let me lick the spoon. She took off her apron and left the kitchen to change clothes before my father got home. I spotted the bowl of frosting up on the counter and realized I could get to it by moving my chair over there. But when I gave the chair legs the usual yank to get it out of its spot, something terrible happened. The cord that plugged in the radio must have gotten in front of one of the chair legs, because the purple plastic Zenith slid off the counter and smashed onto the linoleum. It made a loud, terrible crash, and it was all broken. There were sharp shards of purple plastic, and the metal chassis and broken glass tubes were exposed. Still plugged in, the radio made an angry, urgent hum. Mother appeared in the kitchen tying the sash of her dress behind her. "Jonathan, *what did you do?*"

I didn't know what I did. I said, "The radio fell down." I was still holding onto the legs of my chair. My father had entered the front of the house and was calling out a greeting. Then he was in the kitchen, standing next to my mother, staring at the shattered mess of the radio and at me. "Jonathan," Mother said in a voice I had not heard from her before, "look what you've done." She looked as though she were about to cry. "Now we don't have a radio." The kitchen seemed to grow brighter and brighter. Then my father sprang toward me like an animal. He tore the chair out of my hands. He gripped the back of my neck and turned my head painfully in the direction of the mess on the floor. "Look what the hell you've done!" Jolt, white light—the crack. Then I was up under one of his arms, feet off the ground, as he hauled me through the dark house to my bedroom where he dropped me onto the bed and shut the door. I was left in complete blackness, and the blackness was inside me too. I had broken something of enormous importance from the world of my mother and father, something that could not, I believed, ever be restored. I had been cracked in the head and was now banished to the dark, and the only thing I could think to do was to complete the process, find an even greater darkness and stay in it forever.

Richard Hawley

The darkest abyss I could devise was my closet, and I made my way to it in the dark, pulled the shoes and boxes away from the back wall, shut the closet door and curled into a ball. The misery I felt was like a sickening electric current. It soured what was in my stomach and made me retch. I held myself in the ball and tried to darken the darkness by shutting my eyes tight. I don't know if I slept, but I remember suddenly blinking into the light of the closet, staring up into the enormous standing figures of my mother and father. Mother reached down to pull me up. My father said, "Half wit."

After a few more cracks in the head, I began to wake up in the morning with a different feeling. I did not feel the glad surge that had made me tear the covers away and race out of my room to Mother, breakfast, and bright day. Now I needed to lie there in the warmth. I remember feeling that as long as I could stay there under the covers I was safe, not just safe from cracks in the head, but from doing the things that brought them on. I would not have found the words for it then, but until my loss of confidence, I believed I had a knack for making myself happy. I didn't have to make an effort for interesting things to happen, they just happened, like the appearance of the turtle or of Blackie or Papa walking me down into the basement of my grandparents' house and opening up the old wooden chest and taking out the velvet lined case where he kept his pearl-handled pistols, real pistols, pistols that, if they were loaded, would shoot. The stubby silver barrels and the embossed trigger housings were a little dull with oil and were surprisingly heavy in my hands. I could not get those pistols out of my mind, or their velvet case or the trunk. There were many other treasures in that trunk, treasures from Germany and England, and I was sure that in time Papa would show them to me.

That was just one kind of sign. Nearly any encounter with an animal excited me, but there was no greater happiness than the parties in our living room or at Nana's and Papa's, parties where my mother would wear her sparkly green dress and there would be amber cocktails with sweet cherries for me and delicious cream-filled desserts and always music, music from the

RCA Victor or music around the piano. My uncles would remove the shiny black Gilbert and Sullivan recordings from their brown paper sleeves, and I could not stop watching the gorgeously-scripted green record labels as they circled the Victorola spindle. Papa could play some of the airs from "The Merry Widow" on the piano, and my father would fill in harmonies on his trumpet. My mother's brother, Uncle Desmond, could sing all the words to "I am the Very Model of a Modern Major General." Mother was shy, but she could sometimes be coaxed to sing "You Made Me Love You," and when she finished, Annabel and I would always beg her to sing it again. I remember the buttery lamplight of those parties, the excited talk and shrieks of women's laughter. I can see slivers of light on the cocktail glasses and wine glasses, the amber and reds like jewels in the faceted glassware. I remember my father and his jokes and how his handsome face seemed to shine and that he was always at the center of the music and the laughter.

But after I started getting cracked in the head, all of this seemed spoiled and out of reach. For months and even years, for what seems now like a separate lifetime, there was no gladness at all. I got dumber every day. I had only to take something delicate into my hands, and I would drop it and break it. I spilled my milk, and it slopped down onto my lap, into my socks, down onto the floor. Flash—crack. I could not manage my knife and fork. Big bits of meat would slide over the side of my plate onto the clean tablecloth or onto the floor. Annabel could cut up her food— my father would ask: *what the hell was wrong with me*? Crack. Sometimes, especially at supper, I could not eat, even though I was told I could not leave the table until I cleaned my plate. Gray mounds of meat pooled in dark juice, hard potatoes yellowed with butter and parsley, cooked carrots and sour florets of steamed broccoli loomed horribly before me. "What's the matter," my father would say, "you fill up on a lot of candy and crap?" *Crap*. I could see steaming messes of dog excrement on the pavement. *Filling up on crap*. My stomach clenched like a fist. I repeated the word: crap. Flash—crack. I could taste the sour acidy spit that arose before I threw up. I could not look at my plate. I could not look up at my father's awful face. Annabel was crying. My mother said, "Frank, don't." I wanted dark, I wanted night.

*　*　*

It seemed, especially around adults, I could only say the wrong thing. Uncle Dennis, my father's brother, and Aunt Betty were visiting from St. Louis. I loved Uncle Dennis because he liked to talk to me and play with me. He would get right down on the floor with me and do what I was doing. His voice was soft, and he made a lot of jokes, and I remember wanting him to keep talking to me and never to go home. One morning he taught me how to thumb wrestle, a game in which we would lace our fingers together and each of us would try to pin the other's thumb down with our own. It was an awkward, silly game, and for some reason it made me laugh uncontrollably, which made Uncle Dennis laugh so hard tears came down out of the corners of his eyes, and then when he wasn't paying attention I would clamp my thumb down over his huge bony thumb and win. Uncle Dennis seemed to have all the time in the world to sit on the floor with me, thumb wrestling or just fooling around. Once in that very position I looked into Uncle Dennis's open smile and said, "Why are your teeth like that?" He gave me a funny, questioning look and said, "Like what? They're just teeth," and I said, "They're all yellow and brown." White flash—crack. I didn't even know my father was in the room.

Teddy Weisblatt and I were playing outside in his yard one late cold autumn afternoon. My mother and father had some kind of engagement in the city and would not be home until after supper, so the Weisblatts were watching me until they came home. Annabel had gone to Nana and Papa's. Teddy and I were digging in an untended patch of dirt behind his garage, but the clay was cold and hard to penetrate, and our hands were getting raw and stiff as we took turns with Mr. Weisblatt's big spade. Then I realized I really had to go to the bathroom. Number two. I told Teddy and we left the spade and went to his back door, but it was locked. Mrs. Weisblatt had run out to the store to get something she needed for dinner. She told us she would be right back, but we didn't know the door would be locked. I really had to go, so we ran around to the front of the house, but those doors were locked too.

Teddy told me I'd better hold it, but I knew I couldn't. Something was already happening in my butt. I made my way back to our house, trying as hard as I could not to poop, but the doors were locked there too. I needed to go. I wished Teddy would disappear and leave me alone, but he was right there at my side. "Go away for awhile," I told him, as I waddled back toward his garage. I decided I would go there, someplace behind the garage where no one could see. I barely got around the corner of the garage before I had to unbuckle my belt and unzip my pants and pull them down around my ankles. I pulled my jacket up above my waist so I wouldn't poop on it, squatted down and started to go. It was a big, difficult poop, and it took a long time, because there would be a big plop and then those intervals when nothing more would come out, but I could tell I wasn't done at all. It took forever, and I was cold, and my legs ached from squatting. Teddy had followed me around to the back of the garage, even though I shouted at him not to.

"You shouldn't do that here," I heard him saying. "My dad is going to be really mad." But I was already pooping hard. I thought Teddy might have wandered off. I had forgotten about him when, a few minutes later, I heard his voice behind me saying, "Oh boy, this is really terrible. When are you going to be finished?" I was in a not-done-yet interval, and I didn't know when I would be finished. It seemed like I would never be finished. I wasn't really finished when I finally stood up and pulled up my pants. Teddy saw his mother's car pulling into the drive, and said, "Here's my mom!" and that was enough for me.

Before I could ask him not to, he ran to the car and told his mother. "Jonathan just made a B.M. in the yard!" After that, everything seemed as if it were happening very far away from me, as if I were under dark soupy water. I can't even tell if I remember what happened or whether I have just filled in with pictures from the way my mother and father told the story for years afterward.

I do know that Mrs. Weisblatt used the key my mother had left her and unlocked our house. She turned on the lights and told me I had better go into the bathroom and take a bath. She didn't run the water or help me. She went home to make supper, and I sat in the bathroom by myself for a long time, until my mother and father came home. I may have told them, or tried to tell them, what happened, but I cannot remember succeeding. Mrs. Weisblatt came over later and told my parents what I had done. I remember my mother saying the words, "sick with embarrassment." *Sick with*. My father never got tired of telling the story, which included his cracking me in the head. He always concluded with an account of shoveling up and burying the mess with the Weisblatts' spade. "It must have taken me a half hour," he would say. "It was like something you'd expect from a hippopotamus." Much later, when I was grown up, he would add, "and this is from a man with two college degrees!"

Eventually I learned to laugh along with the others when my father told these stories about me, but every time he did, it was worse than a crack in the head.

I wanted different, better stories.

UNDERGROUND

I was not quite ten when I realized that certain things you felt like doing could, if you actually went ahead and did them, carry you out of the ordinary world altogether. And it wasn't just me. Certain books give you that feeling, too, books about adventures.

I first got the adventure feeling by discovering things. There were indoor discoveries, and there were outdoor discoveries. Each kind was thrilling. My first indoor adventures were in attics and cellars. I can still feel it today. There is something about entering the forgotten, underdeveloped parts of a building that breaks your connection to the ordinary and the expected. True basements carry the dark and damp of the building before it was a building. A true basement can feel as much outdoors and indoors, especially if there is only stone and earth. But even concrete, provided it is not covered over with upstairs finishes and furnishings, can create an earthy effect. People leave their oldest stuff in basements, hardware and machines and tools and gadgets from another time. I loved basements with surprising bins and recesses and dark crawl spaces. In some old houses I played in as a boy there were coal rooms with coal chutes and cold storage cellars timbered like mine shafts right into the earth. A really great basement captures the feeling of a cave. Attics, although they have a different kind of light and an airless, almost unbreatheable atmosphere, can carry the same wonderful sense of a house beyond what anyone living in the house is thinking about. I like attics best that have multiple partitions and tight, complicated crawlways under the eaves. I like attics that are loaded with boxes and chests filled with pictures and treasure somebody wanted to save but forgot about. I like attics and cellars that have trunks in them like my grandfather Papa's basement trunk that had beautiful cloths wrapped around polished wooden boxes lined with green velvet holding old, real pistols. Going down into Nana and Papa's cellar with Papa to look at his heavy, dully-gleaming pistols and to handle them was one of the holiest times of my life.

Those first discoveries create a tremendous longing for adventures, and some of my very best were in the basement of Cyrus Best's house. I met Cyrus when he entered mid-year into the second grade of my primary school, Palatine South, in Palatine, Illinois where we lived after we moved out of Chicago. Cyrus, everyone could tell right away, was a different kind of boy. He had a massive block of a head, and his hair was cut very short. There was a dark thatch on top, but the sides and back were shaved nearly bald. He told me, when I got to know him later, that his brother Len cut his hair. His brother Len and two other older brothers, Cal and Jessie, were teenagers. Len was a big boy at Palatine High School, and Cal and Jessie had dropped out and were working. They looked like men to me, bigger and rougher and older than my Uncle Desmond who was out of college and out of the army and worked for a magazine. Cyrus's brothers had haircuts like Cyrus's.

Cyrus stood out in school. Seated midway down his row of boys and girls, he gave off a kind of vibration. With his huge head and his washed-out flannel shirt buttoned up tight around his throat, he seemed to be beaming out a desperate message from his little blond desk. Part of it, I suppose, was discomfort, as he was always tense and miserable at school. It didn't take long for it to become clear that Cyrus could not read yet. He could not read at all, even "the" or "of." He told me he had been to a different kind of school, a school kept by his church where he used to live which, he told me, was "down state." I actually made a picture of Illinois's arrowhead shape and imagined Cyrus and his people down by the pointed end. He told me he and his people—he didn't say "family"—lived "by the river." That helped explain Cyrus's difference and his special force. He came from another kind of people, downstate river people with small dark eyes set deep behind their big bony foreheads. Cyrus could not read, and I think he was unbearably ashamed that he couldn't. I would ask him about it sometimes, in a nice way. I would say, "Can you really not read?" I thought maybe he could but he was just afraid to do it out loud in class. He just looked at me hard and hunched his neck down into his shoulders and said, "I cain't." He—and his people, when I met them—said "cain't" and "ain't."

I was fascinated that Cyrus could not, or at least would not, read. He didn't even try or stumble when Mrs. Packworth asked him to read a passage in class. He would just hunch his neck into his shoulders and freeze. His small gray eyes seemed to recede even further behind his brow. "Cyrus," Mrs. Packworth would say, "Try sounding it out: wuh-wuh, wih-wih, with-*with*— " Cyrus could have been in another town. He did not look up at Mrs. Packworth or respond to her words. He waited, frozen, until she moved on. Once I took Cyrus aside when a group of us were standing around a big table molding bits of clay for what was supposed to be a colonial fort. "See this," I said to him and drew a large 'A' on a piece of construction paper. I asked him what it was. A look of suspicion flashed across his big face. "You know what it is," I told him. "It's 'A'." He looked hard into my eyes. "A," he said. I was excited. I asked him, "OK, what does that spell?" Cyrus froze. His eyes retreated into his head. He would not read, not even read "A." His refusal was total, and in it there was a force I had not encountered before, a force that I fell under like a spell.

It took me a while to realize that Cyrus, while a special presence in school, was not really himself there. Seated in his assigned row, silent, inert, neck hunched into his shoulders, he was like a photographic negative of his real self. Outside or in his room or in his basement he had a lot to say. He knew about Jesus and hell and sinning. When he and his people lived downstate, he had been baptized in the river with all his clothes on. He told me his preacher had held him down under the brown water for a long time. He said, "I almost drown't." Now he was saved. I never asked him what saved meant, but I kind of knew. Cyrus carried that saved quality with him into our classroom from the first day. He carried it with him everywhere he went. I don't remember him ever laughing or thinking anything was funny. He was always pretty serious, even worried. Once when we turned the corner of his street he pointed up in the direction of the Millers' big stone house and told me the Millers were going to hell. His mother worked for the Millers, and he told me they went around naked there, that it was a "sex house." I didn't know exactly what he meant, but his words carried an electric charge. After that I could never pass the Millers' house or see Freddy Miller at school or see Mrs. Miller at the A&P without picturing them naked, walking around their house naked, walking around in the unbearably charged atmosphere of a sex house.

Cyrus told me about other sins his people knew about. Playing cards and dancing were sins, but knowing this made me feel uneasy because my mother and father went out dancing. On our piano we had a framed picture of them dressed up and dancing. My mother was smiling beautifully in the picture, and it scared me to think of this as being part of a sin that could send her to hell. I could not even imagine my mother in hell. I was sure she was saved. Sometimes in bed at night I would think about playing cards and how that could be a sin. Playing cards seemed to carry none of the tension of being naked in a sex house. Nana and Papa and Uncle Desmond played cards. They played pinochle and cribbage and kept a running score in a leather notebook. Annabel and I played cards sometimes. We played war and crazy eights. Even when I tried to feel bad about the sin of cards, I couldn't. There was no special feeling in it.

* * *

It was more fun to talk to Cyrus about hunting and about guns, especially after we started hunting, with real guns, in his basement. Cyrus had a true basement with a dirt floor and walls of piled stone. A few bulbs on looping wires were suspended from the floor joists overhead, creating a complex impression of islands of light and dark shadowy caverns. The full basement didn't go under all the rooms of the house, but there were crawl spaces of two or three feet under the other rooms, and Cyrus and I were able to wriggle into these through manhole-sized openings in the foundation walls. It was not really like a basement of a house at all. It was a subterranean world. In the winter we could hear the whoosh of the furnace kicking in and water glugging through the overhead pipes, and these sudden, purposeful sounds seemed proof of the secret separateness of the place. The basement, Cyrus warned me, was full of spiders, and we saw quite a few, but even when our faces and hair were filmy with webs, the spiders seemed less dreadful down in this realm where spiders rightly belonged than they did when a frenzied brown centipede would appear in the tub as Mother ran my bath water or when a black spider of any size stood out in stark relief against the white paint of the ceiling above my bed. What was a little frightening, but also alluring, was the prospect of animals in the cellar. Like what, I remember asking Cyrus, when he told me "we got critters." Mice and rats, he said, maybe sometimes a chuck or a possum.

Cyrus's older brothers all hunted and had guns—shotguns, twenty-twos, and pellet rifles—and they had taught Cyrus how to load them and how to shoot. You loaded the twenty-two by pulling back a metal cylinder, slipping in a brass shell, then sliding the cylinder back in place. The pellet rifle had a kind of pump running beneath the length of the barrel. After you loaded a pellet into the chamber, you had to slide back the pump to build up enough compressed air to shoot the pellet. The pump was hard for me to operate. Holding the rifle stock against my shoulder, I wasn't strong enough to pump the rifle with my left arm. Cyrus could do it, but I couldn't. This was a problem because his brother Len would only allow him to shoot his twenty-two. That meant I got the pellet rifle, which Cyrus's brothers thought of as a kid's toy, but I wasn't strong enough to work it. Feeling too weak started to spoil the whole basement adventure. I felt as if I had at last been granted access to a place of limitless adventure, a place Cyrus and I could feel that electric feeling of being armed and on the loose-- but I was too weak to do it. What was wrong with my skinny arms? I could see they were only sticks compared to Cyrus's. I couldn't stand asking Cyrus to help me pump my rifle every time I wanted to shoot. That would mean that he belonged in the adventure, but I did not. I could feel myself starting to lose confidence, the feeling dangerously close to the can't-do-anything feeling that led to cracks in the head I got from my father when I disappointed him. Not being able to pump the rifle was like not being able to hammer a nail straight into the board after my father had shown me how so many times that he started to get mad. It was like the time he asked me to help him wash the windows on the storm doors. He was outside with his ammonia and rags, and I was on the inside with mine. He would wash a square from the outside, and then tap the glass so that I would do my side. When we were both finished, there would still be filmy swirls and streaks. He would swipe at them from his side, but they wouldn't disappear, because they were on my side, and the more I sprayed and wiped, the cloudier it got. It was a curse. I would apply the spray, then pull my rag as evenly and as hard as I could over the glass, and then, just for an instant it would look clear, and then the cloudy swirls would reform. "For Christ sake," my father finally said. He came inside and tore the rag out of my hand and gave me a little shove away from the door. "Get lost. Find something to do. I'll do this myself."

That's what it felt like as I loaded the pellet into the chamber and stood there on the damp floor of the basement unable to slide back the pump of the rifle. Then in a rage that made a bright flash behind my eyes, I knew what to do. I set the heel of the rifle stock against the basement floor, bent down over the barrel and grabbed the pump with both hands. I pressed down with all my strength and all my weight. Then the pump gave way, and I heard a gassy *poof* and then a metallic *ping*. The light bulb over our heads shattered and went dark. "Dang it," Cyrus said. "You shot the light out." It took me a minute to figure out what he meant. Then I realized the rifle had fired. It had gone straight up and broken the light bulb. "Come here," Cyrus said, pulling me by the wrist until we were standing under another light bulb. "Know what else," he said, "You shot yourself in the ear." The tip of my ear was cold. It started to sting. I reached up to touch it, and there was new red blood on my grimy fingers. "Let's go and get you cleaned up," Cyrus said. I didn't know if he was mad or disappointed. We were just getting ready to hunt in one of the crawl spaces. We had shells and pellets in our pockets and a flashlight with new batteries. Upstairs at Cyrus's kitchen sink I washed off my ear with a dishcloth, and Cyrus brought me a bandage. At the door as I was leaving, he said, "You coulda shot yourself in the head and killed yourself."

I thought about that, about having shot myself accidentally in the head or through the eye and being finished with the world at nine years old. Obviously it wasn't to be, but it was a warning of some kind, a message. If it was a message about guns and hunting, I missed it completely, because Cyrus and I went at it every chance we could. We spent many long afternoons after school reclining back against the stone foundation walls of his basement, rifles cocked, a sharp eye out for possum or rat. Or, more uncomfortably, we would lie prone in the damp, buggy earthen floor of one of the crawl spaces, a flashlight beaming a funnel of light through the murk. No critter ever entered those funnels of light, but I spent many wide-eyed nights in my bed at home picturing exactly how it would be. Cyrus and I would be huddled shoulder to shoulder in the dirt, our eyes following the shaft of light, our rifles before us, cocked and ready. Then it would happen. The picture grows larger, the flashlight beam brilliant as a flashbulb as into the white circle of light slithers the ugliest, most menacing creature I had ever seen, yet exactly the kind of creature I imagined when Cyrus had told me we might expect a rat, or maybe a possum. The rat-possum was about the size of a largish, low-slung cat. Its wet fur was silver and black. Its long bald tail was obscenely pink. Spotlighted against a far wall, it turned to us. A circle of green and gold glowed in its black eyes. Looking directly into the light, it bared a line of crooked yellow teeth. It is the time, the exact moment for us to fire. And I am caught there, holding that picture before my mind's eye. I can see it now.

Later, when we got our axes and spears, we took the adventure and the hunt outdoors, which was even better. It may have been a blessing, although it didn't seem like it at the time, that Cyrus's brother Len met us on the basement stairs as we were coming up from a hunt. Cyrus had the pellet rifle, and I had Len's twenty-two, which Cyrus wasn't supposed to let me use, but he did because I couldn't pump the pellet rifle. I loved the twenty-two. I loved that it was the more powerful rifle, a man's rifle, a rifle that, as Cyrus told me, "could kill a man." I loved it so much I would forget that it wasn't mine. It felt like mine. I loved the clean feel of firing it, the little tug I felt through the stock under my arm when I fired. I loved the startling flash of sparks where the bullet met the stones of the foundation wall. I loved the sweet char of gunpowder that hovered around the spent copper-colored shell casings. But Len startled us. Even before he spoke, the adventure was over. He was really mad. What did we think we were doing with those guns in the cellar? What was I doing with his twenty-two? He told us we better not have taken any of his pellets and cartridges. He looked at Cyrus with the same kind of steady, unbearable look Cyrus gave me when he was upset about something. It felt dangerous to be standing on that little wooden stairway. I didn't know what Len was going to do, but I could imagine him doing something terrible. I could imagine him stabbing us or shooting us, and my ears began to ring. He did not look at me, only at Cyrus, and Cyrus's neck was hunched all the way into his shoulders. Len reached down and pulled the twenty-two out of my hands, and then he took the pellet rifle away from Cyrus. "All right, boy, now I know." He took hold of Cyrus's chin and made him look up into his eyes. "I cain't trust you. Now git." After that we had our adventures outside.

* * *

There were a lot of things eight and nine-year-old kids aren't allowed to buy in the hardware store. For instance, Cyrus and I couldn't buy guns, even the Daisy air rifles that other kids in town owned. I wanted a Daisy BB gun, the deluxe model that pumped air into the barrel by cocking a lever beneath the trigger. The Rudd brothers had that gun, and they used to take it out into the fields behind Our Lady of the Wayside school and shoot cans and bottles and birds. Freddy and Eddy Rudd were eleven and thirteen, and their father didn't care if they had guns. Eddy said his father bought him the Daisy deluxe when he was eight. I asked my father if I could ever have a BB gun, and he said, with frightening force, "Never. Absolutely not." The more he thought about it the madder he got. "What would you like to do," he said, "put somebody's eye out?" I told him I would be completely careful, and that I would never shoot it around people or around the house, only way out in the fields, at cans and bottles and maybe birds. I said Freddy and Eddy Rudd had a Daisy and their father got it for them when they were eight. "Then you stay the hell away from them," my father said. "Do you hear me? I *mean* it." I knew he meant it. I thought he was going to crack me in the head.

Even if my father wasn't so against BB guns, I don't think he would have bought me one. I didn't seem to get big presents like that, especially if it wasn't Christmas or my birthday. Even if I had some of my own money stashed away—my sister Annabel had about fifteen dollar bills rolled up in her jewelry box—I could not have bought a BB gun at the hardware store. Once one of the men who worked there saw me looking up at the rack of Daisys on the wall behind the counter, and he asked me if I wanted to hold one. I said yes, I wanted to hold the deluxe. He took it down and handed it to me and showed me how to pull back the spring-coiled slot where you loaded the BBs and how to cock the rifle. He let me try it, and it wasn't too hard. I could feel the air caught in the chamber behind the barrel. The man said go ahead, pull the trigger. I did, and there was a metallic *pfft*. It was a great feeling, a perfect feeling. The Daisy had the look of some of the twenty-twos and shotguns on display, and it was just the right size. It smelled new. The man asked if I was thinking about getting a Daisy one of these days, and I told him yes, definitely, but I knew I would just picture it and picture it, as I pictured certain other things or places that seemed to shine and beckon from a real world not quite connected to mine.

But for some reason there were no rules against the hardware store selling Cyrus and me little hatchets. Cyrus noticed them first. They were in a bin next to the long-handled axes and sledgehammers. The shaft of the little hatchets was not much longer than the one on my father's hammer, but they had real axe heads, painted blue at the fat end, then becoming shiny gray steel as the blade narrowed to a sharp edge. I couldn't believe it. I asked a man who worked there how much the little hatchets cost. He walked over to look and told us, two dollars and ninety-eight cents. That didn't seem like too much. The man didn't say: these aren't for kids. I had two dollars at home in my bank. Cyrus said he had five dollars saved. We could buy two of those axes, and we did.

I don't know what Cyrus did with his, but I hid mine in the garage behind some old coffee cans filled with rusty nails and screws. I knew my mother and father wouldn't like me having a hatchet of my own, and my father would get mad at me for going out and buying it without telling him. So it was a secret, but I pictured it behind the coffee cans in the garage all day long at school, and I pictured it there at night in my bed.

It was fall then. As soon as school let out, Cyrus and I would race back to our houses, put our books inside, grab our hatchets and head for the fields. There was still red and orange in the trees, and out in the fields the tall grasses and corn stalks had dried to the color of khaki. It would get cold enough as the sun started to set that our fingers would get stiff, and we knew we would have to hurry home for supper or we would be in trouble.

Maybe everything we did with those hatchets took place in a single fall, but it felt to me like a whole season of my life. As soon as we turned off the paved street onto the double-rutted tractor path of the fields, we entered the other world. The cool air seemed to go deeper into my lungs. I could smell sweet rot behind the hedgerows and musk from the barns and ruined sheds we passed by or foraged through. The spent grasses were alive with rabbits and the sudden heart-stopping ascent of pheasants. Uncle Desmond had bought me a suede leather cowboy jacket with a row of rawhide fringe along the shoulder line, and this was my field jacket. It enabled me to conceal my hatchet when I emerged from the garage, but when I met Cyrus and we were nearing the tractor path, I would take it out and slide the shaft into the holster of what had been my cap pistol. Cyrus didn't have a holster, but he would stuff the handle of his hatchet under his belt. We would begin each hunt or adventure by snapping down a branch of one of the bushes that lined the path, hacking it free with our hatchets, then whittling one end to a point with our pearl-handled pocket knives. These would be our spears, and although we never came even close to doing it, our hope was to spear some kind of animal that we might scare up out of the bramble. It felt good, it felt just right, to be walking through the empty fields in the autumn chill, the pleasing heft of a spear in one hand, the holstered weight of my hatchet against my thigh, and my knife deep in the pocket of my jeans.

It often felt like a good idea to make a shelter, which we called forts. These became more elaborate and even provided a kind of shelter once we were able to use our hatchets to cut the larger shoots away from the base of shrubs or to hack low lying branches from trees. One afternoon, it occurred to us that we might make something really substantial, a fort that would stand and last. We could do real Work. Maybe it would take days, maybe years. We could build a fort that we could live in. It would take tremendous effort, day after day, and it would take our hatchets. That afternoon and for many afternoons afterward we did nothing but work on that fort. At home I couldn't wait to get away from the table and go to my room where I could picture the fort and make new plans. At school I could only twist around in my chair and look at the big circular face of the clock and watch the agonizingly slow procession of minutes. The clocks were the same in every room in the school. There was a notch for each minute etched into the circumference of the face, and there was a fatter notch to indicate five minutes. When the minute hand was about to move a notch, there would be a cranking sound, and the hand would cock itself backwards a little and then click forward into the next minute. I tried to stop watching the clock and let some other thoughts carry me away so that time would just flow, but I couldn't do it. Every time I looked up it seemed like the clock was on the same minute, and I would keep looking at it until it cranked into the next one. I could not pay attention. I could not sit still. I could see the sun in the trees outside, and I wanted some force to lift me out of my chair and set me down in the fields with my hatchet.

Cyrus and I found a perfect place for our fort. It was down over a rise of a hill not far from an old barn. It was out of the wind and had a protected feeling about it. But the best thing about it was that there were lines of little trees, trees about six or seven feet high with trunks and branches we could, with effort, chop down. Cyrus knew how to cut down trees by hacking a triangular wedge into one side of the trunk, then, when you were almost through, chopping into the other side. Our building plan for the fort was to chop down as many lengths of trunks and branches as we could. Then we would sharpen one end of each pole, dig a little hole and stick them in so they would be standing upright. We would make two rows of these just a little ways apart and then fill in the space between with smaller branches, scrub and grass. These would be the walls. Over the top we'd lay longer branches with the leaves still on them to make a roof, leaving an open space in one corner to let the smoke rise from our fires. We would leave an opening at one end for a door, and maybe later we would get some blankets from our houses for the floor. This was my first real feeling of work, and it connected me to something vast and ancient and great. We chopped and hauled and stacked until we could hear each other panting, but I never wanted to stop or for the sun to get any lower. It seemed to me that the work stimulated ideas and new plans for the fort, and the ideas made me want to work. I remember looking back as we left for home one afternoon and seeing the neat lines of stumps we had left. We had chopped down almost half of that stand of perfect little trees.

    Cyrus and I decided that if we were going to finish the fort and get any use out of it before winter we were going to have to find a way to spend Saturdays on the job. This was hard to arrange because of the things our families wanted us to do on Saturdays, but we finally managed to get together one Saturday. It was cold, and the sky was a solid gray as we made our way into the fields along the tractor path. It felt strange heading out at this different time on a Saturday. We passed Freddy and Eddy Rudd on the path. They had the Daisy with them, and they told us they had shot a bunch of birds but now they were cold. Eddy Rudd said he was "cold as shit." We didn't tell them where we were going. We heard other voices in the distance and the whine of engines as we walked along. After school we never heard anybody else. We were always completely by ourselves.

    We reached the rise just above our fort and were heading down the hillside toward the trees when we heard the sputtering of a motor. We stopped for a minute. It didn't feel right. I decided to go to work anyway. I started chopping a wedge into the trunk of a tree, and the bad feeling opened up into a scream. Cyrus said, "Look *out*," and I looked behind me and saw a man on a tractor heading down the hill straight for us. The tractor motor was deafening, but I could hear some of the things the man was shouting. I could hear *"filthy little bastards,"* and I could hear *"god damned sons of bitches,"* and *"my fruit trees!"*

Cyrus was running ahead of me, and I was right behind him, running in a way I had never run before. This was serious. I heard, *"blow your fuckin' brains out."*

I don't think I turned back to look, but I remember the man's face. He was old. Stringy skin was hanging on his neck. I knew he wanted to catch us and kill us. We ran out of the clearing into the tall grass and scrub. I thought: go where his tractor can't go. I could still hear the motor behind us when we reached a cornfield and charged in between the stalks. Cyrus led the way as we zigzagged through the corn, and when we got out, we were pretty far from the path, but we decided to keep to the high grass and as far from people as we could. It was cold, and it was hard going, hunched down low, finding our footing through the tall grass of the fields. Cyrus said, "He's going to be looking for us. They're going to want to arrest us." *Arrest.* The man had shouted, "my fruit trees." I had never thought of trees way out in the fields belonging to anybody. I thought they were part of nature. "They were his property," Cyrus said, and as he said it I knew, just as surely as I know now, the meaning of *property.*

We escaped from the fields without being arrested, but the closer I got to my house, the sicker I felt inside. I made it into the garage and slipped my hatchet behind the coffee cans. I had the feeling that as soon as I went inside the house everything about what I had done to the fruit trees would be known, and there would be terrible yelling and cracks in the head. Even when that did not happen, I felt it was coming. I waited for it, and it spoiled the days. Cyrus and I never went back to the fort, and then it was winter, and the fields filled up with snow.

The Other World

* * *

For a long time there was nothing close to that feeling of Work, of using our hatchets to make something that was all ours and that would last. But not too long after that something amazing started to happen, and it happened in school. We were leaving the lunch room on our way to the gym for free play when a partly crazy boy in our class, Donny Greener, was trying to get everybody to follow him because he wanted to show them something. The girls didn't even slow down to look at him, and the boys in front of me were laughing at him and saying, "Oh, yeah, Donny, sure, sure. You want us to go down into the basement. Oh, yeah, we really want to go down to the basement." They moved on, and when Cyrus and I got to him, he said, "You got to see this. I went into this little room next to the bathroom downstairs, and there was a tunnel!" When Donny said the word "tunnel," something jumped in my chest. "Where's it go?" Cyrus asked. Donny said he didn't know. He said a janitor came by and told him to get out of there. But he could see it, he said, see the tunnel, and it went on and on. I looked at Cyrus, and he was interested, so we went down the stairs to the basement. Donny shushed us, so the janitor wouldn't hear us, and we tiptoed as quietly as we could past the boys' bathroom. There was always a little time after lunch when you could go to the gym or, in nice weather, out to the playground, but you were supposed to be there or in the cafeteria, not wandering around the halls unless you had a pass. Donny led us down past the bathroom to a grimy metal door. He put his ear against it to listen. "It was open before," he whispered. "The janitor must have shut it. Wait till you see."

Donny pulled open the door. There was a low table with some canisters and bottles on it, and a line of mops was leaning against the wall. It was only a closet, I thought, but then I saw that it kept going to the left. We stepped inside and we could see that under a curved archway cut into the wall on the left was a dark passage of about twenty feet where a bare bulb lit up what looked like a turning to the right. I was absolutely sure that I shouldn't go into that tunnel and absolutely sure that I would. "Let's go," I said, and we ducked under the archway and started making our way over the damp cement floor. When I got to the light, the tunnel turned to the right, and again I felt a tremendous surge in my chest as I saw that it went on as far as I could see, with other light bulbs down the way indicating a complicated system of turns and intersections. My skull and all down my spine was alive with electric tingles. As usual I had no words for it, but it was one of those times something I suddenly saw flowed into something I had always known in a way that felt like a message. There was an elaborate world underneath the world. I heard a muted clank from somewhere in front of us, and then a cough. Then we were running back toward the closet door, and I knew the sound of our rubber sneaker soles slapping on the cement was making a lot of noise. We heard a "hey!" and then a louder "hey!" and then we were out in the hallway and up the stairs.

Cyrus was in a special class now, and I didn't get a chance to talk to him again until after school, but then it was clear. He had seen what I had seen, and we started making plans. Without either one of us having to say it, we made our way from the playground back into the school building, which always seemed to me abandoned and forbidding after school hours. We walked along the waxy-smelling hallways without seeing anybody, but as we were going downstairs to the basement level, we met Lodi, the German janitor who was washing the floor in the boys' bathroom. Lodi had a huge meaty red face that always looked to me as if something terrible had just happened to him, but the kids at school thought he was nice because he liked to talk to us and knew our names. He had big square front teeth like pieces of Chiclets gum, and some kids thought he was funny and even friendly because of the way he looked, but I didn't think he was especially funny or friendly. I thought Lodi was somebody I should stay away from. He didn't look clean.

He asked us what we were looking for, and Cyrus said we needed to use the bathroom. Lodi said we should use the one upstairs because he was washing the floor. We went back upstairs but waited at the top until we saw him go back inside the bathroom with his pail. Then we sneaked back down and found

The Other World

our way to the metal door, opened it as quietly as we could, and slipped inside. It was just as it had been, except now the closet was dark, and the only light I could see was from the bulb down the tunnel to the left. We crept under the arch and moved in the direction of the light. In a minute my eyes were used to the dark, and I could see fine. We reached the bulb where we had to turn back earlier and continued along the passage until we reached the next pool of light, which turned out to be an intersection. The tunnel continued as far as we could see in either direction. It was even better than I imagined. It went on and on. I was moving through the world under the world. We turned left again. The pipes and ducts overhead clicked and hummed, which gave me the feeling that there was an order and a plan to all this. We came to another turn where there were iron rungs of a ladder leading up the cinder block wall. Looking up the ladder I could see a white circle of daylight. We decided to climb up, which turned out to be easy, and with the wall behind us so close, I felt like I couldn't really fall and hurt myself. I was ahead of Cyrus on the ladder, and when I got to the top, I could see the sky and treetops through a screened grate. I pushed out a little into the screening and the grate lifted up in my hand. I climbed up to the last rung and poked my head out of the opening. It was bright daylight, and we were on the flat roof over the cafeteria. I slid over to one side so Cyrus could get up there and see. We considered the perpendicular contours of the school from our perch over the roof. Cyrus said exactly what I was thinking: "This has been here the whole time and we never seen it."

We climbed back down the ladder, silent with the pleasure of knowing what we had discovered, that there was so much more to see, and that nobody but us had any idea of what we had found. It felt to me closer to being in a dream than being awake. I don't know if we discussed it or just felt it, but somehow while we were whispering in that tunnel, we determined that the pleasure of exploring further was exceeded by the greater pleasure of knowing that there were other passages still to be explored. We decided to head back. When we reached the turn that led to the closet, we saw something and stopped still. Lodi was in the closet. He was rinsing out his mop and banging around, making enough noise that he didn't notice us. We stepped back out of sight and waited until we heard the door shut and it was quiet. We peeked down the passage, but it was completely dark at the closet end. Lodi had turned off the lights. We inched our way, very slowly, in the direction of the closet until we could see stripes of light through a vent at the bottom of the door. But then we got a scare. We couldn't open the door. It was locked. We sat down on the cement floor, and I stared hard at the lines of light through the vent. I realized I was sweating. I didn't like the idea at all, but I said, "We could go back and go up the ladder to the roof." At least then we would be outside.

"But then we'd be on the roof," Cyrus said. He was right. How could we get down from the roof? We would have to call out to somebody, and somebody would have to come rescue us, and then we would have to explain about everything, and later at home I would be cracked in the head. Even while I was worrying, I knew there was something right about being in the tunnels, something that felt good even on the floor in the dark. When I am in that kind of mood, the right thing usually happens. As I sat there, my eyes got used to the dark, and I could start to see things, the mops, the pails, the canisters and bottles on the shelves. There was a coat rack with brass hooks that gleamed a little, and on one of the hooks—I stood up to touch them—a ring of keys.

We didn't see anybody as we made our way through the darkening corridors of the empty school. When I said goodbye to Cyrus at the turn off to his street, I had a wonderful feeling, a feeling of almost unbearable expectation. We knew about the tunnels. They were really down there, and we had our own key.

* * *

From then on—it must have been for the whole rest of that school year—I lived for the tunnels. It felt the way my dreams felt, but the tunnels were really there, pulsing like a kind of energy all around and underneath the school. I don't remember anything at all from the regular school day, except for the cranking of minutes on the clock face and moving in packs as we headed to

The Other World

the playground or to the cafeteria or to the gym. There was that little bit of time after lunch when we knew we could go down to the boys' bathroom, then sneak over to the tunnel closet, but since somebody heard us and almost caught us the time we looked inside with Donny Greener, it seemed that either Lodi or the tall, meaner janitor was hanging around the closet during the lunch hour, on the lookout.

Cyrus and I managed some very exciting and very satisfying expeditions after school, but we had to be watchful every second, because we realized that janitors and other workmen used the tunnels. Two different tunnels led into a big boiler room, which was brightly lit from high ceilings. There always seemed to be a janitor or workmen in there, but Cyrus and I would sneak through from time to time because the boiler room was a necessary short cut when we knew we had to get out of the tunnels in a hurry. Some of the tunnels dead-ended into storage spaces, one of them full of old science equipment, including scales and microscopes and chemicals and all kinds of specimen jars capped with cork. That was the room where we found the complicated gadget with brass globes representing the sun and the moon and the earth connected by gears and chains so that they could rotate around each other to show how it got dark and when you could see the moon. This was heavy on its wooden base, and it looked and felt like something valuable and old. It was something Cyrus and I both wanted to keep, but even though it was stashed down in the cement storage room with old jars so gritty with dirt you couldn't see what was inside, we were pretty sure it would be stealing. The piece was also fairly big, and we knew it would be hard to get it out of the tunnels and out of the school and home without anyone noticing. But, like Papa's miniature pistols, it was just one beckoning treasure in a cavernous room full of treasures. Another room was stacked high with old typewriters. Another had two upright pianos with the wires exposed. Our problem was time. We had to be sure to get out of the tunnels before someone found us or before someone locked up the school.

I suppose part of the elevated feeling was knowing that we had to be on the lookout every second. We could never talk in a regular voice. We could never just walk; we either had to creep along in tiny silent steps or else run as fast as we could. Over the course of our time in the tunnels we saw Lodi and the other, mean janitor quite a few times. We'd usually spot them first, and then freeze or hide until they went away. But sometimes they saw us or heard us, and we would run out of there as fast as we could. We were chased a few times, but no one ever caught up with us, and I don't think anybody got close enough to recognize us. But after a close call, Cyrus and I would stay out of the tunnels for a while.

For me staying out of the tunnels every now and then was a kind of pleasure in itself. Knowing I couldn't go down into them made thinking about it even more exciting. I made a few forays by myself, but usually we went in together, and I do not think there was a single excursion or even a single thing we saw or did down there that Cyrus and I did not talk over in exact detail. In my bed at night I pictured the tunnels, the dimly illuminated passage opening up before me under the first bare bulb. After a week or so we knew the underground layout well enough to draw a map, but I always felt that, despite how many times we crept through the same passages and saw the same things, there was always the possibility of finding another opening to what I believed could be network after network of new tunnels and chambers.

Maybe he saw our maps or maybe Cyrus said something to him, but some time that spring in the nice weather as school was about to let out for the summer, Donny Greener found out about our adventures in the tunnels. Cyrus and I liked to make new, revised maps and show them to each other at lunch and then make plans. That is all I can remember talking about. I know it's all I thought about. Still I didn't expect to hear Donny Greener telling everybody about our going down into the tunnels all the time, and I certainly didn't want to take Donny down into them with us. Maybe it was Donny's fault—he never stopped talking, never stopped bugging us to take him along—or maybe the janitors said something to the teachers, but one day after lunch the principal gave a talk to everyone in the cafeteria about staying out of the basement and the "maintenance facilities." She said it was dangerous and discourteous and that if anybody was caught

The Other World

down there our parents would be called and we would be sent home. The principal was saying all of this as Cyrus and I were sitting together leaning over our maps. And of course Donny, who really was partly crazy, stood up at his table and started to look around for Cyrus and me. I glanced up and saw that his face was bright red and he was pointing to us like an idiot, right while the principal was talking. After that it felt hopeless to attempt another trip down to the tunnels. Also, something about the term "maintenance facilities" seemed to cancel out the charged, exciting feeling about the tunnels. I didn't ever want to lose that, so I let the idea of bright summer crowd out everything else, and neither Cyrus nor I ever mentioned the tunnels again.

CLIMBING

That summer I started to climb. I got the idea and the feel of it from a Tarzan double feature my sister Annabel and I saw while we were on vacation in Michigan. For a number of years in a row we would pack up and drive out of Palatine to what my father called the North Woods. We would rent our own cabin, which would be in a line of other cabins along the shore of a lake, and sometimes there was a lodge where the people who stayed in the cabins could get special meals or sit around a fire on rainy days or play cards or ping-pong. Each cabin had its own little dock and a rowboat, and you could fish all day or swim or do anything you wanted. Once or twice we would drive out to a little town and eat chicken-in-a-basket and maybe go to the drive-in. This is where I saw the Tarzan double feature, and after that the idea of climbing up and over things took hold of me the way the building our fort in the fields and hunting and the tunnels had done.

I was just about to say that the Tarzan movies entered right into my brain, but that isn't quite right. It felt more as if I entered the movie, as if somehow I rose up to the bright screen and passed right through into the jungle. Everything about Tarzan was exactly right. I felt as if I had been waiting for that world for a long time. He only had to wear a little leather bathing suit. On anybody else I had ever seen this would have made him look as if he were in his underwear, but Tarzan looked absolutely right and natural. Tarzan movies always had the effect of making me want to get naked outside, or at least almost naked. He was always around water, and he was a terrific swimmer, but it was his climbing that took hold of me. It was not just that he was so comfortable and quick getting up trees; it was that he seemed to belong in trees. He and Jane and a chimpanzee, who I always thought of as Tarzan and Jane's son, lived in a tree fort, and Tarzan would swing from tree to tree, then, when he needed to, down to the

The Other World

ground on a vine. Tarzan moved through the trees the way a person would walk down the road. Watching Tarzan swinging from tree to tree almost naked made me want to walk right out of the theatre and get into some trees myself.

Because we saw the movies at night, I had to wait until the next morning before I could go outside and get at it. But it was nice, driving home from the drive-in, to realize that Annabel had the same kind of reaction to the movie. I could tell she was carried away. She couldn't really explain it. Her feeling wasn't about swinging through the trees nearly naked or being free all day to do whatever you wanted in the jungle. I could tell by the way she talked and by the way she rearranged the stuff in her room that what mattered to her was Jane and how she made a kind of house for herself in the tree fort and how she was somewhere between a mother and a girlfriend to Tarzan. I didn't think about those things all that much, but I remember being glad Annabel had that good feeling about Jane and Tarzan and the jungle.

As it turned out, I was good at climbing. The thing I liked best about it was that I could do it by myself. When I climbed something with other kids, it always turned into a race or a competition—who could get to the top first or who could hang from their knees from a high branch. I don't really mind competition and dares, but they spoiled the climbing. What I liked was the figuring out period and then actually doing what I figured out. Climbing sometimes took me quite a long time, but I liked that too. I could talk to myself, out loud if I was alone, wondering what would happen if I reached out to hang on to a certain branch or if I put all my weight on a dead one. After each advance farther up the tree, I could rest for as long as I felt like. This was very important when I made a mistake and had a close call. I would lose my footing sometimes or something I was holding onto would snap off, and I would fall a little ways before there was something strong enough to grab onto. When this would happen, my heart would feel as if it was flying right out of my chest and I'd be sweating all over until I calmed down. As long as I was by myself, this wasn't too bad. I could just get myself in a comfortable position and talk to myself in a calm way until my heart was back to normal and I got my strength back. I think that climbing was very good for me, because it taught me the way I learn. It helped me understand that I could do practically anything as long as I could do it completely my own way and no one else was around.

I did so much climbing and thought about climbing so much that the second I saw a particular tree, I knew whether I could climb it or not. I could tell by the way the biggest branches came out of the trunk. I could tell in advance whether there would be something to hold onto when you got to the top, whether there would be a place where you could rest and figure things out. I kept my climbing pretty much to myself, and I don't think I talked about it much, but occasionally, if we were on a family trip or a picnic, Annabel or Mother would notice. They'd see that I wasn't around and call out for me, and I would answer them from up in a tree, sometimes practically at the top. A few times Mother was really worried. When she called for me to come down her voice trembled the way it did when she was about to cry. Most of the time, though, she seemed surprised and maybe impressed that I had gotten up there. She would say things like, "Now don't fall and break your neck." The plain, matter-of-fact way she said it let me know she didn't really think I would break my neck and that I could keep climbing.

The hardest thing to figure out about climbing trees was how to get up to the first level of branches when they started high off the ground, which I found was usually the case with the biggest trees. If a tree was right around the house and my father wasn't home, I could drag one of his ladders over to the trunk, but this didn't feel like real climbing. I didn't mind using the seat of my bike or a box or something to boost me up to the first branch, but a ladder seemed too easy. Anybody could climb a ladder up a tree. One time I watched a workman climb up a telephone pole by sliding a leather strap around the pole, then pulling himself up to that level, then sliding the strap up higher and pulling himself up to it until he reached the wires. He went straight up in less than a minute. It was like something Tarzan could do. It was also the kind of climbing I liked to imagine myself being able to do. I didn't have a leather strap like the workman's, but I knew that if I did, I couldn't climb the pole the way he did. I knew I wasn't strong enough, and I started to feel that bad, never-be-able-to-do-things-right feeling, the feeling I got when I couldn't pump the pellet rifle or clear the smudges off my side of the window glass. I remember watching the workman until he came down. I stood practically right underneath him, and then I saw how he did it. He had special spikes, like steel nails, strapped under his boots. I watched the spikes rip into the dark wood of the pole, and I could see how they gave him enough of a foothold to free his arms to slide the strap into the next position. It was good to know that I could do that if I wanted to.

But it wasn't tar-blackened telephone poles I wanted to climb. I wanted to be up in the leafy breezes of treetops. I wanted to rest in the safe bowered crook of trunk and limb, high up over the lawns and garage roofs, unknown and invisible to kids playing on the sidewalk and to mothers talking to each other over their fences while they pinned billowing sheets and pillow cases onto their clothes lines. I wanted to be able to think about things for as long as I wanted up there, to talk to myself out loud. Sometimes when I was up in a tree I knew really well, and I was having a good day, I could feel my climbing become so effortless and sure it didn't feel like climbing at all, but like floating. It was what Tarzan must have felt flying on his vines from tree to tree. When I would get that feeling, everything I did turned out right. I didn't have to grip anything tight with my hands or strain to hold myself in position while my feet found a place to rest. I could just let everything go loose, so that climbing down from a perch at the top of a tree was just like shinnying down a pole. I'd barely hold onto things as my body slid into place from higher branch to lower branch. My body just seemed to know what to do and where to go.

Once I got the knack of climbing, I started picturing practically everything I saw as climbable or not climbable, and the more time I had to talk to myself and figure things out, the fewer things seemed not climbable. I would look at the way people's awnings were attached to their porches by poles and wonder how I could shinny up those poles and get on top of the porch. When I saw a

Richard Hawley

garage roof or a house extension that had a flat roof with railings, I would immediately start to figure out how I could get up there. That turned out to be pretty easy, provided there was a window with a ledge underneath it. If there was, I just had to pull my bike below the window, stand on the seat, and get a foothold on the window ledge. Then, leaning into the side of the building just enough to keep my balance, I would feel overhead for the roofline or, if I could reach it, the bottom of the railing. When I got a decent handhold, I could pull myself bit by bit up to where I could really get hold of the railing, then hoist myself onto the roof. If the building had gutters with sturdy down spouts, I could use those as hand holds when I climbed down. The more I climbed the more everything turned out to be climbable.

On Christmas Eve and other special days my father would take Annabel and me with him on the train downtown to Chicago, and we would ride the elevator of his bank up to the top floor where his office was. Out the window I could see the roofs and top floors of the skyscrapers across the street, and it seemed obvious that once you got a story or two above the street, these buildings would be easy to climb. There were big, deep ledges beneath all the windows and lots of obvious handholds and footholds into the decorative tracery. Not only that, the highest buildings tapered to a point, which would make the climbing a lot easier as you started getting to the top. I found I couldn't get those Chicago skyscrapers out of my head. From the minute we got out of the train station and stepped out onto the windy street, my eyes would scan the walls of the Wrigley Building looking for a way to get up past the first floor, where the really good footholds started. I remember thinking that the builders must have had climbing in mind when they put in all the special ledges and extra stonework. Once I heard Nana, who didn't like downtown Chicago, say something about "the unearthly canyons" of LaSalle Street, where my father's bank was. I realized that the word was just right. *Canyons*. Those streets really were canyons, and they made you feel like climbing.

I knew that if I was ever going to able to do that kind of climbing, I would need practice and confidence. There were heavy ceramic downspouts and good window ledges at my school, and I had many times worked my way up onto the ledges of the first floor windows. These were only about four feet off the ground, but they were really higher than that, because directly below each window was a concrete window well that went down three or our feet. I knew falling down into one of the window wells would be serious. There was good footing, though, on the ledges, and some of the down spouts were just the right distance from the window so that you could lean into the column of the spout and hold onto it while you worked your feet up along the window trim. One time I started going up a little ways toward the second floor, but it was mid-afternoon and I was on the front wall of the school, and somebody on the street saw me and shouted at me to get down. I realized that I could do it, though, and that felt good.

It turned out that Nana and Papa's house was a better place to practice. Their house in Palatine was bigger and more solid than ours. The walls were made of rough brown bricks, and I noticed that at the corners of the house, every other brick was slightly recessed into the wall. It was probably a decorative touch, but I could tell right away that the indentations might make handholds and footholds. As soon as I could, I tried climbing up the corner of the house. It almost worked, but the indentations were only about an inch deep, and it was hard to hold on for more than a few seconds. But around one of the corners there was a corrugated metal downspout running from the gutter line to the ground. The downspout was only a couple of feet from the corner bricks, and I could see that it would provide the extra handhold I needed. It was getting dark, and my parents were already in the car getting ready to drive home to our house, but I slipped around the corner and tried it. It worked perfectly, just as I had thought. I climbed up three or four feet, heard the car horn honk, and jumped down. As I ran to the car, I was already making plans. I pictured myself standing at the peak of Nana and Papa's roof. I was leaning back against the chimney, holding onto the TV antenna with one hand for support.

I lay awake in the dark of my room, picturing my climb. I could feel the rough little ridges of brick against the pads of my fingers and pressing up into the soles of my sneakers. I would start up the wall, but then I would be back on the ground where I would start up again. I never got to the top, or even most of the way. I just kept starting my climb, knowing that I could do it.

A few weekends later Annabel and I went to stay at Nana and Papa's house for the night. On Saturday afternoon when Nana and Papa went to the store and Annabel was playing inside the house, I had all the time I needed to figure things out and start my climb. The corner of the house with the good downspout was in a side yard surrounded by high hedges, so I didn't have to worry about neighbors or kids on the street bothering me. The first three or four feet went easily, just like before, but when I got up above the level of the first floor windows, it started to get hard. I think I was getting a little scared, but it was harder to calm down on the wall than up in a tree where you can usually find a comfortable place to stop and rest. In order to keep a firm hold on the downspout, I could only wedge a little bit of the sole of my sneaker into the indentation in the brick. When I stopped to rest, I could feel the sharp edge of the brick digging into the bottom of my foot. The longer I stood still, the more uncomfortable and more cramped my foot felt. If I took my foot away from the little ledge to shake out the cramps, I was pretty sure the other foot wouldn't hold me, and I'd fall. I tried taking a step down, but my sneaker slipped off the ledge, and the only way I kept from falling off was by hanging onto the downspout with all my weight until I could reposition my feet. When I did that, the metal column of the downspout moved a little in my hands, and I could hear something scraping above me at the gutter line. Sweat started pouring out of my head and neck. If I pulled the downspout off, I was going to fall for sure. This was bad. This was a lot worse than a tree. My foot was really starting to ache, so I decided in a flash that since I had almost fallen trying to step down, I'd just continue up, with no pauses, so I could maybe get up to the roof and rest. I knew I couldn't think about the downspout anymore. Either it was going to hold me, or it wasn't. I had to stop thinking about it.

I just climbed, one indentation after the next, until I was at the level of the bedroom windows on the second floor. I had to rest a minute because my feet and calves were aching with cramps. There were just a few more steps up to where I could reach the gutter and grab onto something that would let me pull myself onto the roof. It didn't make my legs feel any better to rest like that, so I stepped up until I could feel the rim of the gutter with my hand. I looked up and with a sickening feeling saw that the woodwork below the gutter actually jutted out away from the house. If I grabbed onto something up there and tried to pull myself up, my legs would have to come away from the wall, and I would be dangling by my fingers. This was the electric shock moment in a dream when you know you are going to wake up or you are going to die. But I couldn't make it be a dream. The sweat was cold in my hair and on my neck, and I know I was talking out loud. I must have been leaning with all my weight on the downspout because it made another scraping sound and slid a little way from the corner of the house.

Then I was yelling *Help me! Help me!* My voice didn't even sound like me. It sounded like some kind of gargling, and I realized it wasn't really loud enough. I would have to relax a little. I would have to tilt back my head and let my throat open up. Then I started yelling really loud. My legs were getting wobbly against the brick. I looked down and saw Annabel's beautiful little face looking up at me. I could tell that she knew just what I was feeling. She pushed her way through the base of the hedge and ran screaming for help.

A man in a white shirt appeared in the yard where Annabel had been standing. He was asking me questions, but I couldn't make sense of them. Then he was gone, and Papa was standing there, telling me to hold still. This I understood. It was a relief to have something I thought I could do: hold still. A few times while I was holding still the downspout scraped a little further away from the corner of the house. Pretty soon I was going to be spread out horizontally. If the downspout broke away from the wall, I was sure I would fall down headfirst. I wanted to fall feet first.

The man in the white shirt was back, and he was pulling a ladder into the yard. Then the ladder was next to me up against the brick, and I knew I was going to be all right. I wanted to laugh out loud. I wanted to sing. I tried to tell Papa not to worry, because I knew that if I let go of the downspout and got a grip on the ladder, I could easily swing my legs over to the rungs and climb down. I had done that kind of thing many times in trees. I was actually hoping to show Papa that I could do this, that I could manage something impressive as a climber. But he said *hold still!* in a voice so sharp I knew he meant it. Then he was up on the ladder right next to me. The man in the white shirt held the base of the ladder in place, and Papa looped one arm around my waist and told me to let go of the downspout. Holding me tight in the crook of his arm, he backed down the ladder and set me down on the ground.

I did not feel glad or relieved anymore, because I knew I had caused trouble. The air in the yard was charged with trouble. I almost never caused trouble at Nana and Papa's, only at home and at school. If I were home, my father would be cracking me in the head, and he would mean it. I knew that when Papa told my father what happened, he would crack me in the head. I was starting to feel sad and ashamed.

Papa finished talking to the man in the white shirt, and the man dragged his ladder out of the yard. Annabel had come back. She was standing just behind Papa, looking as if she might start crying.

"Jonathan," Papa said, "you come here."

I approached him, and he took me by the shoulders and turned me away from him. I felt a firm loud whack on my bottom. Then he was stooped low in front of me looking into my eyes, and I started to cry. "That was very, very stupid what you did," he said. "That was unnecessary." Papa looked as though he might start to cry himself. "You could have been *kilt.*"

* * *

I knew what Papa meant. He meant he didn't want me to be killed, that it would make the family sad. But deep down I knew just the opposite, that I could not have been killed, that it just wasn't meant to turn out that way. I could have shot myself through the head with the pellet rifle in Cyrus's basement. I had lost my footing and started falling down from trees so many times I couldn't even remember them all. The man on the tractor said he wanted to blow my brains out. In the summers ahead I would not go for a week without some car or truck's brakes screaming as they approached an intersection where I had coasted through on my bike, thinking hard about other things, not paying attention. If I could have been killed, I would have been.

That bad time at the top of Nana's and Papa's house put me off the idea of climbing buildings, but the climbing urge rose up again whenever I saw a formation of rock out in nature. It started with the western shows I watched on TV in the afternoons, Hopalong Cassidy or The Cisco Kid or The Lone Ranger. There was usually a part of each episode when somebody was being chased on horseback along a dusty trail that cut through formations of rock. Sometimes the riders would dismount and climb up into the rocks and have a gunfight, the bullets of the missed shots singing and whistling off the stones. There were no places like that in Palatine, which was completely flat, but when we went up to the North Woods for our summer vacation, there were rock formations that carried me up to the other world. I remember hearing my mother say the word for them: bluffs. The word, like the bluffs themselves, seemed too charged with feeling to belong in the regular world. There were bluffs over Devil's Lake in Wisconsin, and there were bluffs overlooking Lake Superior in Michigan, and there were lots of high stone ridges that Mother told me had been carved over many, many centuries by the clear rushing streams which in sunlight turned the rocky stream beds the color of honey. The bluffs and ledges were made of granite or limestone or sandstone, each with its special feel and its own kind of weight. When we drove up north, as soon as I would see an outcropping of rock along the side of the road through the car window, I would start making plans. I liked to think that most rock faces would be possible to climb. There had to be at least a little inward taper and some crevices or plants growing out of the rock for handholds and footholds. All I could think about was climbing rock ledges. I thought about it so much and made so many plans that I was able to label instantly every new rock formation I saw as Possible, Impossible, or Perfect.

One morning in the North Woods we took a day trip to a state park, and as soon as we settled our stuff in a picnic area along a rushing river, I saw a Perfect ledge. You had to cross the river over the dry tops of the stones to get to it, but after looking at it for a while, I figured out which stones would get me there. As soon as I could get free, I made my way to the opposite bank where the granite ledge rose up to a piney ridge overhead. I don't know exactly how high it went. It could have been five houses high, or maybe ten. I looked back across the river to our blankets and table and saw that my parents and Annabel had started on a hike. This was a relief, because I didn't want anybody watching me or calling for me to come down. The ledge was ridged and creased in such a perfect way I didn't have to stop and plan. The footholds and handholds were just there where I expected them to be, and as I made my way up along the warm stone, I could hear the river whooshing in my ears and feel the white force of the sun on my cheeks.

The climb went fast, and when I paused to look down to the water, I saw that I was much higher up than I pictured I would be. I didn't want to think about getting scared, so I kept going, but leaning harder into the rock face. The good footholds continued, but the higher I got, the more I thought I should take smaller, slower steps. I don't know if it was because I was up so high, or whether there is just something about sound and rock, but the river seemed to get louder the higher I got, and for some reason it sounded like it was warning me. I was not far from the top, and I could feel no-energy tingles in my calf muscles, so I paused to rest. A bee was buzzing around my sweaty hair, so I raised up my arm to swat it away, but the motion of doing that upset my balance just a little, and I glanced down again at the river which now seemed tremendously far below the white rubber soles of my sneakers. The bee wouldn't let me alone, but I knew I had to let it do whatever it was going to do, because I needed to hold on.

The next ten feet up would not be gradual. The narrow indented ridge I had been moving along came to an end, and I would have to step up to a series of parallel ridges above me. But at this height it did not feel good to lift either foot from the rock. And if I did lift a foot to step up to the next level, I would need a handhold, and I couldn't see one in the rock, only some green scrub growing out of cracks. Back, I thought. I would inch my way backwards and back down. But after a few little steps I realized it wouldn't work. I could not see where I was going, and the ledge was too narrow for me to turn my feet around. Then I knew. I was too high. I was in trouble again, the way I was at the top of Nana and Papa's house, only this time there were no people, no safe yard, no ladder. The horrible feeling started and I was saying out loud: *this is really happening*, and then the sound of the river exploded in my ears.

At those moments when you can feel your pulse pounding along the side of your head and your heart is pumping so hard, you stop thinking and move. I was crying, but I was also shrieking. I was shrieking to myself to *go! Goddamnit, go!go!go!*

I don't really know what I did or how I did it. I remember stepping up onto each new ledge without stopping, even if there was only an inch or two to catch the sole of my shoe. The only thing I could see overhead was bits of green scrub, and I grabbed for it, and when it started to come away from the stone I grabbed the plant just above it, and I knew that I was not going to stop moving no matter what my legs felt like. I was snuffling and swearing out loud, and if there had been a living being in my way between me and the crest of that ledge, I would have killed it.

I jackknifed my upper body over the lip of the last ridge and wriggled forward until my whole body was on flat ground. For a while I just lay there sweating and panting, my breath honking out of me in a way that burned my lungs. When my chest stopped heaving, I stood up. A family hiking on the trail along the crest stopped and stared at me. I could see their faces were full of questions, but I knew I could never explain. I sat down where I was, turned my back to them and looked over the river. When Papa carried me down the ladder from the top of his house, he told me that my climb had been unnecessary. But it was necessary. This ledge too was necessary, even more necessary. I was still shaking with it. I could tell that the family who watched me crawl over the top of the ledge was still looking at me, but I could not bear to turn around and face them. I knew they had no idea about the other world, and no idea about me.

FOR LOVE

Not long after I started going to kindergarten, a feeling came over me that something was trying to reach me, a message I was almost but not quite getting, although there was a clue. A phrase from a song on one of Uncle Desmond's records would pop up in my thoughts before I would go to sleep at night, or I would find myself singing it out loud as I walked to school in the morning: *there's oh such a hungry yearning burning inside of me.* A man's voice sang this on Uncle Desmond's record, and it sounded to me like he really had the feeling. I started to feel it, too, but I didn't realize what I had it for, until I heard Nana and Papa's recordings of "The Chocolate Soldier."

This happened in Nana and Papa's living room on a Sunday night in winter. It was snowing outside, and there was a fire in the fireplace. Nana and Papa were in their armchairs, my mother and father were lying back together on the sofa, and my sister Annabel, Uncle Desmond and I were lying on the carpet in front of the fire. Papa suggested that we change the music and listen to "The Chocolate Soldier," which I had never heard before. I pictured a full-grown soldier made of chocolate, and I wanted to laugh, but the feeling was more than just funny. "The Chocolate Soldier" was a story, a whole operetta on three records, and I wanted to hear it. Papa showed me the illustration on the cover of the album. Against a chocolate brown background were the golden faces of a soldier and his bride. The soldier's golden hair flowed back from his forehead in waves, and the same kind of golden light lit up the hair and on the cheeks of the bride. The soldier held the tips of the bride's fingers in his hands, and they both looked out ahead of them with expressions showing that they were overwhelmed by something beyond them. These, I would learn later, were the faces of the singers Nelson Eddy and Rise Stephens, and though I had never seen them before, I recognized them immediately.

The Chocolate Soldier isn't really a soldier at all. He's a clown, and he doesn't think he's really strong or brave. But he meets the Lady, and he is completely in love with her. Many other soldiers love the Lady, and she wonders if she should really love such a foolish soldier, but as they tease and play with each other, she knows that he is her love. When the Chocolate Soldier thinks he has lost her, it is worse than if she had died. He sings that there isn't really a world, not even a night-world "while my lady sleeps." But she wakes up, and all the Chocolate Soldier's silliness and play have been good enough, and she realizes she does love him, and, finally, they both know it and sing, "Come, come, I love you dearly." The Lady sees that his clowning has been his secret way of making himself known to her, and that he is really a hero, and in the duet that ends the operetta, they sing together, "Come, come, I love you only, my hero, mine!" They have the hungry yearning burning feeling, and they will have it forever.

I realized this love feeling had always been around me, and not just in stories and in songs. I think sometimes my mother and father had it, even Nana and Papa. There had to be a hero and a lady the hero loved and who loved the hero. I was small and thin and dark, and nothing at all like Nelson Eddy with wavy blond hair and handsome man's jaw and the gold braid crossing the chest of his soldier's uniform, but when the romantic love feeling rose up in me, it was as if I swelled up inside Nelson Eddy and really was a hero. It made me different, braver and more serious. I pictured myself giving off a golden glow. It also made me sing. I used to sing a lot anyway, but now all I wanted to do was sing the love songs in "The Chocolate Soldier." But to really sing them the way I felt them, I had to sing them loud, which meant I had to be all by myself somewhere. To sing out the way I wanted to, I needed a lot of space.

As soon as I got the romantic love feeling and started singing like a hero, I pictured myself singing to—"serenading" (another word I automatically knew)—my Lady. I knew that if I sang my "Chocolate Soldier" songs to the right girl in the right situation, she would feel what I felt and we would have romance. At first she would think I was just funny, just a clown, but she would secretly like that, and if I could get to certain songs, she would see me as a hero.

In bed at night and whenever I could, I thought about how I would set up the love singing. It could only be outside, not in somebody's house. Most of the girls who lived on our street were older than I was, some of them even teenagers. The littler ones I knew did not seem to go out of their houses much. At least they didn't wander down around my house where I could see them. Sometimes on warm summer nights during Daylight Saving Time, a whole bunch of neighborhood kids would come together in somebody's yard, and we would play a chasing game like tag or capture the flag. It was very nice running around together in the soft air. As it got darker and hazier, fireflies would come out, and just running through that smoky light whooping and shrieking felt very close to the other world.

On those evenings the kids were different than they were at school, wilder, happier. You could talk to anybody. You could grab somebody's wrist you didn't even know and twirl them around. Somebody might run up and knock you down for the fun of it, but not hurt you. You got to find out the people you liked. One night when it was almost dark I realized I liked Beth Bartell, who lived about a block and a half down our street and who was in Annabel's grade. Even though she was older than I was, Beth Bartell was very small and delicate and her brown hair went out from the sides of her head like a round bubble and tucked in somehow under her ears. She had a little nose and bright eyes, and she was cute the way a kitten or a puppy is cute. She was also very shy, and she never seemed to say anything or run very fast to get away during the games. I had a strong feeling that night when I went home that Beth Bartell could be my Lady. I started to have the hungry yearning burning feeling. I started planning how I would sing to her.

Beth Bartell was hard to find. I was allowed to go out and play on my own in the neighborhood, and I took to walking down the Bartells' end of our street. I got to be very familiar with their house, which was a ranch house, and how the bushes were arranged around the front windows and how easy it would be to climb up on their garage and walk around anywhere I wanted to on their roof. In my plans, Beth would wander outside by herself one Saturday morning. I would happen to be there, and I might have my axe in my holster or maybe my knife out while I was carving the end of a spear. I would be behind some hedges, or maybe completely hidden inside, and when she got close enough, I would start to sing.

I am just a Chocolate Soldier man

For me you feel great pity

Just a funny Chocolate Soldier man

In a uniform so pretty

A silly Chocolate Soldier Man

Just made to tease the misses

So sweet I'd melt

If e'er I felt

A full-grown maiden's kisses

In my plans, if she heard me sing enough songs and got used to it, then it might be possible, although I was not completely clear about this, that she might sing back to me in a duet. I wanted this to happen very much, but I wasn't sure I could set it up. It was hard to picture Beth Bartell singing. I had hardly ever heard her talk. My feeling was that if it was going to work, she would first have to get used to me and my songs. Then maybe there could be the duet I was hoping for:

Jonathan: *To tell the truth I never knew*
There were maidens such as you

Beth Bartell: *Do you mean that I am charming?*

Jonathan: *In a manner most alarming*

Beth Bartell: *Each time we meet you're someone new*
How can I be sure of you?

Beth Bartell would not come out of her house. I watched her mother and father come and go. I watched her sister and her friends sun bathing on their lawn. Every now and then I would hear the old lady who lived in the house with the hedge I was hiding in tapping at her window and shaking her head at me. She wanted me to get out of there. I tried some other bushes, and then I sat on the curb for a long time, waiting.

Then one day I just decided to sing it. I was across the street and a little way down from the Bartells' house. I thought maybe she would hear me and come out. It actually felt good to let it out. I thought I sounded better than usual, very loud and very high.

I am — just a Chocolate Soldier Man

For me you feel great pity

Beth Bartell never did come out, and after a while I stopped thinking about her as my Lady. By this time school had started again, and there was a real Lady in my class, a new girl named Gwendolyn Bliss. The second I heard the teacher read her name and turned around to see who it was, I felt the hungry yearning burning.

Gwendolyn Bliss was the smallest girl in the class. She was so slender and delicate that she seemed almost breakable. She had blue watery eyes and frizzy blond hair that caught the sunlight like spun glass. When she was called on in class, she spoke so softly Mrs. Roederer had to ask her to speak up. "Gwendolyn," she would say, "you are *whispering*." But whispering was as loud as Gwendolyn could get. I knew this right away, and I knew Gwendolyn could not bear to be called on. I don't really know how I got to know her so well, but after a few days I felt I knew her completely. She didn't really talk, to me or to anybody else. But at recess I tried to be around her as much as I could, and she didn't mind. I did not have words for it then, but I knew something had happened to Gwendolyn that made going to school and reciting and talking to other kids almost impossible. When I could get her to look at me, her eyes seemed to be saying, "Don't you *know*?" I thought I did know, and I wanted to protect her. Somehow I knew that this is what a hero did, and I wanted Gwendolyn to be my Lady. She didn't say anything about it, but I think she wanted this too. She let me be around her. I could talk to her, but she didn't talk back. She didn't have to.

On our playground there were two jungle gyms, a new big one with complicated extensions and inner chambers and an old one, which was just a simple box with evenly spaced bars going up and down every few feet. The kids only wanted to play on the new one, and since Gwendolyn never wanted to be with the kids, especially at noisy, wild times like recess and lunch, she would stand way off to the side by the old one. Sometimes a boy from our class would approach Gwendolyn and start to tease her, and I would go over and give him a shove. Then maybe he and his friends would come over to me and start saying, *"Jonathan likes Gwendolyn, Jonathan likes Gwendolyn,"* but I would just stand there looking at them until they went away. I knew I was protecting Gwendolyn and that she was glad. It was working. It occurred to me that the old jungle gym was perfect for protection, so I led Gwendolyn inside, ducking under the bars, until she was right in the center where she could sit on the ground in the inmost square. From the outside it looked a little like she was in jail in there, but she was always willing to go inside and sit quietly until the bell rang and we had to go back to class. It felt lonely, but in a good way, to be standing guard next to the old jungle gym, not running around or playing with the other kids. Protecting Gwendolyn felt important. It felt like my job.

The more days I spent standing close to where Gwendolyn was squatting and guarding her, the more I felt the love feeling, even though she never talked. It seemed that every minute of the day, no matter where I was, I could see her just behind my eyes. I couldn't see her clearly, just an impression of her pale little knees and wrists, the delicate point of her chin, her wet, worried eyes, and the bright frizz of her hair. After school at home I couldn't get her out of my mind. I felt the hungry yearning burning feeling.

I was starting to want to sing my love songs to Gwendolyn, but it never felt right out there on the playground. I had barely been able to talk to her, and I was pretty sure it would frighten her if I started singing my songs, especially if it was loud. But at night in my dark room I could picture it. Gwendolyn would be squatting in the innermost square of the old jungle gym, and I would be guarding her. Something would have happened, and the other kids would have gone away somewhere, and I would sing.

Ah---sweet mystery of life at last I've found you

For---at last I know the secret of it all

Then one day Gwendolyn was gone. For several days her chair had been empty in her row, and then Mrs. Roederer told us that Gwendolyn had moved away. *Moved away.* It is hard to explain the kind of sadness I felt. It was as if someone had lifted something solid up out of my chest, leaving just a weak, airy space. Later I would understand how suddenly and completely you can lose a beloved person, but Gwendolyn, I realized, had been lost to me even when I thought I had her. That's what the hurt, worried look in her eyes had been saying. The worst thing had already happened to her. There was no protecting her. She could only keep moving away.

It must have been at about this time that I asked Annabel to marry me. I realized now that people you felt the love feeling for could move away, and it was at least possible that you could go the rest of your life without having that feeling with somebody else who had it at the same time. The idea of that made me really sad. Annabel was safe. She was my sister. I knew I could never feel too lonely with Annabel. She told me that brothers couldn't marry their sisters, which I kind of knew, but she understood what I meant. She told me she hoped she could marry Burt Lancaster or somebody just like him, but that when we were grown-ups and if there was nobody else to marry, we could live together on a ranch.

The next year I had the love feeling for Linda Bluestone. It was very different from my feeling for Gwendolyn. It was much livelier. Linda Bluestone had been in my class since kindergarten, and she didn't live far from my street. I just hadn't paid very much attention to her before, but a few days into the new school year she was standing in front of our class giving a report, and I realized that she was beautiful. She was beautiful the way the stars on the covers of Annabel's movie magazines were beautiful. She had thick shiny black hair, which was braided into pigtails tied in bright bows. She was always happy, so happy that as soon as you even started to talk to her she would laugh, which crinkled up the corners of her eyes in a way that made you want to laugh too. Probably the reason I didn't love her before is that she was so happy she just went along with everything and blended in, or maybe she became beautiful all of a sudden.

I wanted to be around Linda Bluestone as much as possible. Whenever I could I would twist myself around at my desk to look at her or to whisper something funny. My teacher, Miss Rodd, told my mother I was being a problem, and when Mother mentioned this at the table, I got a crack in the head from my father. But I couldn't stop paying attention to Linda Bluestone. She liked me. She laughed at everything I said, and this made me want to be funnier than ever. I practiced making certain faces in the mirror at home, and I learned how to cross my eyes, which always made me feel a little car sick. At recess the boys played with the boys, and the girls played with the girls, but I couldn't stop myself from looking over every few seconds to see what she was doing. The girls mainly skipped rope on long, extra thick ropes the teachers handed out at recess. A girl would hold each end of the rope and swing it around in loops while another girl would step in and jump. They would jump in rhythm to chants they all knew, like "my boyfriend's name is Fatty, he lives in Cincinnati." It seemed like every time I looked over, it was Linda's turn to jump, and she would go on and on without stopping the rope. It looked to me as if she was barely lifting her shoes off the pavement, but she seemed to know exactly how and when to make a little hop. When Linda Bluestone was skipping rope, she looked like she was in a happy trance, and I wanted to be in a trance like that.

The best thing I could do was to make her laugh. She laughed at everything. The more serious she tried to be, the easier it was to crack her up. Sometimes Miss Rodd would have been mad at us in class, and there would be a hush in the room, with everybody keeping our heads down close to our desks while we did our work. This was always the time to catch Linda's attention. If I could just twist my head around and get low so she couldn't help seeing me from her seat, which was a couple places behind me in the next row, I had her. I could cross my eyes or put the eraser end of my pencil up my nose and she would erupt. I loved watching her try not to laugh. She would clamp her mouth shut tight and close her eyes so hard her nose crinkled, but then it would just come out of her, a sound like steam from a kettle at first, then her gasps and high giggles which got me and everyone around her going too. I knew I was being a problem, and it was getting worse, but there was nothing I could do.

I think Mrs. Bluestone drove Linda to school in the morning, because I never saw her on the way, even though I changed my route to go close to her house. But she and her friends walked home after school, and I got my chance to be as funny as I wanted. It felt so good making those plans. There were a bunch of trees between the school and her house that were perfect for climbing and hiding in. I liked to run out ahead of everybody after school and get up on a branch that went over the sidewalk where she and her friends would pass by. Just as they were going under me, I would let out one of my high hooting sounds. I might even make it say *Leeeeeeeeeendaaa Bloooooooooostone*. This really worked, especially the first time. Linda and her friends stopped still on the walk. They looked behind them and all around, but no one looked up. I could hardly keep quiet watching them. After a while they caught on, and I could see them looking up ahead into the trees as they walked. They would see where I was, and when they passed under me, they would say, "Hello, Jonathan. Up in the tree again, Jonathan? Har-dee-har-har-har." But I could tell from the way Linda acted at school that she liked it and she liked me.

At night in my room I liked thinking up new plans for Linda Bluestone. One that I really wanted to try but couldn't figure out how to do was to fall down wounded, really hurt but not too bad, at her feet. I was pretty sure this would make her feel worried and want to take care of me. It would have to happen on the playground or on her way home from school. Somebody might have hit me in the forehead with a rock and made a gash, or maybe I fell out of a tree just as she was getting close. The problem was that in my plan, Linda would be by herself, but she was never by herself. She was always with two or three other girls, and I didn't want them in on taking care of me, so my idea of being wounded was just something I thought about a lot.

At school I wanted to be as funny as possible, but Miss Rodd was completely against it. I think she thought I wanted to make trouble just to bother her, but I didn't want that at all. I kind of liked Miss Rodd. She seemed young and nice for a teacher, although her clothes had a sour little smell when you got up close to her. Actually, I wished Miss Rodd thought I was funny. I wished she liked me. I just liked being funny. Certain remarks and sayings came right out of me, without any planning. Of course the best feeling was to hear Linda Bluestone's high giggles from her desk behind me, but most of the time the whole class laughed when I got off a good one. Miss Rodd told me that my good ones were "unnecessary." She said it very slowly. She said that if I kept talking without raising my hand, "there would be trouble." Most of the kids thought trouble meant going to the principal, Mrs. Gilooley, which actually wasn't too bad, but I knew Miss Rodd could call my mother again, and I would end up getting cracked in the head.

Miss Rodd kept me after school one afternoon and told me I had to learn to keep my comments to myself. I knew I did, too, and most of the time I did, but that did not stop them from coming up into my mind. In fact, knowing I couldn't get off a good one out loud only made a lot more good ones come up. Having to be quiet made me funnier and funnier, and sometimes I had to duck my whole head under the lid of my desk because trying not to laugh at my good ones made me make faces and made me start to laugh in a way I knew would make Miss Rodd mad. The only thing that helped, finally, was imagining my glass booth.

Not only in Miss Rodd's class but for several years to come, I pictured a glassed-in booth up toward the ceiling at the rear of the classroom. The booth was very realistic. You'd get up to it through a trap door over a wooden ladder built permanently into the wall. The booth was built specially for me, and I had the only key. The arrangement was that I could leave my seat whenever I felt like it and go up to the glass booth where nobody could see what I was doing, but I could see and hear what was going on in class, if I wanted to. Inside the booth was a chair where I could sit and look out over the class, and there was a microphone next to the chair. Anytime I was up there and came up with a good one, I could say it over the microphone, and everyone would hear it. It would not be making trouble, just a regular part of class. There was plenty of room in the booth for me to lie out on the floor when I wanted and to think about other things, or just rest.

It really helped, picturing the glass booth. I thought about being up there even when I was at home after school. If people had asked me about it then, I probably would have told them there really was a glass booth like that in my room at school. Most of the time it felt like there was.

I was going to have to wait awhile before getting off good ones could be part of my regular personality. I needed to find other ways to express my love feeling to Linda Bluestone. It didn't take long to decide that she would probably like presents. I thought a lot about giving her presents and what kind of presents I wanted her to have. I don't think my first ones were very good. They were mainly old things that I used to like. I put a bunch of them—a sheriff's badge that would pin onto your shirt, some little metal army men from a whole huge set of army men Uncle Desmond gave me, and some loose sticks of gum, which I put into an envelope—into a shoe box, which I wanted to wrap with wrapping paper, but I couldn't find any. Something told me that this present wasn't going to be right, at least not right for a girl, so I went into Annabel's room and looked around for something. I knew I shouldn't take her stuff, especially her important stuff, but I thought maybe I could find something she didn't care about anymore. I decided that she might not care about a little china cardinal, which she probably got at the Ben Franklin in town. It was cute, but pretty small, and it wasn't on her main shelf. I felt bad about taking the cardinal, because Annabel was pretty careful about her things, but I needed something I thought a girl would like for the shoebox.

My plan was to give Linda Bluestone the presents first thing in the morning when she came into the room before school started. She would take her seat, and there I would be and I'd plunk the shoebox down in front of her, and she'd be surprised. But the more I thought about it while I was lying in my bed, the more it seemed the shoebox wasn't right. It was too big. The things inside didn't take up very much room. I could picture them sliding into a corner and not looking very good. I needed some tissue paper, the kind that filled up Christmas boxes. I could crumple up the tissue paper and separate the different presents and fill up the box. Early in the morning, before my father and mother got up, I went down to the pantry and looked for tissue paper, but I there wasn't any. There were plenty of old newspapers, but they wouldn't be right for a present. It seemed to me there was not much difference between tissue paper and toilet paper, so I unrolled a lot of it from the bathroom and rearranged the shoebox. It looked a lot better. Just before I left the house after breakfast, I took a few packs of Kool-Aid from the cupboard and lay them in the box on top of the toilet paper. I don't even know what made me think of that. I just came up with it.

That morning at school it didn't work out the way I thought. Linda did not come into the room until class was just about to start. There was no time for me to visit with her by the coats or in front of her desk. Miss Rodd was already telling us to take our seats when Linda walked by my desk. "Hey," I said to her, "got you something," and I handed her the shoebox. I couldn't see her reaction because I had to pay attention. But as soon as I could, when we were doing silent reading, I looked back and caught her eye. She had a funny look, as if she wanted to ask me something. She was mouthing some words but not making any sound. She was mouthing "Kool-Aid" and "toilet paper." I could tell she didn't think of it as a present. She wanted it to be funny, and I saw right away that it wasn't really a present at all, at least not a good present, to a girl. After lunch the shoebox was on my desk with all the stuff in it. That felt really bad.

I needed to get the right kind of present. I wanted Linda to be surprised and amazed. Just by luck I got another good idea. My mother had two jewelry boxes, a little green leather one where she kept her rings and what she called her good jewelry and a big one full of what she called "costume jewelry." I always thought the big box was the good one, because the necklaces and bracelets and pins in it were bigger and shinier and more colorful. The glass stones were bright green and red and deep blue like the jewels in the strongboxes in a pirate movie. When you opened the top of the big jewelry box and saw the light flashing on all of it tangled up together, it looked like treasure. Mother used to let Annabel play with her costume jewelry. She and her friends would put it on when they played dress up. I knew it was all right for me to go into the big box, so I did, and I took out some things for Linda Bluestone. I took out two necklaces, a bracelet and a big pin. Each piece was a different color. One of the necklaces was ruby, the other one emerald, the bracelet was diamond, and the pin had orange stones, the color of apricots. I thought they looked beautiful lying next to each other, and even without them, the big jewelry box still looked full. That night when I pictured Linda looking at the sparkling jewelry, I got a very excited feeling.

I knew the shoebox was all wrong, so in the morning before I left for school, I tore a section of aluminum foil off the roll in the kitchen and wrapped up the jewelry. This time I waited for recess to give Linda the present. I wanted to give it to her when she was by herself, but she was never by herself, so I gave it to her while she was standing in a line of her friends waiting for her turn to skip rope. I just wanted to hand it to her and get out of there, but I had to say something, so I said, "here you go," and ran away. At

The Other World

lunchtime, Linda walked over to my table and said, "Are they for keeps?" I told her they were, and after lunch her friends followed me all over the playground singing, "Someone's got a girlfriend."

That didn't stop me from wanting to give Linda presents. My friend Cyrus and I were out in the fields one bright afternoon, and we made our way down into a grove of overgrown sumac where there was sometimes standing water and frogs. I looked overhead and saw that there were puffy clusters of what looked like red velvet pouches attached to the sumac leaves. I picked one and saw that it was like a mitten, and with the sun shining on its red and purple folds, it was very beautiful. I could imagine seeing velvet like that in a pirate chest along with the jewels and coins. I knew right away I wanted Linda Bluestone to have these, so I picked a bunch of them and wedged them into my holster. I thought they might amaze her because they were not only beautiful, they were from nature.

In the morning I got a pillowcase out of the linen closet and folded the red velvet pouches inside of it and took them to school. I waited till after lunch, when she was at her desk and her friends weren't right there, but something had gone wrong with the package. There were dark red sticky stains all over the pillowcase, and when we looked inside, the fruits weren't puffy and velvety anymore. They were dark and wet. Linda stepped back when she looked inside the pillowcase. She said, *"Oooh,"* and I could see she was really scared. She said, "Are they *alive?*" I thought she was starting to cry. I grabbed the pillowcase up off her desk and stuffed it into the wastebasket next to Miss Rodd's desk. I couldn't stand even to think about the slimy red fruits stuck together like leeches. It also made me mad that my hands and arms and the front of my shirt were stained and sticky. It was one of those times when I knew that even more things were about to go wrong, and they did.

As soon as Miss Rodd came into the room, she asked if she could see me out in the hall. This was always bad. I was sure she was going to tell me I shouldn't have brought the spoiled sumac pouches to school, and that she was going to call home, and I would have to explain about the pillow case. But that was not it. She had just gotten a telephone call from Mrs. Bluestone who wanted to know about some jewelry that Linda had brought home from school. Miss Rodd said that Linda told her mother I had given her the jewelry. She asked me if this was true, and I said yes. The skin around Miss Rodd's mouth pulled in tight around her teeth. She asked me where I got the jewelry. I said I just had it, it was mine. I meant that I got it at home, out of the big box we were allowed to use and play with. "Jonathan," Miss Rodd said, "Did you *steal* that jewelry?" I said no, but I said it way too loud, and Miss Rodd said she didn't believe me, and she took me by the hand down to Mrs. Gilooley.

My mother usually didn't get really mad at me, just my father. But that afternoon she was really mad. I don't think it was that I had given her jewelry to Linda. She was mad and embarrassed that Mrs. Bluestone had to call the school about me. She told me Mrs. Bluestone had almost called the police. *The police.* My mother put her face down close to mine. She was angrier than I had ever seen her. Her chin was trembling. "Jonathan Force," she said, "why can't you behave?" When my father got home, he talked to Mother and then he talked to me. He would ask me a question, I would answer him, and then he gave me a crack in the head. It went on and on, until Mother was crying and made him stop.

After that it was harder to feel the love feeling for Linda Bluestone, and it went away. It didn't feel too bad, because I could see that she was always so happy. There just wasn't anything I could give her.

THE END OF BASEBALL

When you are a kid you never think about things suddenly changing. Maybe you do if your mother dies or if you have to move to a different state, but usually you just wake up in the morning and expect things are going to stay the way they were when you went to bed. But in the summer between fifth grade and Junior High, something, what felt like the biggest thing in my life, came to an end, and only now, in the declining years of my life, have I begun to find words for it.

That summer there were no words, just sensations and urgent impulses. I would awake to a flash of sky and sun, my eyes barely open before I could feel myself pedaling my fat tired bike to the park where there would still be dew on the infield grass and the faintly sweet, faintly sour smell of the mustard colored dirt. The airless necessities of school had at last opened up into summer, and summer was baseball.

Baseball was not a game I played. It was not a diversion or even a vivid preoccupation. Baseball was an enchanted realm in which I was at once eager explorer and captive, a realm as numinous and charged with feeling as Pan's Arcady or the Garden of Eden. By the time I was eight I was held fast and rapt in the rhythms and textures of baseball—the smack of the ball in the oiled pocket of my mitt, the dink, pop, or crack of the bat striking the ball, the dark dot of a fly ball's arc against sky as I braced to sense its trajectory and took off to get under it, the target, the orange pancake target of the catcher's mitt behind the plate, and I, squinting down from the mound at that target, fingers caressing the raised seams of the ball, savoring, like an assassin, the pause before rocking into my windup.

That summer between fifth grade and junior high would mark a change in all of this, a world opening up to still greater worlds as my friends and I advanced from Junior Little League to the Ten-to-Twelve division—Little League itself. This meant you got to play on the good diamond, which had lights at night. You also got full uniforms with white or gray jerseys and pants, long socks with a loop on the bottom that went over your other socks, and a hat which was just like the real hat of a major league team.

There were try-outs for the ten-to-twelve teams, and the managers picked you. All the teams were supposed to be equal, but they really weren't. The Indians and the Cubs were the best teams every year, because Mr. Hightower and Mr. Spinks were the best managers, and they always knew who the kids were and who was good, and they always ended up with the best players. I wanted to get on a pretty good team, but I didn't care too much which one, except the Padres, which had the worst uniforms. I was one of the best players in the eight-and nines, but I was a pitcher and also one of the smallest kids, and the pitching rubber in ten-to-twelves was ten feet farther away from the plate and it was up on a little mound.

The tryouts were on a really hot Saturday morning. The managers got everybody signed up for their positions and then had each group go out to a base or to the outfield somewhere and take turns fielding balls. I was with the pitchers and catchers, and after we warmed up for a while, I got in a line behind the pitcher's mound and waited for my turn to pitch to a catcher behind the plate. One of the dads stood in the batter's box, but he didn't swing.

Mr. Hightower, the manager of the Indians, was in charge of the pitcher tryouts, and I was nervous waiting for my turn, because he had a voice like someone with laryngitis, and I thought he might turn out to be kind of mean. "Okay, Force," he said, when it was my turn. He already knew who I was. "I hear you're the strike out king. Let's see what you can do." The mound on the good diamond was built up on a little hill, so you actually looked down at the batter and the catcher. Something about it made the catcher's mitt look really far away, not just ten extra feet.

I threw a pitch, and it was pretty good. It made the right kind of smack in the glove, and I started to feel better. Mr. Hightower said, "That's good, now see if you can bring that down a little bit, right at the knees." I was starting to like the way he talked, and I liked that he thought I knew how to throw my pitch a little lower. I threw the next pitch as hard as I could, and it was lower, but right over the plate. Mr. Hightower didn't say anything for a while, and I kept pitching to the target. Wayne Stegner, my old eight-and-nines coach, was standing behind the backstop, and he was shouting things like, "You're throwing smoke, Lefty, you're burning them in." I didn't look up at him, and I really wished he would go away.

After I had thrown a bunch of pitches Mr. Hightower said, "Nice job," and asked me if I had any other pitches. I said I did. I had a curve, which my father taught me how to throw by putting my first two fingers right next to the seam, and then twisting my wrist as I let go of the ball. I thought my curve was amazing because it would go straight, but with a funny spin on it, until about ten feet before it got to the target. Then it would seem almost to stop in mid-air and float over to the right. My father laughed when he caught my curves. He said I had "a big hook."

I actually wanted to show Mr. Hightower my curve, but I had never thrown one with a batter standing there. The dad was batting on the left side of the plate now, and I was trying to figure out where to aim in order to make my curve end up in the target. I decided that if I threw it toward his hip, it might end up over the plate. I tried it, and for a second I thought the ball might actually go behind the batter's back, but it kind of hesitated, the way I hoped it would, and started floating over to the right. The extra distance from the new mound made it curve even more than usual, and the ball went from almost behind the batter's butt to the front of his pants and then over to the far side of the plate. The dad batting laughed and said something, and behind the backstop Wayne Stegner shouted, "Hey, Lefty, where'd *that* come from?" Mr. Hightower said, "That's a helluva hook," and let the next kid in line pitch.

That night after supper, some kids called me up and said they heard I made the Indians, which made me feel excited but also nervous, and then Mr. Hightower called up and told me I really was on the Indians and that I was going to be the only ten-year-old pitcher. I had a funny feeling about being picked for the Indians. I knew they were the best team and they had most of the best play-

The Other World

ers, but when I pictured those kids in my mind, they were all big kids, and I didn't know them very well. I pictured the best pitcher on the Indians, Craig Cummerford. He was twelve and really big. The kids said he was five feet nine. His legs and arms were at least twice as big around as mine. I wasn't even five feet yet.

Later, when practices started and I came up to bat against Craig Cummerford, his pitches would seem to hiss past me before I could even think about swinging. They cracked into the catcher's mitt with such force I felt jittery in my stomach. I couldn't stand to think about what it would feel like if one of Craig Cummerford's pitches hit me. My father would always tell me that the worst thing in baseball was to be afraid of the ball. When I stood up to bat and Craig Cummerford was going through his wind up, I tried to squint back at him and tighten my grip on the bat like I was ready to take a big swing, but I knew I wasn't going to do it. I wanted him to throw balls and walk me. The truth was that I didn't want to get hit. He was a really good pitcher, and he almost always threw strikes, so I knew I had to swing, but I also knew I could never hit a pitch from Craig Cummerford. From the dugout Mr. Hightower would say, "You're late, you're swinging late." From behind the backstop my father would call out, "You're waving at the ball," and I was.

The kids in my grade I played baseball with were kind of jealous that I got on the Indians, but for some reason I wasn't that glad about it. I was pretty excited before the first game, mainly because of the new uniform and the way INDIANS was written in orange and black letters across the chest of the jersey. Also, my father took me to the sporting goods store and bought me a pair of spikes and a leather pitching toe that screwed in over the front of my left shoe. The smallest pair of spikes they had were one size too big for me, but my father bought them anyway. He said I would grow into them and that we could stuff some cloth up into the toe area where the extra room was. I was glad they were too big, because they made my feet look bigger.

Even when we were warming up before our first game, I could tell something was wrong. I didn't really know the other kids on the Indians very well, and the one kid I did know, Gary Spender, wasn't much fun to be around. He was also the worst player on the team, and the only reason he was on the Indians was because his dad was one of the managers with Mr. Hightower. Just before the game started, Mr. Hightower called us over and read out the starting lineup. It was the opening game, and I knew Craig Cummerford was going to pitch and that I wasn't going to be playing any other position, but it still surprised me for some reason that my name wasn't called and I wasn't going to play. I felt like I might even cry, which would have been really embarrassing, so I started walking fast out toward the outfield.

Maybe my face looked funny, because Mr. Hightower called after me and said I was going to be his fireman. I asked him what that was, and he said fireman was a name for a relief pitcher, a pitcher who came in and put the fire out. I liked the idea of being a fireman for the Indians, but after the game got started, I realized that there wasn't going to be any fire. Craig Cummerford was striking out just about every batter, and the Indians were getting a lot of hits and scoring runs in every inning. The games were six innings long, and by the fifth inning the Indians were winning by about sixteen to nothing. There was no reason for Mr. Hightower to take out Craig Cummerford and put me in, but I wanted him to do it anyway.

I started to make a plan to slip away behind the bench and go home, but I knew my father was somewhere in the stands watching the game and that I would really get it if I went home without him. When it got to be the last half of the sixth inning, Mr. Hightower decided to put in a lot of subs. I was sent out to play right field, and Gary Spender was put in center, which made it worse. It was practically dark, and I'm not sure I would have been able to see a ball if it came out to me, but I could see Craig Cummerford winding up and then hear the ball smacking into the catcher's mitt. When the inning was over, I hadn't even moved. As I ran back to the bench, I saw that our team was forming a big huddle. They started the cheer, "Two, four, six, eight, who do we appreciate..." and I ran right past them into the parking lot to look for our car. I felt really terrible, and I hoped my father wouldn't make me talk to him, because I didn't want to start to cry.

A few games after that, Mr. Hightower told me I was going to pitch against the Dodgers. It was going to be a Saturday afternoon game, which felt to me less important than a night game, because there wouldn't be the fuzzed, golden look of everything under the lights. The Dodgers were supposed to be a pretty crummy team, but I kind of liked them because of the bright blue color of their hats and letters. Also, some of my friends from school were on the Dodgers. As soon as Mr. Hightower told me I was going to pitch, I started making pictures of myself up on the mound against the Dodgers on a bright, hot Saturday afternoon, but I couldn't make the pictures seem any good. I knew when the time came I would probably go into my trance, but when I thought about the game in advance, it just seemed like a lot of effort to be throwing all those pitches.

Even so, the night before the game, I did not sleep for one minute. All I could do was make pictures of myself going through my wind-up on the mound and throwing toward the target, but every time something was a little off. I wouldn't shift my weight forward enough, so I would be off balance when I let go of the ball, or I'd be so off balance at the end of my wind-up that I couldn't throw at all. I wondered for a while in the dark whether I might completely forget how to pitch. I pictured myself being totally wild, throwing the ball way behind the batters' backs and over the umpire's head into the backstop. As it was started to get light out, I could hear it begin to rain. At first there was the tapping and hissing of a drizzle, then the splat of the big drops. I really didn't want the game to be rained out. I wanted to be able to stop picturing bad things.

It stopped raining by the middle of the morning, but the sky did not clear up. When I went over to the park at noon to warm up, the light outside was so strange, it almost didn't seem like the regular world. The clouds overhead were black and purple, making the sky look more like night than day, but it wasn't dark at all on the field. In fact, everything kind of glowed. The dirt of the infield, which was usually just dusty and gray, was moist and black, and the wet grass beyond the infield was a sparkly green. The white in our uniforms really did glow in that light, and the color of the letters and numbers—bright blue, black and gold—flashed in your eye the way bluebirds and orioles look in the woods. I had thrown plenty of new baseballs before, but I had never seen anything whiter and redder than the leather and the stitched seams of the ball they gave me to warm up with.

    Warming up was nothing like my night pictures. My wind-up was fine, and each white pitch went right into the target exactly the same way. I wanted to relax into my trance, and I'm sure I would have, but Mr. Hightower and the other managers kept talking to the umpires about whether we should play. They thought there might be a storm, but finally, because there was no lightning or thunder, they decided we could play the game.

    We were the home team, so the Dodgers batted first. Because of the dark sky and the glowing colors, I went into a different kind of trance than usual. I wasn't thinking or planning at all, and if somebody had spoken to me or asked me something, I'm pretty sure I wouldn't have been able to answer. My warm up pitches were just like the ones I had been throwing on the sidelines, right in the target, hitting the catcher's mitt with a terrific *smack*.

    Then the first hitter came up, Russell Weeks, a kid from my class. He was tall but skinny like me. He stood up straight in the batter's box and looked out at me with an expression that let me know he was never going to hit the ball. I threw three identical strikes to him, and he struck out, swinging at the third one, actually just waving at it. The next two batters also struck out. Mr. Hightower said nice going, and I stayed in my trance while we batted, then I was up on the mound again under the dark sky in the glowing light. I knew most of the other Dodgers. They weren't that good, and they didn't look as if they thought they would hit the ball. This was probably because the first three kids struck out. The next two kids did too, and it felt a little like pitching in the eight-and-nines, except the sixth batter swung and hit a ball pretty hard which bounced chest-high into the glove of our first baseman who trotted over to his base for the out.

    When we were up again, I got to bat and walked and then scored. We were winning, but it never occurred to me that we wouldn't be. Then, in what seemed like a second, everything changed. The swollen dark clouds moved on, and the sky was just gray. The color of everything faded back to normal, and when I got back up on the mound to pitch again, there was a wind blowing into my face. I know you can't blame something like the wind, but I remember getting mad at it, because now it seemed like there was something in the way between me and the target.

The first batter of the inning was a big fat kid named Stu Freyberg, another kid from my fifth grade class. He acted big and tough, and some of the dads thought he was really good because of his size, but I knew he wasn't that good, at anything. He was making a fierce-looking face at me, and he twirled his bat in little circles as he waited for me to pitch. I felt myself getting mad at the expression on his face, and I was already mad at the wind. I threw a pretty good pitch, and Stu took a big swing and hit it really far down the third base line. It went foul, but his hitting it like that all of a sudden made everyone on the Dodgers' bench start yelling and cheering. This made me mad too. I wouldn't have minded throwing one right into Stu Freyberg's fat stomach, but that would have been bad sportsmanship, and I wanted him to strike out.

He hit the next pitch even harder, and this time it was fair, into left center field between the two outfielders, who had to chase after it. It was a triple, and it probably would have been a homer if Stu Freyberg wasn't so fat and slow. The kids on the Dodgers bench and now a lot of the dads were whooping it up, and I started to feel really bad, a combination of still being mad and being ashamed that a kid like Stu Freyberg got a triple off me. Then I walked a kid, and the people on the Dodgers side started yelling and jeering. The next kid up was left-handed, and I knew a left-handed kid would have a hard time hitting my curve ball. So I threw one, and it was perfect. It started off headed straight for his butt, then it did its little wiggle and started floating to the right. It ended up right in the middle of the target. The umpire called out, "*Ball!*" I felt an electric shock behind my eyes. It wasn't a ball. I walked toward the umpire and said, "That wasn't a ball," and our catcher, Steve Minz, was standing up saying the pitch was right in there. But the umpire shouted right back at me. He said the ball was inside when it passed the plate and only ended up in the target. I looked up at him in a way that I hoped would let him see how mad I was, and as I was walking back to the mound, he came out after me and grabbed my shoulder and said, "What did you say, young man?" I told him I didn't say anything. I did say "total jerk" to myself, but without making any sound. He said he heard me say something and that I should watch my mouth. Then he told me again how my curve was inside when it passed the plate.

Now there was just crazy yelling and the wind and names I was saying to myself inside my head. I threw another curve, which started off toward the kid's butt, which I wouldn't have minded hitting, but then it floated even farther to the right than the last one. Steve Minz had to move the target outside to catch it, but I was pretty sure it was a strike when it crossed the plate. The umpire said, *"Ball two!"* I said, *"What?"* — I didn't plan it, it just came out. The umpire said it was a ball, outside, and that I better watch my mouth or I could watch the game from the bench. Mr. Hightower came out to the mound and squeezed my shoulders with his hands. He said to cool off. He said to just throw strikes. I couldn't think. I decided to pitch as hard as I could and not say anything. I threw the next pitch at the left-handed kid's butt, but I forgot to make it a curve, and it hit him. I pretended to be really calm. I walked over to the kid I hit, who was sniffling a little, and I said I was sorry and that I didn't mean it. He was okay, and when he went down to first, all the Dodgers people cheered.

Now the bases were loaded, and Russell Weeks was up again. My first pitch missed the target, and then I threw two good strikes. The next pitch was going to be a strike too, but Russell swung and hit the ball over the shortstop's head into the outfield. The Dodgers were scoring runs, and I went back into my trance, but in a different way, because now I was secretly crying the whole time. I didn't say anything bad. I watched my mouth and threw pitches, but my trance didn't work anymore. The Dodgers kept getting hits off me, and Stu Freyberg got a hit every time. The kids coming up to bat, even quiet kids like Russell Weeks, weren't afraid of the ball. They looked like they wanted to hit it, and they did.

I pitched the whole game, and we lost, nine to four. I knew I wasn't going to be amazing on the Indians. Something final had happened when the field stopped glowing and the wind came up. Mr. Hightower said I could be his fireman again, but I only got to pitch when we were way ahead, usually for just one inning. He also let me play right field a few times, but I almost never had to make any plays. I just stood out there, picturing things, like the night my father taught me how to catch fly balls.

Nobody my age could hit balls like that yet, but one night after supper my father got a bat and sent me down over the slope of our yard, through the bushes and scrub and up over the far side onto the flat place on the Metzgers' vacant lot. We were so far away from each other that I could barely hear what he was saying. He would toss the ball up with one hand and then hit it way up in the air out toward me. I didn't get it at all at first. I just stood there trying to track the black dot of the ball against the sky until it thudded down somewhere, and I would run and get it. I could hear my father shouting at me. He said, "*Get under it! Get under the ball!*" He was getting mad, but I saw what he meant. I got so I could get under where the ball was coming down, but I had a feeling that because it was coming from so high up and so far away, it would have a terrific force behind it, and it would shatter my hand inside the glove. When I got under one of the fly balls, I would offer up a stiff arm and make a tight face. I kept missing, and then I saw my father walking down the lawn toward me holding the bat. I started to feel the can't-do-anything feeling, and I thought I was going to get a crack in the head.

But my father wasn't even mad. He talked to me in a slow, nice way. He said that catching a long fly ball was the same as catching a pop-up. I just had to keep my eye on it, get under it and gather it in. When he said "gather it in," he showed me how to bring the glove down into my body as the ball fell into it. He showed me what I was doing with my stiff arm and how that didn't work. I had to gather the ball into the pocket and seal it with my other hand. He made it look slow and smooth and graceful. He said to imagine that it was a bird I was taking into my glove. I should take it in firmly enough to keep it, but not to hurt it. He threw me a couple of pop-ups to let me get used to the bird idea, then he walked back over to our yard and started hitting me long flies.

After one or two, I got it. I heard the pop of the bat against the ball and tracked the dark dot. I ran a few yards to my right, got under it, and gathered it into the pocket of my glove. The ball made just the right smack in the mitt, and it didn't feel any harder than a pop-up. I heard *"Atta boy! Atta boy"!* and I couldn't stop the waves of tingling in my neck. I caught all of the next ones, and in a few minutes I couldn't wait for my father to hit the next ball. I was tracking and getting under everything, including a few that started going way over my head. My father shouted, "Wait a minute!" and went inside the house and got my mother. Then he was hitting me more balls, and I got under them and gathered them in. I knew where the ball was going the second I heard the crack of the bat. I was talking to God out loud, saying please don't let it get dark.

I am not sure those were my precise recollections as I idled in the right field twilight during those seasons with the Indians, but I remember the feeling of being out there, alone and distanced from the action, half fearing and yet desperately wanting to get back inside the bright, pulsing baseball world that had held me in such thrall.

It would not happen. I suppose I became a serviceable player in the summer leagues and then, for a while, in high school. I had gained what I suppose was necessary perspective. I had a pretty clear idea where I stood, what I could contribute. But although I could not have articulated it then, I felt *diminished* when baseball came to feel like another thing I was expected to do, like taking piano lessons and serving as an acolyte at the early service once a month.

But while I hardened and distanced myself from the game, I did not grow out of baseball—I forsook it, or perhaps just lost it, lost access to its mythy tug. But there had been that tug, that realm. Its intimation has not dimmed in the slightest. At my advanced age I am open to the possibility that its beckoning insistence may be more than baseball, that baseball may have been a mere vestibule to another, still greater world, but it was in baseball that I sensed and for a time dwelled within that world. Far from relegating it to a faded preserve of my boyhood, I find myself coming back to baseball, to what it was trying to tell me, to that time, like the darkening evening in our back lot when my father hit me fly balls and I was talking to God out loud.

TEN

There are times when your life gets small and you can hardly remember the other world. Almost no pictures come up, except sitting at my desk in school, trying to develop a secret handwriting or trying to learn to write with my right hand, so that the work I handed in wasn't always smudged with pencil lead or ink from the heel of my left hand. That whole period seemed to be cold weather, and I was usually sick, either just getting bronchitis or getting over it, or having it so bad I had to stay home from school coughing up blood-streaked phlegm into the toilet or blowing it out my nose into tissues that turned hard overnight. I hated the honking sound of my coughing and the raw feeling it made in my chest. Diane Fuerst, who because of alphabetical order always sat next to me, would get mad at me for coughing all the time. She told me it was "disgusting." I got mad at her right back and told her I couldn't help it, but I actually knew what she meant. Sometimes the stuff would shoot out of my nose and my mouth and I'd have it on my hands or it would get on my work. We sat side by side at tables that year, not desks, and Diane Fuerst would slide her chair as far away from me as she could get. Once she turned back to me and said, in the meanest way she could, "I bet you have T.B."

I wasn't going to explain to Diane Fuerst, who wasn't even nice, about having pneumonia when I was born and because of that always having bronchitis, but I really did want to stop coughing all the time in school. And although I didn't show it, when Diane Fuerst said she bet I had T.B., it really scared me. T.B. was on our minds because one of the P.E. teachers, Mr. Kiner, got T.B. that year and had to leave school and go away to a sanatorium. After he left and Mrs. Gilooley told us about it at lunch hour, we all had to get T.B. tests, which involved every kid in the school lining up, one class at a time in the main lobby, to get a shot on the inside of our arms. I hated this for two reasons. First, I couldn't stand

The Other World

the idea of shots. I'd rather just get a terrible cut all of a sudden by accident than sit there watching someone sticking a needle in very slowly on purpose. Second, Mrs. Gilooley told us what went into you from the shot was a tiny bit of tuberculosis called bacilli. The idea was that the tiny bit would cause our body's immune system to rise up and resist real tuberculosis. It made me sick to think about this. I couldn't stand picturing little brown drops of tuberculosis squirting into my blood. I could picture the theory not working and the bacilli taking over. This is one of the reasons I wanted to stop coughing so much, not to please Diane Fuerst. What I actually told her was, "Yeah I've got T.B., and now you've got it, too," and then maybe I coughed at her.

When I got to be ten, everything got better. I had always wanted to be ten, and now I was. That was the year of fifth grade, the best grade and the last one before Junior High. I had Mr. Click for homeroom and I loved Patsy Prentiss. I remember thinking that if there were ever a time I could go back into and stay forever, it would be ten.

I was so lucky to get Mr. Click, but maybe it wasn't luck. I had been waiting a long time to feel something from the other world again. Sometimes, like when I was sick, I wondered if I ever would. So when I got Mr. Click, it actually felt like it was planned. There were three sections of fifth grade, Mr. Click's, Mrs. Mellors's, and Mrs. Goodroe's. People hated Mrs. Mellors because she was strict and had a really sour expression on her face all the time. Annabel had Mrs. Mellors and was so scared and unhappy that she would beg our mother to let her stay home from school. I hated Mrs. Mellors for making Annabel feel like that, especially since Annabel usually loved her teachers and would write really nice private notes about them in her diary. I had already decided that if I got Mrs. Mellors, I was going to be a problem. Mrs. Goodroe was tall and tired looking. Her hair and skin were the same grayish color, and on one side of her face she had some kind of purple growth or stain that started from under her hair and went all across her cheek.

Mr. Click not only turned out to be just as much fun as everybody said, he really liked me. He didn't care if I got off a good one every now and then, and sometimes he would get off a good one about me. He was really tall and not too old. He had short curly black hair and wore glasses with thick black frames that kind of went with his hair. He didn't dress like a teacher. He wore loose old corduroy coats and pants, with usually a dark green or a black shirt and a tie with bright swirls. He had a bunch of different pairs of suede shoes with dark rubber soles, and there was something extra exciting about his wearing those shoes because Elvis Presley had a hit song called "Blue Suede Shoes," and something about Mr. Click just went with the feeling of Elvis Presley. Mr. Click had a yellow Pontiac convertible, and sometimes when we were driving somewhere in town, we'd see Mr. Click heading somewhere with his top down. Mother would say, "Look, there's your teacher," and almost laugh. When she talked about Mr. Click with her friends she called him "a real character."

Being in Mr. Click's class was just as relaxing as not being in school. We did the same kind of work that the other sections did, but there was nothing tense about it. He was a good explainer, especially in math, and he always knew when to stop when somebody couldn't do a problem on the board and ask the whole class questions until everybody, even the kid at the board, got the idea. I think Mr. Click liked literature and social studies best, because that's what we spent the most time on. He liked to give us funny composition assignments, like "What is the Stupidest Thing You Have Ever Done?" or "Describe a Place That Couldn't Possibly Be." Sometimes he would just talk to us in a personal way and tell us stories about things that happened to him when he was young. Before he handed back our compositions, he would sit on the front of his desk and read parts that he liked out loud to the class. He wouldn't say whose composition it was until he was finished. The first time he did it, the first week of school, he read practically all of mine. The assignment was to write about the best thing we did over the summer, and I wrote about going into the woods behind our cabin in Michigan and trying to spot a bear. I actually did that, but it didn't work, because I'm sure bears didn't want to hang around close to resorts during the day, and also it was sticky and airless in the woods. There was no path, and I was getting a lot of mosquito bites, so I cut it pretty short. But I decided to make my composition funny, with a lot of exaggerations and some made up stuff thrown in. I wrote how I thought I would be protected if the bear attacked me because I had my pearl-handled pocketknife with me. I really did think that at the time, but the way I wrote about it made me seem like a real dork, but in a funny way. When I wrote about doing really stupid things, I liked to use very intellectual expressions, like "and this turned out to be not a particularly good idea" or "you can imagine my mother's surprise" because it had a funny effect. Mr. Click always read my good parts to the class, and sometimes he would laugh out loud. From then on, no matter what the assignment was, I couldn't wait to get going on it and to come up with something that would make Mr. Click and everybody laugh.

You couldn't make Mr. Click lose his temper. He could get everybody to quiet down just by standing up and saying, "*People—?*" When a kid got mad at somebody and was doing mean teasing or got in a fight, Mr. Click would just lead him away to some place quiet and ask him what was wrong and what the kid could do to make it better. He had to talk to me once when I got mad at Scott Overman for smashing into me while we were playing dodge ball. I called Scott Overman a fat, stupid slob, and Mr. Click heard me, and he came over and led me away. He leaned forward in front of me, so he was looking right into my eyes, and he asked me how I thought it made Scott Overman feel to be called fat. Mr. Click was calm and nice, not mad. I told him I thought it would make Scott Overman mad. Mr. Click asked me what else Scott Overman might feel, and I actually started to picture it. I'm not sure if Mr. Click explained it or if I figured it out, but I started feeling really bad about what I said, because Scott Overman really was fat. His tee shirts would come up out of his pants when he was out on the playground, and his fat stomach hung out over his belt, and I know he felt bad about it. I wasn't one of the kids who called him Fatso everyday, but I could see that calling him a fat slob when he smashed into me could really hurt his feelings. Mr. Click asked me what I thought I could do about that, and I went right over to Scott Overman and told him I didn't mean it. I told him I didn't think he was fat.

Mr. Click always had a sense of what we were up to, who our friends were and who we didn't like, even things we did outside of school. He knew about Patsy Prentiss and me, not just that we were boyfriend and girlfriend and that we were together all the time, but the exact way I felt about her. In a way, I was glad he did, because that made it seem important.

Patsy Prentiss was the first person I had the love feeling for who loved me back in exactly the same way. It wasn't anything like the way I felt about Beth Bartell or Gwendolyn Bliss or Linda Bluestone when I wanted them to be the Lady in a romance with me. Patsy Prentiss was a girl I really got to know. She entered our school in the fourth grade, but she was not in my section, so I barely knew who she was. At the end of the summer my mother told me we got an invitation to a barbecue picnic and pool party at the Prentisses' house. It was for all the kids and families who were going to be in Mr. Click's class. I didn't think very much about it, except that I liked hot dogs cooked on a grill. I didn't quite understand the part about its being a pool party. It didn't seem much like a party to eat in somebody's yard and then go over to the town pool and swim. I didn't realize until we got to their house that the Prentisses had their own swimming pool. I didn't think anybody in Palatine had their own swimming pool. It was nice, too, a lot smaller than the town pool, but completely closed in with a high wooden fence. Patsy was already in her bathing suit when we got there. She stood there in the driveway with her parents saying hello and shaking everybody's hand as they arrived. I thought it was going to be embarrassing saying hello to her and shaking the hand of a girl in my own grade, but she was in such a good mood and so natural about it that it was fine.

Inside, the Prentisses' house was huge and ritzy. You couldn't even see all the rooms. You went into a big hallway with shiny wooden floors, and on each side there were fancy living rooms with white carpets and light blue chairs and couches. It took me a minute to realize the thing that was so different from other houses was that the ceilings were really high, like at school or the post office. Mrs. Prentiss took me to a bedroom with its own bathroom and told me I could change into my suit in there if I wanted.

The Other World

When I went in there and locked the door, I had to sit on the bed for a minute and think about being rich. But I also wanted to get outside and get in that pool.

I had a good feeling the second I saw Patsy in the driveway smiling and talking to everybody. Her hair was a mixture of brown and blond, messy but interesting to look at. It was cut almost as short as a boy's if he didn't get a haircut for a long time. Patsy must have been in her pool all summer, or else she just got outside a lot, because she was brown and shiny all over from the sun. She was so tan the skin between her fingers and toes was bright white. When I got out of the changing room and found my way to the door to the pool, Patsy was standing at the edge of the diving board talking to the kids who were treading water below her. I loved Patsy Prentiss's voice. It sounded a little hoarse, the way you get when you've been shouting for a long time or when you've got a certain kind of cold and everything sounds lower and scratchy, but in a lovable way. When she was really excited about something, Patsy's voice would break into croaks and squeaks.

She was really good at thinking up things to do and setting up games. "Come on," she said in her croaking voice to the kids in the pool, "let's have a contest to see who can make the biggest splash off the diving board." We all wanted to do that. Then she set up contests to see who could do the biggest belly flop and who could swim the farthest under water. The sparkly blue-green water of that pool was the best water I ever swam in. It would hold you up even without dog-paddling. When it started to get dark, lights went on underneath, and the pool glowed like a huge blue-green jewel. I never went out to the yard to get anything to eat, because I wanted to stay in that pool, as close to Patsy Prentiss as I could get.

* * *

It was one of those great swimming nights when the water felt warmer than the air, making you want to stay in and keep fooling around. When it was time to get dressed and go home, Patsy and I and two or three other kids were still in the water. We were crouched in the shallow end up to our chins, and everybody had been in the water so long, our voices shivered when we talked. This made us laugh, but everything was making us laugh, and I got off some really good ones. When I got home, I couldn't stop telling my sister Annabel about everything that happened, the Prentisses' ritzy house and the pool and how great it was that we were all going to be in Mr. Click's class for the whole year. I didn't even try to tell her about Patsy, because I actually had too much feeling to express, but I think it came out in what I was saying about everything else.

Because of her pool party, Patsy and I already knew each other when school started. On the first day when Mr. Click read off her name, Patricia Prentiss, I turned around to look at her, and she was already looking at me. She had the same great smiling expression she had when we were fooling around in her pool. It was an expression that said *let's go, let's do something,* and that's pretty much what we did. The second we got out after school, we headed off somewhere to try something Patsy or I happened to think up. Patsy always liked there to be a lot of kids, and she was nice about asking everybody, even kids nobody ever talked to or who were never allowed to do anything and never came along. A lot of the best things we did involved jumping and falling.

In the town park closest to her house they put in a really high new slide. It was so steep, especially up at the top, that a lot of kids, even big kids, wouldn't go down it. But we figured out every possible way to go down, on our stomachs, sideways with our legs over the sides, two people back-to-back, two people face-to-face, and lying down backwards. Going down the slide in a tricky position could be really dangerous because unless you knew how to slow down by making friction with your legs against the sides when the slide started to level off toward the bottom, you'd just shoot out onto the gravel in whatever position you were in. That happened to Larry Landis when he went down backwards, headfirst. I was just about to go up the ladder when I saw him do it. Going down backwards headfirst made it hard to get friction and slow down at the end. Larry Landis's legs were hanging over the rails of the slide, so he couldn't get any friction at all. When he got to the bottom, he flew through the air for a little way, and then his head and back hit the gravel really hard. I ran over and wondered if he would be dead. His eyes were open and he looked confused, and then he started to cry really hard, like a much younger kid. His voice went up really high, and he lost his breath and started slobbering and choking. It was terrible looking at him. Patsy ran home and got her mother, who helped Larry sit up. The hair on the back of his head was all bloody, and some of the blood was drying and turning black. Mrs. Prentiss had a towel with her, and she wetted it in the drinking fountain and held it against the back of Larry's head. She helped him to get up and walked him over to her station wagon where he and Patsy got in, and Mrs. Prentiss drove to the doctor's. The next day Larry came to school with six stitches sown into the back of his head. You could see them perfectly, like a spongy black zipper against the white circle of his scalp where the doctor shaved his head.

    After that we still liked trying things on the new slide, but Patsy decided to make it safer by having a bunch of us drag an old mattress from the back of her garage over to the park. We put it right at the bottom of the slide to break our falls. It felt really good landing on the mattress, no matter what position you were in. You didn't even have to make friction with your legs and slow down at the end. One time Patsy and I went down face-to-face, with her frontward and me backward. This meant we were looking right into each other's eyes the whole way down, which made both of us scream with laughter. The next thing I knew we were at the leveling off place at the bottom, and then I was falling over backward in a kind of somersault with Patsy smashed up into me. I landed on my bottom, and her forehead hit my upper lip really hard. When we got untangled on the mattress and I sat up, I had pins and needles in the space between my upper lip and my nose. Patsy looked confused and was feeling her forehead with her hand. There were two white dents above her eyebrows, and while I was staring at them, they filled up with bright red blood. Patsy said, "Look at you!" I knew there was something wrong because my upper lip felt numb the way it did when the dentist gave me Novocain. Something metallic tasting was pooling in my mouth, and when I wiped it with my hand, my hand was all bloody. Somebody ran off to get Patsy's mother, and I sat there holding my throbbing mouth, hoping Patty was going to be okay and that my teeth wouldn't come out. They were my second teeth.

Mrs. Prentiss took us to their doctor's office, and in different little rooms Patsy and I both got Novocain and stitches. Mine were inside my mouth between my gums and my teeth, and when I got home I couldn't eat anything except cold soup. When the Novocain wore off, I felt like the front of my mouth was on fire. The next morning when I got up and looked in the bathroom mirror, I looked like a clown. It hurt to talk, and my front lip was so puffed up it looked like I was making a duck face. I didn't want to go to school looking like that, but Mother said I had to. One of my front teeth was a little loose, and Mother said I was lucky it didn't get knocked out. She was mad at me for fooling around on the slide. Patsy came to school with just a regular bandage on her head, and she looked even prettier and livelier than usual. That made the love feeling swell up inside me, and I really wished I didn't look so bad. I wanted Patsy to look at me and feel what I felt when I looked at her.

We weren't always trying dangerous things and getting hurt. Some of the things we thought up were just fun. By fifth grade we were old enough to walk into town after school and, if we had any money, buy a coke or an ice cream or maybe Hostess Cupcakes at the Creamery soda fountain. It always felt good to be sitting at the soda fountain, getting off good ones with Patsy and a lot of kids. Sometimes there would be ten or twelve of us at once, and it was hard to get that many empty stools, especially next to each other. The ladies who worked behind the counter at the Creamery were usually mad at us, because the whole time we were there we'd only spend one dime on a small coke or a small chocolate phosphate, the cheapest things you could order. They kept telling us to keep it down or to go outside. They thought we were too loud, which we probably were, but I couldn't help it. Doing things with Patsy and other kids after school always put me in a great mood, and I would get off good ones without even trying.

The Other World

It was Patsy's idea to see if we could get all the way to the Creamery from school going only through people's back yards. It was about five or six blocks into town from school, but the first few times it took so long to get over all the fences that by the time we made it to the Creamery, it was time to go home for supper. But we modified the rules a little so it worked. We said that if there were two fenced-in yards in a row, you could just do the first yard and then go along the fence to the sidewalk and skip the next house. If the next fenced-in yard had a dog in it, you could go straight back and continue along the yards of the next street over. Only one or two kids stuck with Patsy and me in the back yards game, because it could get scary. Sometimes an old man or an old lady would look through their window and see us running through their yard, and they would bang on the glass and yell at us to get out of there. One old lady, who had a fence, always yelled the same thing: "You're *trespassing!*" That got to seem really funny to me, although I was scared the first time I heard her. When we were sitting around at the Creamery or at the lunch table at school and somebody would say something just right, like "can I come over to your house after school?" I would go into my high crackling voice and say, "No, you're *trespassing!*" One day in class when we were discussing the Dakota Indians and how setting up railroads and towns and fences made it impossible for the Indians to keep hunting buffaloes, Mr. Click asked the class how we would feel if we were the Dakota Indians and people started settling right in the places where we had always been able to hunt. I didn't even have to think. I just croaked out, "You're *trespassing!*" It got to be one of my main jokes.

Patsy liked to lead the way when we'd go by back yards to the Creamery. She was good luck, too, and nothing bad ever seemed to happen when I was running along close to her. Once we were sneaking through a yard, and just when we got to the garage, a car pulled up and a man and woman got out with groceries. I thought the man was going to get mad, but Patsy said in a loud, friendly way, "Excuse me, sir, may we cut across your lawn?" They didn't mind at all, and we just kept going. I had never thought of getting permission. In spite of the scary times when somebody might be yelling at you or there were fences with barbs at the top or mean dogs, I really liked the back yards game. Besides the risks, there was something interesting about seeing a familiar street in a completely different way, seeing the kinds of things people kept in their yards or behind their garages, seeing that some of the back yards were still kind of wild, or that some had little barns or a cement pond with fish in it. In the winter it was dark by the time I left Patsy's house or the Creamery, and I would even go home through people's back yards. This was easier and less scary because I was alone and no one could see me in the dark, and I wasn't in any hurry. The better I got to know everybody's property, moving from yard to yard in the dark, the more I felt I knew the town better than anyone else ever could. It was like the town was now arranged inside me.

Two of the times I had with Patsy Prentiss that year were like nothing that had ever happened to me before. I saw Patsy for most of the time every day. I got to school early so I could fool around with her in the main lobby or at her desk. We always had lunch together, and after school everybody would go over to her house, which had a ping-pong table and an electronic bowling machine in a big paneled room in her basement, or we'd go to the Creamery, or just think something up. Mr. Click called us the Bobbsey Twins, and without anyone having to say it, all the kids linked us up as boyfriend and girlfriend.

The first great thing with Patsy happened the afternoon we went out to look at the new housing development site at the edge of the fields. All week huge tractors and bulldozers had been roaring through town, past the school and past our house. It felt a little as if some kind of army was passing through on the way to a war. At the edge of the fields, where the new houses were going to go, the earthmovers had already dug deep pits for the foundations, and the dirt was piled up in a line of connected little hills. The weather was starting to get cold, and I remember hoping the hills would still be there when it snowed, so we could go down them on our sleds. Patsy and I and a bunch of other kids made our way up to the top of the side of one of the hills and walked along the ridgeline. About half way down the slope of the last hill, the packed dirt leveled off a little to form a kind of landing, and below that was a pile of straw. Patsy and I sidestepped down to the landing, and I was looking down into the straw when Patsy tapped me on the shoulder. Her eyes were wide, and she looked like she was trying to hold in a laugh, and then, still looking me in the eye, she stepped off the landing. I don't know how far down it really was, probably a few feet, but it seemed at that moment like a long way. She landed on her heels and then, still looking up at me, let herself fall backwards into the straw. Then there was the rattle of her laughter, and she was saying, "Jonathan, *come on!*"

Then we were all jumping down into the straw. We were jumping into it the way we would jump into a pool, legs crossed, tucked into a ball, as if we would make a splash when we landed. It felt really comfortable when you hit the straw. I could just tell that I wasn't going to get hurt. I really wanted everybody to watch my jumps, and I couldn't help screaming as soon as I took off. I rolled out of the straw and raced up the side of the hill as fast as I could to get back up on top and jump again. The air felt cold in my lungs, and I was just about out of breath every second, but it felt so good I couldn't stop. The clear sky overhead was getting rosy and gold and was starting to lose its light, which made landing in the straw feel like sinking into smoky cushions. The other kids were beginning to leave for home, and I was getting the sad, desperate feeling of not wanting it to be over.

When it was practically dark and Patsy and I were the only ones left, we decided to do one last jump, but together at the same time. We stood side by side at the lip of the landing, not looking at each other. I said, "One, two, three," and as I was saying it Patsy took my hand, and then we jumped. I shut my eyes and didn't open them until we landed in the crunch and crackle. We were partly buried in the straw, and I could see bits of it in the tousles of Patsy's hair, and I could feel it down the collar of my coat. We were kind of tangled up, and it was going to take some effort to get up and get out, but I didn't want to move. I just wanted to stay there tangled up with Patsy in the half dark. I was glad that she wasn't moving either. I realized what felt so good: the side of her skull was touching the side of mine. Patsy said, "That was really fun."

That feeling was completely new, and I will never forget it. It was like a swelling inside my chest that kept opening and opening. You couldn't describe it in words. It was more like a kind of music, or the way certain colors grow out of each other in a sunset near the horizon. I walked Patsy all the way back to her house, then walked home in the dark. Supper was almost over, and I got yelled at and cracked in the head for being so late and for being so dirty and full of little bits of straw. For once, though, it didn't feel like the worst thing in the world to be in trouble, and even getting cracked in the head didn't bother me for more than a minute. I knew that as soon as I could be by myself in my room, I could get back to that feeling of being skull to skull with Patsy in the straw.

The second great thing with Patsy was even better. It was like the completion of the first thing, which let me know it was real and would always be a part of the world inside me. It happened at the end of Donna Madden's Shock Theater party. Shock Theater was a new TV show that came on late on Saturday night. It started at ten and went till about midnight. There was a host named The Creep who wore a monster wig and black eye makeup and lipstick, and he would introduce famous old horror movies like *Frankenstein* or *The Thing.* During the commercial breaks The Creep would tell jokes and set up little skits with people in the TV studio. We didn't watch Shock Theater in our house because Annabel got really scared of the movies, so scared that it made you feel terrible to watch her. She couldn't even watch The Creep. But kids started having Shock Theater parties on Saturday nights when the show was on. You'd usually go over to the kid's house and play whatever games they had in the basement, then come up for pizza or something and then sit around on the floor in the living room to watch Shock Theater. A lot of kids got tired and went to sleep before it was over, and some kids' parents picked them up early, but at Donna Madden's Patsy and I and maybe three other kids were still awake as the movie was ending up. The movie was *The Invisible Man,* which I didn't think was very interesting or very scary, but I was in a good mood because I was sitting with Patsy, and I was getting off good ones.

The Other World

People always turned out the lights to watch Shock Theater in order to make it scarier. Patsy and I were sitting on the floor leaning back against the front of the sofa, and it seemed like we were sitting there for hours. As it got later, the bits from the movie got shorter, and The Creep and the commercials got longer. The other kids started to get up and call their parents to take them home. Even Donna Madden stood up and said she was going to bed. By the end of the movie Patsy and I were in the dark, flickering living room alone. Without the other kids around, I didn't feel like getting off good ones. At the exact second I realized that being by ourselves was what I was hoping would happen, Patsy leaned into me a little and rested the side of her head against mine. It was the same ringing pleasure as when we were tangled in the straw after our last jump. We were skull to skull, and it made a low ringing tone inside my head. Without even planning it, I wedged my arm out from between us and rested it over Patsy's shoulder. She made a beautiful little humming sound and scrunched a little closer into me, to get more comfortable. I knew I was feeling as much as I could possibly feel and that I needed to hold perfectly still. I could not talk or think or even move my eyes to look around. My body felt frozen, except for a pulsing line where Patsy's head and shoulder and side pressed in on mine. I was aware that the final frantic scenes of *The Invisible Man* were flashing in front of me in a grainy old-fashioned way, but it could have been anything. There was only the swelling feeling, opening and opening. It was happening again, and I knew there would be no end to it. Then the lights were on, and Mr. Madden was hooting and joking, yelling to his wife, "Hey, we got two left!" Mr. Madden was being very cheerful. He looked down at Patsy and me and said, "looks like somebody got mighty sleepy," and all I wanted was to go home, get into my bed, and start thinking about everything that had happened.

* * *

I wish I could go back into every one of those days and open them up the way you might take old photographs out of an envelope. Some of the moments, like jumping into the straw or the Shock Theater party, are as vivid and clear as they were at the actual time, but so much of the rest of that year is a blur. I can feel the mood of it, the skull-to-skull love feeling for Patsy, but the procession of days and all the things we did seem like a kind of floating, with a sweet, achy feeling in my chest. I do remember, though, that when it got warm again at the end of our fifth grade year, Patsy and I started going to the country club for lunch.

Barrington Lakes Country Club was at the north end of town where the fields stopped. I never knew anything about it, except to see its green sign with gold letters when we would drive by it in the car. The Prentisses were members of the country club, and on the night of the Fifth Grade Easter Dance, Patsy invited me to have supper there with her parents. I wasn't nervous about it when she asked me, although I didn't know what sitting around eating supper with her parents would be like. But something about going to the country club made my mother tense, and then I started to get nervous. Mother told me the country club would be "dressy," a term I had never heard before. It meant not only dressed up, but really dressed up. When I got dressed up for Sunday school, I would wear my checkered sports jacket, a white shirt, one of my father's ties, my gabardine pants, and my good shoes. Mother said she thought my checkered jacket wasn't dressy enough and that we needed to go shopping to get a new one. We went to Zimmerman's department store downtown, and I had to try on all the jackets that were around my size. Mother didn't like any of them, and neither did I. They either had stiff shoulders that stuck out past where mine were or they were made out of ugly cloth, and just about every one of them looked too big in the mirror. They went down too far over my legs, and the sleeves went down to where my fingers started. So we had to drive out to a bunch of big stores in Chicago, which took the whole afternoon, and we didn't get home until after supper.

Getting me a dressy outfit made Mother tense. I got really tired going into the stores and waiting around until Mother found somebody to help us, then trying on all the jackets, and going into the changing closets to try on pants that went with the jackets.

Each time I went in I had to untie my shoes and take them off, put the new pants on, then put my shoes back on, tie them back up, and go out there for Mother and the salesman to look. Finally, at the last store, Mother decided to get a dark blue jacket, which she called a blazer. We also got a new pair of pants made out of scratchy gray wool, which Mother said looked dressy with the blazer, and my own tie. The tie had slanted blue and red stripes going down it, which I really liked. Actually, except that the pants felt like they were too long, so that I had to buckle them way up on my chest, I liked the feeling of getting dressy. Looking into the long mirror on the closet door of my mother and father's bedroom, I liked the way the dark wool of the blazer made my shirt look extra white, which made the stripes of the tie really bright. Mother told me that I should always button the middle button of the blazer, which covered up how high my pants were. I looked really different, almost like another person, a person who belonged in cities or catalogs, and I couldn't stop looking at myself.

The idea of getting dressy didn't make me nervous, but the other things Mother started talking about did. She told me that dinner at the country club would probably be formal, which was another term I hadn't heard, and I thought it had a dark, unpleasant sound to it. I had pictured the country club as a big ritzy restaurant, but Mother thought it might be more formal. She told me I should remember to do certain things at the table and to practice them at supper. She told me not to say things like "pass the butter" or even "please pass the butter," but always to make it a question, "could you please pass the butter?" She told me to be sure not to start eating anything that came to me until Mrs. Prentiss started eating hers. She told me to pass things to the person next to me, not to skip a person or reach across the table. From there it started to feel like too much to remember. She told me when we got to the table to keep standing up until all the ladies and girls sat down. She said if there was a lady or girl next to me, to pull her chair out a little and then slide it in behind her legs. She made me practice this a few times on Annabel. She said the first thing I should do when I sat down was to unfold my napkin and put it on my lap. She told me not to put my elbows or arms on the table while I ate. There were a lot more things, but I couldn't keep track of them. She said not to cut up all my meat at once, just the bite I was going to eat. She told me that I should put my knife and fork down during each mouthful, not to hold onto them while I was chewing. She told me there might be a lot more pieces of silverware than I expected, what each piece was supposed to be used for, and how usually it was a good idea to move from the outside in. I started to lose my confidence. The idea of going to the country club with the Prentisses started to feel a little sickening, like having to go to the dentist.

The night I went, it wasn't as bad as I thought. When I got into the back seat of the Prentisses' car with Patsy, Mrs. Prentiss smiled at me and said, in a really nice way, "don't you look nice." The country club dining room was crowded and bright. The tables had thick white tablecloths and napkins and extra heavy plates and silverware. Mr. and Mrs. Prentiss were friendly and relaxed, and they joked around a lot, which made me less nervous. I was sitting next to Patsy and remembered to pull her chair out and slide it into the back of her legs, but that seemed to surprise her, and her mother laughed and told her just to sit down. There were, as Mother told me, way more forks and spoons than I needed, but I just looked over every now and then and used the one Patsy was using. The only time I was really nervous was when it came time to order my food. I couldn't understand a lot of the things on the menu, and Mr. Prentiss asked me if I wanted to have a shrimp cocktail. I had never heard of that, but I had a feeling if I saw an actual shrimp on my plate and tried to eat it, it would be sickening. I said no thank you to the shrimp cocktail and to anything else I didn't understand. I listened to what Patsy ordered and then ordered that. I said I wanted a thousand islands dressing on my salad, and I was pretty nervous wondering what that would be. It was just friendly, regular talking until dessert, but then the waiter came back and said what they had and asked me what I would like. I might not have been listening very well, because I couldn't make a picture of any desserts from what he was saying. I kept waiting for something familiar, like "pie" or "cake," but there was nothing like that, so I said no thank you again. Mr.

The Other World

Prentiss said, "Not even a little ice cream, Jonathan?" and I said yes, please. When the ice cream came in a little glass dish, it was vanilla, which was fine, even though the Prentisses all got what looked to me like big delicious pieces of cake.

By the time we left the country club to get in the car and drive to the dance, I wasn't nervous at all. The only reason I even bring it up is that, after that night, Patsy and I started going to the country club all the time.

We never would have thought about going to the country club by ourselves if we hadn't already started going into town for lunch, and the reason we started doing that was the weather. After Easter and all through May was the softest, most beautiful weather I can ever remember. Even if it rained a little, the sun would come right back, and make everything pale green and a little steamy, and as you walked along the damp sidewalks, the air was sweet with lilacs and honeysuckle and the pink and white blossoms of the fruit trees. I remember deciding on one of those days that I was going to stay outside, even if I got in trouble. It was during lunch period at school, and Patsy and I were taking a walk around the edge of the playground before going in to eat. There wasn't a rule against this, but nobody ever did it because people were usually hungry and wanted to eat lunch before they went outside to play for the rest of the period. The air was so green and bright, and the wind was so soft, I realized I didn't want to go back inside, and before I could even say it, Patsy said, "I've got an idea."

Patsy's idea was to slip through the hedges and go into town and have lunch at a restaurant. I couldn't quite imagine it. I had never gone to a restaurant in town during the day. I was pretty sure it wasn't allowed, but Patsy said that kids who lived close to the school were allowed to walk home for lunch, so this was really no different from that. We were already walking toward town, and I wondered how long it would take to get to a restaurant, eat our stuff, and walk back. Lunch period was forty-five minutes, and we had already been out for a while. Patsy said not to worry, it would be fun. Then I thought about money. I felt in my pocket and remembered I had a quarter and a dime, which was probably enough for something in a restaurant, at least a toasted cheese. I told Patsy I had thirty-five cents, and she told me not to worry, she was loaded. We ran the rest of the way into town as fast as we could, partly because we didn't know how much time we had, but mainly because we just felt like it.

We were winded but in a really good mood when we got downtown. We decided to go to June's, which was a long, thin place with wooden booths running along each wall. My father had taken me there for a hot dog after Little League games, and I liked it. It was pretty crowded and noisy when we walked in, and we had to wait for a few minutes to get a booth. I got nervous while we were waiting, because there were no other kids around, only grownups, people I recognized from the stores. I looked around for a clock and tried to figure out how much time we would have. It felt to me like we had already been gone a long time. Patsy didn't care. She was in a good mood and told me not to worry, we'd think up a good excuse. When we got into our booth it felt much better, like we belonged in there. You could see out onto the street and all the people walking by, and past them the green park in front of the train station. Patsy said I should order whatever I wanted and not to worry about spending just thirty-five cents, so I ordered a BLT with potato chips and a chocolate malt. Patsy ordered a whole bunch of things, including soup. Before our food came, the waitress brought us chilled glasses of water and a basket full of rolls and crackers and butter. By the time our food came, the whole tabletop was filled with dishes and bowls and glasses, and all of it looked really good. The waitress filled up my glass with chocolate malt and left the huge silver container next to my plate. I picked it up and saw that it was practically full of extra chocolate malt. I couldn't believe it. The bright sun outside and the people walking by and all the food made me feel like I was in a new, much bigger world. Patsy was probably used to places like June's, but she seemed excited too, so I started getting off good ones.

I could tell that the people in the other booths were looking at us, but I don't think we were making trouble. I think they probably thought we were cute. Our waitress was really friendly and called us honey. When she first came over, she said, "Call off school today?" and Patsy looked right up at her and said, "Parent conferences." Patsy could always do that, come up with tremendous fibs, and she was always in such a cheerful mood, she never ended up in trouble. By the time we finally finished our food and the rest of my chocolate malt, I knew it was way past lunch period at school. I knew we should hurry back as fast as we could, but I just couldn't force myself to do it in that soft breezy air. When you feel really good in a certain way, partly in a trance but still aware of what you are doing, you almost never get in trouble. That's what happened to Patsy and me when we got back to school. It turned out it was even later than I thought. It was almost two o'clock, which was only an hour before school was over, when we got back to the building and started walking down the empty corridor to Mr. Click's room. I opened the door without making any noise and looked inside. It was quiet, and the kids were reading by themselves. I looked around for Mr. Click, but he wasn't at his desk, and I couldn't see him. Patsy and I gave each other a look and walked over to our desks and sat down. I could hear Patsy's friends whispering, "Where *were* you?" and Patsy whispering back, "We had an *appointment.*" After a while Mr. Click came back into the room. He stood at the doorway for a minute and looked around. I glanced up from my book, and he was looking at me, his eyes extra big behind the black frames of his glasses. He smiled a little and said, "So you're back."

I loved that time at June's, and because it was so exciting and because there was that sweet, soft air practically every day, Patsy and I never wanted to eat cooped up in the cafeteria. We went to June's a few more times, which was kind of fun, but we had to run all the way there and all the way back, and even when we ate as fast as we could, we were always at least a little bit late. We were also running out of things to tell the waitress about why we weren't at school, which is when Patsy thought of the country club. She said they had great lunches at the country club, and we wouldn't even have to pay, because they were members and she could charge it. It made me a little nervous to think about sitting around the country club dining room in my school clothes. The country club was also twice as far away as June's downtown. Patsy said we should bring our bikes, and it would actually be faster than June's. So the next day I rode my bike to school, and as soon as we got out for lunch period, we rode out to the country club really fast. It felt so good, riding hard like that in the middle of the day, with the warm breeze blowing past my face and through my hair.

Lunch at the country club turned out to be much more fun than I thought it would be. It wasn't in the big dining room inside. It was in a low, screened-in building between a bunch of tennis courts and the swimming pool. There was a counter where you ordered your food, and then a man would bring it over to your table. Because it wasn't summer yet, there were hardly any other people in the snack bar, just a few ladies wearing short white tennis dresses that showed their bumpy legs. We would sit as far away from them as we could, at a table close to the pool. With the breezes coming through the screens and the white sun sparkling on the pool water, it was even better than June's. For one thing it was much quieter, and Patsy and I could really talk to each other. We talked about everything. I told her about going to the north woods in the summer and about hunting with Cyrus and about the tunnels and our fort, and Patsy told me about going to her family's cabin on its own island on Lake Superior. Patsy had a way of talking about the things she did that made you feel like you were there, and it always made me wish I had done all those things with her. In bed at night I stopped thinking about my own things and started picturing Patsy's island and how the water was so clear you could see the rocks and sand thirty feet below on the bottom. I could actually see that water and the bright sky and feel the wind off the lake, but I was also mixing it up with sitting with Patsy at the country club and the sunlight sparkling on the pool.

I can hardly remember anything about school that spring, except that I knew it was going to be sad to end the year and not have Mr. Click anymore. All I remember is sitting across the table from Patsy at the country club snack bar. The sun would come out from behind a cloud, and in a second the whole side of my face would be warm. I would have a BLT on toast and a chocolate malt, and Patsy would have a bowl of clam chowder and a mound of chicken salad on top of lettuce. We must have been thinking about having to get back to school, but I can only remember feeling that we had all the time we could ever want and that I had so much to tell her. But mostly I remember looking across at her face and at the way the messy waves of her straw-colored hair framed her beautiful brown cheeks and the white teeth of her smile when she leaned forward to tell me something special. That's the picture I would make at night in the dark of my room.

The last day of fifth grade was a half-day, and there was no lunch at school, which meant Patsy and I would have all the time we wanted to have lunch at the country club. That's the only thing I could think of all morning, and then Mr. Click was saying goodbye to us and that he had really enjoyed getting to know us, and I wished there was something I could have given him, like a present.

Then we were all outside in the blinding sun, and before I went over to the bike rack to get my bike, I took all the books and graded work and supplies from my desk and threw them into the trash bin. Then I met Patsy, and we rode our bikes across town to the country club. I had made a plan, and when I got to the path in front of the snack bar, I parked my bike and took the shopping bag out of my bike basket. That morning I had put my blue blazer in there. It wasn't too wrinkled, and I put it on. Patsy was waiting for me at the door. She was smiling so hard I thought she had a secret, and she did. She had a box from a store under her arm, and she said, "Wait a second," and went to the bathroom. When she came out, she had changed her clothes. She was wearing a stiff light pink dress with no sleeves. Her face was extra beautiful, and I noticed she had also put on a pink band to hold down her hair in the front. She had thought of the same thing I did, getting dressed up. That turned out to be our best lunch. We didn't have to hurry, and we could lean back in our chairs. After a while we were the only people left in the snack bar, and the breezes were blowing through the screens, and we could hear the plip plip of the water against the side of the swimming pool. I know I was paying attention to Patsy and what she was saying, but I was aware of something else at the same time. I was watching myself from some other place, and I realized that I wasn't ten years old, that I had somehow skipped ahead to someone I would be later, or maybe even into a completely different person. That happens sometimes in the other world.

THE OTTAWANNA WAY

When my mother realized I didn't like Little League anymore, that it was actually making me sad, she decided to send me to Camp Ottawanna at the end of the summer. Camp Ottawanna was an overnight camp on a big lake in Wisconsin. Mother told me that when she was a girl she had wanted to go to Girl Scout Camp more than anything in the world, but Nana and Papa couldn't afford it. She told me Camp Ottawanna would be wonderful. I would sleep in a cabin, and there would be boating and swimming and camping out in tents. She said there would also be sports, including baseball, and that I could bring my glove. I really didn't want to go. I wanted to go on our regular vacation with everybody else up to our own cabin in the north woods. I could see that saying this was hurting Mother's feelings, so I stopped, but I really did not want to go to that camp.

Mother found out another boy from my school, Patrick Dannehey, was also going to Camp Ottawanna. She told me about it to make me feel better about going. She said, "You'll have a friend." I knew Patrick Dannehey was not going to be my friend. He was a grade behind me, and he had white hair and pale skin, and he was really weak. Thinking about Patrick Dannehey trying to hang around me for three weeks made me feel terrible.

I was right about it, too. Camp Ottawanna was completely terrible. The bad feeling I had about it right away was just a tiny hint of how terrible it would get. Mother took me to the train station on a Saturday morning where a special train just for the camp was going to take all the kids to Wisconsin. Mother said she thought it sounded like so much fun, but I didn't think it would be fun. The train started out in Chicago, and it was about half filled with kids by the time it got to town. Patrick Dannehey and his mother and father were waiting on the platform when we got there. Mother went right over to them and started talking and laughing with Mr. and Mrs. Dannehey. She was always cheerful and polite with other people. I said hi to Patrick Dannehey, who looked weak and sick, and he started talking to me. He asked me if I had been to camp before and what I thought the kids would be like. I knew Mother and the Danneheys were watching us, wanting us to get along and be friends. This made me not want to talk to Patrick at all. I didn't want to be mean to him, but I couldn't help feeling mean. I said no, I never went to the camp before and that I didn't know how the kids would be. I felt bad about not being nice, but when I looked at Patrick Dannehey's weak face and his soft white arms, I got even madder about having to go off to a camp I never wanted to go to and that nobody even asked me about before signing me up.

Two big boys from the camp who might have been in college or even men came up to us and told us which car to get into, and I realized that Patrick Dannehey was going to get on the same car with me and sit next to me in the double seat all the way up to Wisconsin. Mother helped me lift my suitcase, which was a huge blue plastic one of Nana's, up the steps of my car, and then she gave me a long hug and said goodbye. She was crying a little and being really nice, so I tried not to show her how mean I was feeling. I dragged my suitcase to the seat where Patrick was already sitting by the window. I lifted it up onto the seat so there could it be a wall between us, and then I sat back and got as mad as I could.

The train seemed to stop every three minutes to pick up more kids, and our car got noisier and noisier. Some of the kids who must have gone to the camp before were singing songs about Camp Ottawanna, which got me to hate those songs right away, songs like

We welcome you to Otta-wan-nay
On the sandy banks of Lake Hathaway,
Where hearty braves can swim and play
In the old Ottawanna way

The songs were supposed to sound like real Indian songs with a *boom*ba-*boom*ba rhythm, but they mainly sounded corny, and most of the kids couldn't sing at all, so they just shouted. For as much of the trip as I could, I shut my eyes and tried to look like I was sleeping, so I wouldn't have to talk to Patrick Dannehey.

When the train finally got to the last stop, I opened my eyes and looked out the window, but there was no camp or lake, just a station platform and some stores of a little town. From the train we all had to get in old yellow buses, which smelled like gasoline and sour sweat and throw-up. The ride was bumpy and kind of sickening, which made people stop talking and singing. The bus turned off the paved road and went through the woods for a while down a rutted dirt lane that came to a big clearing with a line of log cabins and behind them a big, shimmering lake. Seeing the lake got the other kids excited again, and they started talking about camp things they knew and remembered from last year and the names of the cabins and the counselors. We were about the third bus in, and when it came time for us to get out, one of the counselors who helped get us onto the train stood on the bus steps and blew a loud whistle. He said his name really fast, but told us to call him either Kip or Mr. K. He told us we were all going to have a lot of fun, provided we did one thing, and that was to do what he told us to do, right away with no lip. He told us to get off the bus and form a circle around a log bench he pointed to. When we were all off the bus, standing around the bench with our suitcases, he looked at us for a long time and didn't say anything. Then he got up on the bench and turned slowly around, still not saying anything. He blew his whistle again, which was unbelievably loud, and said, "I hope we're not off to a bad start here. I hope we're not off to a bad start. Because it would be a very bad thing to get off to a bad start, because a bad start is a very bad thing." Somebody laughed, and Kip jumped down from the bench and went over in that direction. He looked mad. He was standing right in front of Patrick Dannehey. "Was that *you?*" he shouted at Patrick. "Did I say something *funny?*" I could see Patrick Dannehey say "no" but it didn't make any sound. "Well, I hope not," Kip said, and he clapped his hands down really hard on Patrick Dannehey's shoulders. "Because that would get us off to a bad start, and that would be a bad thing."

I felt terrible looking at Patrick Dannehey's scared white face. I knew he wasn't the one who laughed, and that made me start to like him.

The Other World

"We're off to a bad start," Kip said, "because you guys didn't listen to the one important thing I told you." I couldn't stand this. I wished I could turn completely invisible and pick up a rock and throw it at his head. "I told you to make a *circle* around this bench, and would anyone call this a *circle?*" He blew his whistle and clapped his hands, and kids started moving around trying to form a circle. Pretty soon everybody got the idea, and we were all standing in a pretty good circle. "Well what do you know," Kip said, "so it's true, chimpanzees really can learn." Some kids laughed, and Kip didn't mind. He looked like he was in a good mood now and told us the first thing we were going to do before we went to our cabins was to learn the Camp Ottawanna song.

Kip said, "Here's what we're going to do. I'm going to sing this song for you, one line at a time, and you are going to listen to it and remember it. Then I'm going to ask some *volunteers*"—he looked around the circle. "I'm going to ask some *volunteers* from last year to demonstrate how it goes, and then we're all going to sing. *Because*, my little monkey friends, nobody is going anywhere until we can sing Ottawanna Way by heart. Got that? No suppy, no beddy-bye until we sing it loud and clear. Okay!"

Kip said a line of the song in his talking voice, and then he sang it. When he was done, he sang the whole song through.

On the banks of great Lake Hathaway
Where chief Black Wing once came to stay
We will pitch our tent and stake our camp
In the old Ottawanna way.

At Ottowan-nay where we work and play
The weak go home but the strong ones stay
To greet the sun at the break of day
In the old Ottawanna way.

Undabunda dee, undabunda ray
Kowakumpa ree, kowakumpa kay
This is what the young braves say
In the old Ottawanna way.

And now you know our sacred song
And evermore can sing along
In joyful voices clear and strong
In the old Ottawanna way.

Kip sang the song in a loud goofy voice that wasn't really like singing, more like making fun of singing, and while he was doing it, I realized who he kept reminding me of—my little league coach, Wayne Stegner. It seemed like there was a certain kind of person, like Wayne Stegner or Kip or Lodi the German janitor at school, who were in charge of kids or who worked around kids and everyone was supposed to like them because they wanted to be with kids. They all had that exaggerated way of acting and talking that kids were supposed to like but I never liked at all. Something, though, about that kind of person seemed to hypnotize a lot of kids, and they talked about people like Kip as if they were really funny or really great guys, even though they were actually pretty mean and sometimes got way too personal. Our Youth Outreach minister at church was like that too. Reverend Klug. He was still partly in college, and you could see practically his whole scalp under the long strands of his hair, which made me wish he was just bald. Reverend Klug told all the kids in Youth Outreach that he believed God called him to work with us. He told Youth Outreach that we could tell him anything at any time and he would keep it to himself. Sometimes he was kind of interesting, like when he would tell us things he did when he was a kid in Duluth, Minnesota, but he wasn't very good at organizing us to do things or getting us to be quiet. It seemed like the main thing he wanted to do was talk to us while we sat and listened to him. Everything took him forever to explain before we could get up and actually do anything. Also, I didn't like looking directly in his face because he had some kind of extra lip behind his upper lip, and it would show a little when he said certain words. He wasn't very good at keeping us quiet, either. We would be fooling around, talking to each other while he was explaining something, and he would just stop talking and stare out at us, looking sad. I remember wondering what it felt like for him to be called by God to work with us in Youth Outreach. It was hard for me to picture, but it seemed to go with a lot of other church things like Sunday picnics and pancake breakfasts, which we went to but were never any fun. Almost everything about Reverend Klug made me want to get out of Youth Outreach as soon as I could.

We stayed in the circle and practiced singing Ottawanna Way about fifty times. Even after we knew it, Kip said it wasn't loud enough. He made us count off in threes, and had the ones and twos and threes sing it separately to see who could do it the loudest. By the end, everybody was practically screaming the words, so there was hardly any tune to it. Finally we were loud enough, and Kip led us over to our cabins so we could unpack and wash up before supper in Black Wing Lodge. My cabin was Laughing Bear, and there were twelve kids in it and six bunk beds. A big kid named Warren Keener was in charge of our cabin and had his own bed. Warren Keener was thirteen, and he got to be junior counselor by going to Camp Ottawanna for three years in a row and winning a bunch of Achievement Awards at the final Pow-Wow. Kip was in charge of Warren and the other junior counselors, but you could tell they were extra friendly and that he wouldn't make Warren do the kinds of things he would make the regular kids do. Kip told us Warren was our "lord and master" when we were in the cabin, and that if any of us gave him trouble, we would be spending time, he said, "with Mr. K.," and that we wouldn't enjoy it very much. Then he went away to the next cabin and left us with Warren Keener, who told us to form pairs and choose a bunk and decide who was on top and who was on the bottom. He said we had to keep our suitcases under the bed and out of sight and to keep our bed made all day and to leave the bathroom neat and clean. He said it should be "spotless." He said there were cabin inspections every now and then, and he wanted Laughing Bear to get a lot of Achievement Points, so we could win the special banquet, which was steak, on the last day of camp.

Warren Keener was tall and bony. His chest was caved in a little, and he slouched forward while he talked to us. He had dark hair in a short crew cut with a funny dent in the front. He didn't seem like a nice kid at all, even though he got chosen to be a junior counselor. He liked using dirty words like "piss" for peeing and "crapper" for the toilet. He told us things like, "We'll get along great if you don't give me any shit."

He told us to let him know if kids from the other cabins gave us any shit. He said sometimes there were midnight raids on the cabin from kids in other cabins. The purpose was to mess up your cabin and get away before anybody got caught. The other thing he said kids from other cabins might do is pants you when you were walking back to the cabin after Camp Fire or some other time when they could get away with it. Somebody asked what pantsing was, and Warren Keener said it was a kid holding you from behind while another kid pulled your pants down or even off. He said sometimes when you got pantsed they might goose your balls, sometimes not. He said most of the pantsing was for fun, and it helped keep up the competition between the cabins. He said the best way not to get pantsed was to stick together.

A big blond kid named Wally Kanicky said he would share a bunk with me and that he wanted the bottom. I said fine. We were supposed to take the things we needed from our suitcases, like our toothbrushes and toothpaste, and put them under our pillows, then to stow our suitcases under the bottom bunk so they wouldn't show during inspection. Nana's big blue suitcase was too big to fit under the bunk, so I asked Warren Keener what to do. He said "Figure it out," and gave me a mean look. I had to keep looking at him, because I didn't know what to do with the suitcase. Finally he said, "Why'd you bring such a big suitcase?" and told me he didn't care what I did with it, just to put it somewhere.

That turned out to be the way everything was at Camp Ottawanna. Everything was supposed to be all set up on a schedule, which was out to the flagpole in the morning when the bugle went off, breakfast at the lodge, getting into our bathing suits and going to the lake for swimming practice and races, changing back into our clothes for field sports, then lunch, then back to the lake for sailing or kayaking lessons, then cabin hour, then to the ball fields for volley ball or softball, then supper, then Campfire, then either back to the cabin to bed or go somewhere for an overnight in a tent. After a day or two, I realized that each thing we did was terrible, and it wasn't going to get any better. The system was to make everything a little too hard or too rushed. For instance, when the bugle blew out at the flagpole in the morning, each cabin had to have every kid there in formation in ten minutes. This never worked, because some kids were so sound asleep they couldn't get moving even when someone pulled them out of their bunk onto the floor. Also there were only two toilet seats and two sinks in the bathroom, and everybody had to go and most kids wanted to brush their teeth, and there was no room, so most kids, including me, would go out and pee behind the cabin. I hated having to run out to the flagpole in my wrinkly clothes when the grass was still so wet my sneakers would get soaked through. Some kids were always late, and Kip would make them and sometimes their whole cabins do push-ups in the wet grass while everybody watched. Kids who made their cabins get push-ups would usually get pantsed on the way to breakfast.

The counselors worked it so that nothing could be fun or relaxing. The meals were terrible, especially breakfast, which was always the same, sour juice, cold toast, and eggs which were between scrambled and fried with streaky brown marks on them from the grill. They turned cold in your mouth, and there was no salt or pepper because when they used to have it, kids would unscrew the tops of the shakers so that the whole thing would come out on your food.

I hated swimming the most, because it was right after breakfast when it wasn't really warm yet, and when it wasn't sunny, I would get so cold in the water my jaw would start shaking on its own, so I couldn't even talk. We'd have to start out swimming laps doing the crawl, breaststroke and backstroke, and then we'd have races against the other cabins, keeping score. There was a lot of screaming during the races, and if you didn't win your laps or fell behind during your lap of a relay, Warren Keener, who always had on dry clothes and a sweatshirt, would stand over you on the dock and say something like, "Thanks a lot, now we're in fourth" or "great speed." Some kids, like Wally Kanicky, could barely swim at all and were in a special beginners group during laps, but when races started everybody was supposed to swim for the cabin. Warren Keener would cheat every now and then by skipping Wally Kanicky and having some good swimmer go twice, but sometimes Wally had to swim, and Warren Keener would say something like, "Great, now we're in last," before Wally even started.

One of the main counselors, Mort Emerson, was in charge of all the boats, and when Kip introduced him the first day, he said Mort Emerson had been on a boat racing team in the Olympics. Mort Emerson was pretty serious and quiet, and he didn't seem to like teaching kids about sailing and kayaking. He talked in a quiet voice and kept the same expression on his face. He didn't seem actually mad, but you could tell he didn't really want to be around a bunch of kids, especially on the camp's big sailboat, *The Ottawanna*. Mort Emerson was really strict, and he meant it. He wouldn't let any kid sail by himself, even in one of the dinghies, until he could pass a test of boating terms and then prove he could tack, jibe, and land a boat without smashing the bow into the dock. This was actually pretty hard, so only about four kids got Sailing Privileges the whole time we were there. There was also kayaking, which seemed to me like it should have been simple, but Mort Emerson told us it was really dangerous, and that we had to learn safety techniques like rolling completely over underwater before we could take out a kayak by ourselves. In order to roll the kayak, we had to be strapped inside in a very complicated way, which I couldn't keep track of, and most of the kayaks were missing some strap or buckle or something, so almost no one got certified to kayak by himself. That actually disappointed me, because I liked the feeling of paddling the kayak through the water and it would have been nice to be able to take off somewhere by myself.

The big treat in the boating program was supposed to be the day you got to sail out on Lake Hathaway in *The Ottawanna*. Starting the last few days of camp, each cabin got a turn, and even though I should have known better, I was kind of excited when it was time for Laughing Bear to go out. For one thing, *The Ottawanna* had a downstairs cabin with beds and sinks and cabinets and instruments built into the walls, and kids got to go "below" to see it. What I always liked best about ships in the pirate movies was that down inside they had big rooms with heavy dark furniture, like a house. The cabin of *The Ottawanna* was a little like that. All the woodwork and brass was polished and shiny, and it would have been nice staying down there, but something about being down out of the air while the boat was moving up and down made you automatically feel a little sick. Even if it didn't, we weren't allowed to stay down there or to do anything, just to look around. We were all supposed to do certain jobs on deck, things we practiced during boating instruction, like trimming the main sheet or raising the jib or setting the spinnaker. The afternoon of our sail was pretty windy, and none of us was strong enough to pull in the ropes that adjusted the sails by ourselves, so Mort Emerson had to step in and do practically everything. I mainly just stood there, holding onto a rope, feeling the boat dip down into a pocket then rising up to meet the wall of a wave, spraying me with cold water. As I stood there holding on and squinting at the shore, I kept thinking that if you took a picture of me and the other kids out on the lake sailing *The Ottawanna*, it would look exactly the way my mother pictured it when she decided to send me to camp, but thinking about Mother only made me feel sad.

I don't think Mother even believed in people like Warren Keener, people that mean. He wasn't mean every now and then or mean just to some kids. He was the kind of kid who tried to make you feel as bad as possible, no matter what it was about. If a kid got homesick and started to cry during cabin hour when the mail came, Warren Keener would go over to the kid's bunk and tease him. He'd say, "What's the matter? You miss your mommy and daddy?" He'd keep going until the kid was really crying, until maybe the kid would start yelling swear words and swinging at him, and then he would jerk the kid around by the front of his shirt and tell him he was in big trouble. If Warren Keener was making fun of a kid, he tried to get other kids in on it, and some kids would join in, to get in good with Warren Keener for a while. Most kids, though, tried to stay away from him as much as possible. You just didn't want him to notice you, which was hard when he was with our cabin for most of the day.

You were supposed to be really excited and try really hard to get a lot of Achievement Points in everything, including inspections, swimming, boating skills, and crafts. The junior counselors reported each cabin's total Achievement Points at morning flagpole, but because Warren Keener was our junior counselor and got to give Laughing Bear's report, we pretty much stopped trying to get a lot of Achievement Points, which made Warren Keener start calling us "losers" when he talked to us after Lights Out.

Lights Out was really unfair, because the campers weren't supposed to be allowed to talk, only the junior counselor. But Warren Keener would get kids to talk by teasing them or by asking questions, and then, whenever he felt like it, he'd get mad at them and tell them he was reporting them to Kip. Sometimes he did report them, and they'd have to do push-ups or laps at morning flagpole, and sometimes he didn't. You never knew. Sometimes everybody was talking and laughing and screwing around after Lights Out, and Warren Keener wouldn't care. He would use really dirty words and let other kids use them, and this would get kids laughing, and it would get louder and dirtier until I had to go into a certain kind of trance. I hated talking and screwing around during Lights Out more than I hated anything else at the camp. At night in my bunk was the one time I had to make my pictures and tell my stories, but I couldn't do it with everyone making farting noises and Warren Keener talking about everybody's private parts and getting kids to laugh at him. Whenever he felt like it Warren Keener could tell people to shut up and if they didn't, he said he would make sure something would happen to them on our next tent overnight.

Tent overnights were supposed to be where we learned camping and wilderness survival, but there was an old tradition where kids from a certain cabin were allowed to go out after Lights Out with their junior counselor and ransack the tents and scare the kids from the cabin that was camping out. Kip and the main counselors were in on it, and it was supposed to be fun because it was a tradition, but on our cabin's tent nights, some kids got into real fights. Weak kids got pantsed and tied up to trees, and some kids got their sleeping bags peed on. I think something bad happened to Patrick Dannehey on his cabin's first tent night, because a kid told me his parents drove up and took him home.

The final two days of camp were supposed to be the most fun. In the morning, instead of races and relays, there was free swimming. Kids who got certified in boating were allowed to take the sailing dinghies and kayaks out by themselves. Before supper on the second-to-last night was the Radio Show, which was supposed to be an actual program that went out over the radio in Wisconsin. Some of the cabins worked up skits, and kids who could play instruments or sing or do imitations performed at a big microphone in front of the whole camp. Before the show started, the kids in the audience had to practice clapping and laughing when the counselors held up a sign saying APPLAUSE or LAUGH. Almost from the time we sat down, kids started leaning over to other kids and saying it wasn't real, because the big microphone looked fake, and the headphones Kip was wearing didn't have wires connected to anything, but the kids went along with it, laughing and clapping when the signs went up. I couldn't understand what anybody was saying during the skits, and most of the kids who sang or played their instruments weren't as good as the kids at school. One kid was really good, though. He played a boogie-woogie on the piano, which was as good as an actual record. Toward the end of it, Kip stood up in front and made a big face and started clapping in rhythm to the boogie-woogie beat. Everybody joined in, but in my opinion it spoiled the song.

That night they put paper tablecloths on the tables for supper, and we got fried chicken. For the next-to-last Campfire everybody got marshmallows to toast in the fire, but the final Campfire was supposed to be the biggest tradition in the camp and people said that it made some kids cry. As I walked over to the fire pit from Black Wing, I wondered if they could actually do anything that would make me cry in a good way, but nothing like that happened. There were mainly a bunch of awards. You got a certificate for everything you did, for swimming, for boating, for softball, even if you didn't advance to a higher level. Kids got special awards for being the best in each thing. I had a feeling I might get the softball award, because I was one of the best players and was one of the captains, but I didn't get it. It went on and on, and even though you got up about every two minutes to get another certificate with your group, it was hard to keep paying attention and to keep clapping for everybody. When it was almost over, Kip gave special certificates and hunting knives to the junior counselors. Warren Keener went up to get his knife just like everyone else, and when he shook hands with Kip, he smiled and looked glad, just like a regular nice kid. It was like another awful thing he knew how to do. I knew that in a little while he would be lying close by in the dark after Lights Out talking about people's private parts.

Usually after Camp Fire the kids lined up behind their junior counselor, and he would turn on his flashlight and lead them back to the cabin. But the tradition for Last Camp Fire was for each kid to get his own candle, and Kip would light the junior counselor's candle, and the junior counselor would light the candle of the first kid in his line, and that kid would light the next kid's until everybody's candle was lit. Then they would walk single file through the trees singing *Fair Ottawanna.*

> *Though in the years to come*
> *Our paths will surely stray*
> *The sons of noble Dark Wing*
> *Will softly make their way*
> *Yes softly make their way*
> *To our fair Otta-wan-nay.*

I held my candle out in front of me so I could see the path, and I tried to hear if anybody was crying. I hoped they weren't. I hoped that when I got back to the cabin and everybody was finally quiet, I could start thinking up things I could tell Mother about the camp that wouldn't make her feel bad.

THE REAL THING

At the beginning of the summer I thought going to Junior High would be the most exciting thing that was going to happen to me, but then the real thing happened.

Junior High meant going across town to a new, bigger building, and the whole setup was different. You didn't have your own homeroom with your own teacher and the same kids for most of the day. You went to a different class with a different teacher each period. You got a locker, and you had periods that were just study halls when you didn't have to do anything. When I was in fifth grade class with all my friends, I liked picturing Junior High and all the new arrangements. I already had some good pictures in my mind from the times I would go to the Junior High with Mother to pick up my sister Annabel after school or to see one of her choir concerts. I liked the way the seventh and eighth graders looked. Some of the boys were really tall and dressed like high school boys with white buck shoes and khaki pants and crewneck sweaters. Those big kids laughing and horsing around in the lobby or shooting baskets on the paved courts outside seemed like they had their own secret world, and it made me start hoping really hard that I would get taller.

The week before I went to camp, Mother took me to Zimmerman's department store to buy me school clothes for Junior High. I was secretly hoping she would get me khaki pants and crewneck sweaters, but I didn't see any in the part of the store that had my size, and I didn't really know the names of what to ask for, so I ended up getting some new jeans and corduroys and more plaid flannel shirts like my old ones. I did ask Mother if I could get white buck shoes, but she didn't think I was serious. She said white buck shoes got dirty and ratty looking after a while and that mine would get dirty right away.

In Junior High there was no recess, but a separate class called Gym, and boys had to have their own gym shorts, gym shirt and sweat suit. The shorts and shirts and sweat suits said PALATINE PHYSICAL EDUCATION on them, and there was a box below the letters for your name. The gym uniforms stayed the same all the way through high school. I had seen lots of Palatine gym shorts and sweat suits because big kids wore them all the time in the summer when they played basketball under the lights at the park. Zimmerman's had a special room just for school gym uniforms, and there were high stacks of new-smelling tee shirts and shorts and gray sweat suits on the tables. The sizes were Small, Medium, and Large, and Mother thought even the Smalls looked like they would be too big for me. She held up a pair of size Small gym shorts and tried to figure out if the waist was too big. She told me to go into one of the changing closets and try them on. I knew I could figure out a way to wear them no matter how big the waist was, but I tried them on anyway, and they were fine because there was an elastic band puckered into the cloth that held them up over my hips.

The first thing I did when I got back to my room was to try on my whole gym uniform, starting with my athletic supporter, which had the effect of making me feel kind of nude. Then I put on the shorts and the tee shirt, which was so long it came down lower than the shorts. I decided to put on my sneakers too, so I could see what I would actually look like for Gym. I went into my mother and father's room to look at myself in the long mirror. It wasn't good. The shirt was way too big, and the tops of my arms coming out the sleeve holes looked smaller and bonier than usual. The shirt came down so far it looked like a dress, and even when I tucked it in, the white cloth came down and showed below the bottom of the shorts. Finally I got the shirt not to show by wedging a lot of it inside the elastic of my athletic supporter. It still didn't look good, though. The shorts seemed too stiff and new. I wanted them just to hang down straight along the tops of my legs, but they flared out on each side, which made my legs look extra small.

My mother called up from downstairs and asked me what I was doing, and I shouted down that I was trying on my gym suit. I heard her move to the bottom of the stairs. She said, "Let's see."

So I went over to the top of the stairs and stood there. I knew the gym suit wasn't right and that I felt skinny wearing it, but I didn't know Mother was going to laugh. She wasn't mean at all and never tried to hurt my feelings on purpose, but she couldn't help it. She looked up at me and started laughing. She had to bend over at the waist and was kind of snorting trying to make herself stop, but that made her laugh even harder. I couldn't move or say anything. I just stood there, feeling cold and tingly, feeling the air blowing right up through the huge leg holes of the gym shorts. Mother caught her breath and tried to make me feel better. She said she was sorry. "It's just those... enormous shorts and your little knees." She was still laughing. She couldn't stop.

I wished she hadn't seen me, because even if I disappeared forever that second, it had already happened. She saw me and knew how skinny and ridiculous I looked, which was something I knew I couldn't fix. It was the way I really was, and it felt terrible. I had a feeling that from now on everything that happened was going to be terrible, like camp.

* * *

A few days before school was supposed to begin, I started praying, in a new way I came up with, that I wouldn't have to go to Junior High. In my method I would shut my eyes and make a picture of some sunny place in nature, like the fields or the north woods around one of our cabins. I'd hold the picture still for as long as I could, and then I'd make my mind as tense as possible and say to myself PLEASE GOD KEEP THIS. Then I'd open my eyes. The idea was that maybe I would be pulled up into the bright picture and stay there. It was a little like waking up on certain Saturday mornings and realizing the dream I just woke up from was so good I wanted to go right back to sleep to keep it going. I never figured out how to do it, but I wanted to so much. I knew that if my prayer method ever worked, I'd be gone from the regular world, and that would upset my mother and probably Annabel, but it would be worth it to be back in nature forever and not have to go to Junior High and come out from the locker room and show up in the gymnasium in front of everybody with my little stick arms and legs coming out of my gym uniform.

I don't think it was because of my praying method, but on the Saturday afternoon before school started, I did get pulled up into the other world. Nana and Papa invited me to spend the day and sleep over at their house, and then Annabel would get to do it on Sunday. I always liked sleeping overnight at Nana and Papa's because it took me completely out of my regular life and reminded me of the best things from when I was little. There were a lot of great things to look at in their house, like painted scenes of German towns Papa had wood-burned into a piece of wood, then painted and varnished. Nana had glassed-in cabinets full of fancy china plates with scenes on them, and in Papa's study upstairs there was a shelf full of old-looking beer steins with painted scenes around the sides and pointed metal lids. He also had a rack of carved pipes on his desk and a huge dagger in a green leather sheath that he used as a letter opener. There was one whole bookcase full of big leather volumes of his stamp collections, which I was allowed to look at if he was there with me. Sometimes when he got a new packet of stamps in the mail, he would turn on a special lamp on his desk and let me stand next to him while he took the new stamps out of their little onionskin holders and set them into the albums next to the other stamps from that country. I never got tired of looking at the colored inks and the engraved letters and the little heads of the kings and the queens on the stamps, especially when there was a whole page of them lined up together.

Everything at Nana's and Papa's was like that. You just wanted to look around at the things they had. The big sofa and chairs in their living room were extra comfortable, and Nana always cooked the things she knew were your favorites. There was a bowl of M&Ms on the kitchen table, and I could have as many as I felt like. Maybe the best thing about being over at Nana and Papa's was that you were always allowed to do what you wanted, and there was always enough time. Nana would play Monopoly or cards or Chinese checkers if I asked her to, and she was always in a calm mood about it, kind of pretending to be mad or glad

Richard Hawley

about how she was doing, but she really wasn't. If I felt like playing by myself, Nana would give me a pad of paper and pencils and crayons to draw with and let me alone. She seemed to know in advance the things I wanted to do.

The Saturday before school started was really hot and muggy. I was drawing by myself on the screened-in porch, and Nana came out and asked me if I wanted to go upstairs and change into some cooler clothes, like my shorts and sandals. I actually did feel pretty sticky, so I went up to change. The only pair of shorts I had with me was a too-big pair that we got from my cousin Gordon in a package of hand-me-downs. I knew they looked terrible, and I never would have worn them at home or around other kids, but I knew no one would see me and that Nana and Papa wouldn't care what I put on, so I changed into the shorts. My underpants were sweaty and were sticking to my skin, so I decided to take them off and not wear any. Gordon's old shorts were so baggy and loose, I could feel the air moving around the tops of my legs all the way up to my thing. This felt uncomfortable but also good at the same time, and all of a sudden I wanted to get outside, to get into nature, to get past the houses and into the fields right away. It was a very strong feeling, nervous and exciting all at once. It would be a long time until supper, and I decided not to tell Nana I was going out. I just left and started walking.

The fields were only about three streets away from Nana and Papa's house. The road going in was paved with gravel, and there were some houses along the way before the road changed to a dirt path and the actual fields began. Sometimes Nana and I would take a hike down this path, but it wouldn't last very long, because the path came to an end in high grass that sloped down to a swampy place. Nana didn't like hiking off the path, so we'd turn around and head back.

Today I wasn't even thinking about what was along the path. I just needed to get past the houses and be by myself in the hot fields. By the time I got to the dirt path, I was really hot. I had to keep swatting at bugs buzzing around the back of my head, and my face got so sweaty I had to stop every now and then and wipe my eyes. It was the kind of hot day that made everything in the

123

fields come to life. Big grasshoppers were making rattling arcs across the path, and crickets and peepers were screeching in a way that seemed to be coming from inside my own skull. There was no breeze at all, just the hot, heavy air. The excited feeling I got when I first put on the shorts kept building and building. I could feel the cloth brushing against my thing, and I not only didn't mind, it made me feel even more excited. I started to feel like getting naked somewhere all by myself. I had never felt anything like this before, and I knew that something even greater was coming. I took off my sweaty tee shirt and stuffed it into the pocket of my shorts, which made them slide down further on my hips. My thing started to rise up and in a minute it felt as hard as a bone. When I got to the end of the path, the waves of screeching from the fields and the pulsing in my chest felt like they were the same thing. It felt like the sticky air wasn't outside my skin anymore, as if I had somehow spilled out of myself and was all mixed up in everything. I just kept moving into the high grass and didn't care about it tickling against my bare arms and legs and belly. I was too excited to make a picture of where I was going or even to think. I just forced my way through the heavy grass until I was under the dark branches of sumac trees. I felt my feet sink down into something cold, and both sneakers filled up with water.

 I had reached the edge of a still black pool. Sumac and other trees with long slender trunks grew up out of the water, and the branches overhead made a dark leafy dome that only let in a few patches of sunlight. It was airless and a little cooler under the cover of the dome. I was aware of the hot white light outside, and I could still hear the waves of screeching from the fields, but, except for the plop and croak of a frog every now and then, it was a dark and quiet place, and it had called me there. I knew I was in another time in another world, the world before the regular world, and even though I knew in my mind it was afternoon, it was somehow also twilight. I untied my sneakers and took them off. Then I unbuttoned my shorts and let them slide down around my ankles. The back of my neck and skull and all down my spine started tingling, and then the tingling took over my whole body. I didn't know if I was dead or already in heaven. All I could do was stand still and feel everything, feel each wave of tingling give way to a stronger one until I was held in a spiral of all of them at once. Then the pleasure erupted. It came throbbing out of my thing, and then everywhere. It was everything I could feel, everything there was. It rose and fell, rose and fell, until it was gone.

The first thing I thought was that I did not ever want to leave. I wanted it to happen again, but the longer I stood there, the more I knew I was just standing in muck with my shorts down around my ankles. I knew I had been taken up into the other world and that I had felt everything there was, but I also knew that even now, even right afterward, I couldn't connect what happened to the regular world. There was no way to talk about it and nobody I could tell. By the time I was dressed and sloshing along the path in my mucky sneakers, I was so far back in the regular world that I couldn't even tell myself what had just happened to me.

JUNIOR HIGH

The farthest you can get from the other world is school. Even the first days, which used to be the best days, I could see that something was wrong with Junior High. Almost nobody from my fifth grade section was in any of my classes, and I could go practically all day without really talking to anybody. Every fifty-two minutes we went to a different room for a different subject, and we were supposed to have a different section of our notebook for each subject. Math was just a lot of problems, and in most of the other classes the teachers taught us how to take notes and make outlines, because we were going to have to make a lot of outlines of big topics like lumber and transportation and then do reports on them, along with maps and articles you cut out of newspapers and certain other things you could do for extra credit. At the end of the unit, you handed everything in to the teacher in a colored folder and then got a grade on the whole thing. I knew all about it from Annabel, who kept all her old units in her desk drawer. Annabel had beautiful, perfect handwriting, and she copied over all her written work in ink. She was right-handed, so she didn't make a smeary mess of everything with the edge of her hand the way I did. Also, her extra credit drawings, especially in the Birds of the Americas unit, were really beautiful, as good as the ones in books, but in crayon. Annabel did her extra credit and her other work in her room by herself. She hardly ever talked about her units or about school. In Junior High you got graded on everything, and three times a year you got report cards with a list of your grades in each subject, along with a 1, 2, or 3 in effort and conduct, 1 being excellent, 2 being satisfactory, and 3 being unsatisfactory. Annabel got Bs on all her units, and underneath the B her teacher would maybe write "Good" or "Good Work." I asked her if B was pretty good, and she said it was okay, that it was average. Annabel was always quiet, but she got really quiet in Junior High. She did her work at night, and she got Bs on her units, and when her report card came, she and Mother would go over it, and Mother would ask me to leave the table so they could have some privacy, because Annabel was getting Ds and Fs in math.

I had always been one of the smallest kids, but in Junior High I also started to feel small. Gym didn't turn out to be as bad as I thought, though. I didn't know most of the kids in my section, and because I was one of the kids who was really good at sports, nobody made any bad comments. I also noticed that some of the kids wore kneepads in Gym, and I thought the kneepads would make my legs look bigger. What bothered me the most was that my lower leg looked so small and skinny below my knee. Most kids' legs just tapered down gradually down to their ankles, and there would be a kind of bulge of muscle in the calf, but below my knee there was a big indentation and then just my skinny shin bone. It looked really terrible in the mirror, like the legs of starving kids in Africa. I knew the kneepads would sort of fill in the indentation, so I told Mother they were required, and we got a pair at the sporting goods store. After that, I started to be able to relax in Gym.

Sixth grade was supposed to be the first grade of Junior High, but in a way it was separate. Palatine Central Junior High had sports teams with uniforms and played games across town with Palatine South and Palatine North and other places, but only seventh and eighth graders could be on the teams. Sixth graders just had Gym teams. Some sixth graders could be on Student Council if they got nominated and the whole class voted on them, but there were mostly new kids from the other elementary schools in my classes, so nobody nominated me, even though I secretly wanted them to, because in Mr. Click's fifth grade class I got to be president and captain of just about everything. I didn't tell anyone, but it made me sad not to be one of the sixth graders on Student Council, because I could see that in seventh and eighth grade, the kids who got nominated and elected were the kids who got elected in sixth grade because they were the kids everybody knew, so I would never be on Student Council. That whole feeling of being elected and sitting up in front of everybody wasn't going to happen anymore.

But a much worse thing than that happened a few weeks later. It gave me the worst, most miserable feeling I ever felt, and it never really went away.

After lunch in the cafeteria you could buy candy bars at a special Student Council table. Members of the Student Council got to collect the money, which went for things like dances and foster children. Anybody with any money always got in line after lunch and bought candy bars. One day as I was about to stack up my tray and get in line, I looked up in front of me to where the Student Council kids were standing around, and I saw the back of Patsy Prentiss's head. I actually felt a kind of clout in my chest even before I recognized her. There was the crinkly swirl of blonde and brown hair, and then she turned around a little, and I could see her sunburned cheeks. She was talking to a bunch of seventh and eighth grade Student Council kids who were sitting on the edge of the candy table. I could see her start to laugh, and I remembered the sound of it, the helpless machine-gun rattle that came out of her. I remembered her husky voice and how it felt to be around her, the way she was always just about to do something I didn't expect.

Patsy. How could I have forgotten her? Then everything from fifth grade came back in a rush, running through people's back yards in the cold fall air, lying tangled in the straw, looking up into the darkening sky and feeling her skull against mine, sitting back in the breezy snack bar of the Country Club, seeing the crinkles in the corners of her eyes as she was telling me something funny. There were a lot of kids in line between me and where Patsy was standing. I kept watching her as I moved up, and the closer I got the worse I felt. It would take me a long time before I could understand it or explain it in words, but before I even got close enough to her to wave and say hi, I knew I wasn't going to be important enough. I was going to be too small, and I wouldn't know enough, and there was going to be something that wasn't right about my clothes. Maybe Patsy grew a lot over the summer, or maybe it just seemed like she did, but by the time I got up to her, she seemed not only much bigger, but a completely different kind of person, almost not even a kid.

She had on different clothes than I had ever seen her wear. She was wearing a gray skirt and a soft gray sweater under another sweater just like it but with buttons up the front. She had on white buck shoes and new white sweat socks, which made the skin on her calves look extra brown and shiny. Her calves were just the right size and looked really nice. I bought a candy bar and walked up next to her. She was telling a story and had just said, "We all practically broke our necks," when she noticed me. She said, "*Hey*, Jonathan!" She was being really nice. "Hey, this is Jonathan Force, my old bud." *Old bud.* The seventh and eighth graders looked at me, and then Patsy finished her story. It felt all wrong to be standing there. I was the smallest kid by a lot. I just had on my regular clothes, and the seventh and eighth graders had on khaki pants and nice shirts with button-down collars and white bucks. They were supposed to be around the candy table, and I wasn't.

All that fall I would lie in the dark at night and try to understand what had happened, how Patsy could have changed into a new kind of person, a person I knew I didn't even belong with but still wanted to be with. I wanted to get back that feeling when we were running somewhere side by side. I wanted the skull-to-skull feeling, and the thought that it was gone and I'd never have it again made me too sad to cry. Before that day in the candy line I wasn't thinking about her at all. I had forgotten her. After that, I couldn't get her out of my head for a second. I figured out where each of her classes was and knew where she was every minute of the school day. Two or three times every day I would pass her in the corridor between classes or going up the stairs while she was coming down. For a while I tried hanging around where she was standing after lunch or on the playground, but that only made me feel worse, because she was always with a bunch of bigger kids I didn't know, and some of the boys were the tallest kids in the school.

A few days after I saw her in the candy line, I called her on the telephone. I didn't really know what I wanted to say, but I ended up asking her if I could come over to her house after school and do something. She said sure, but even though she was nice, I could tell that she didn't think my coming over was going to be anything special, probably because I didn't think it would be either. I knew I was too small. But I still loved to think about her. Even though she was bigger and was starting to have that teenager look, I couldn't wait to catch sight of her in the corridor, to see the way her hair bounced around her head when she walked, the brown and peach color of her cheeks. There are some people, and Patsy was one of them, who just cause your cells to change when you get near them.

The afternoon I went to Patsy's house after school wasn't much of anything. She met me on her front stoop, and we sat down and talked about school and the teachers we had. She said she liked Junior High so far but really missed the kids she was with over the summer on their island. She asked me about camp, and I said it was slightly crummy but okay. We played the bowling game in her basement for a while, and even though I kept feeling I wanted to talk to her more than anything and figure out a way that she would only want to be with me after school so we could do everything together like last year, I couldn't do it. Everything I thought of to say was boring, even to me. I couldn't even imagine getting off a good one. We talked a little more on her front stoop, and then I walked home and let the sadness take over.

* * *

In some ways Junior High was even more terrible than camp. There was nobody who wanted to hurt you all the time or who was as dirty-minded as my junior counselor Warren Keener, but the days were organized pretty much the same way. You went to a new class every period, and you handed in homework from the day before for a check mark, and then the teacher explained something new, and then you had homework about that. Most of the teachers seemed to be in a hurry, and they acted like we were already behind in whatever we were supposed to be doing. The main classes like English and math and science were grouped by ability: Accelerated, Fast, and Average. In Art and Music and Gym ability didn't matter, and anybody could be in your section. I was in Accelerated everything except math, where I was in Fast.

The Other World

We got put in ability-grouped classes based on how we did on tests we took in fifth grade, the Iowa Standard Achievements. I couldn't remember taking the tests and wondered if I was even there on those days. I especially wondered how they figured out I was only Fast in math. I always thought I was one of the smartest kids in math, one of the kids who figured everything out right away and got problems right on the board and on tests. Somebody must have known something, though, because when we got into algebra later, I started getting things wrong even in Fast.

It was fine to be in Fast classes, but nobody wanted to be in Average. You weren't supposed to look down on kids who had all Average classes, but you couldn't help thinking about them in a different way and feeling sorry for them. Sometimes a kid would drop out of an Accelerated class into Fast or a smart Fast kid would go up to Accelerated, but no Average kids ever got moved up. They pretty much stayed in their own groups, and then in high school you would almost never see them because they would be in Vocational Ed, which prepared you for life in minor jobs.

Except for algebra later, I didn't think any of the work in Junior High was very hard, but there was always something you had to do. There were books and printed articles we had to read and outline for Social Studies, and the outlines would be part of our units. There was no Reading for Life competition anymore. Everybody in Accelerated English read the same books, books Junior High kids had always read, such as *Johnny Tremain, Julius Caesar,* and *The Diary of Anne Frank.* I got all of them from Annabel, and I had read most of them already. I ended up reading *Diary of Anne Frank* a bunch of times. I read it the first time because when Annabel read it, she was so upset she cried really hard and had to be alone with Mother. After that she had nightmares. When I read it, I saw why she had that reaction. A story like that is too mean for a girl like Annabel, not that Anne Frank herself was mean in any way. She was actually tremendous and the kind of person I know I would have had the love feeling for if I ever met her, but knowing that the Nazis crashed into their family's upstairs hiding place and took them away to the concentration camps where they died was something Annabel couldn't stand to picture.

I didn't read *Julius Caesar* in advance, because when I started to read it, I couldn't understand a single thing. Not only could I not understand the way the words went together, I couldn't figure out who the people were whose names kept being mentioned. *Julius Caesar* was the kind of book the teacher had to tell you everything about in advance, and even then you weren't sure you were getting anything out of the actual words. It felt important to be reading something by William Shakespeare, and I could never get some of the phrases out of my head, like "yon Cassius has a lean and hungry look" or "lend me your ears," but for a play that was supposed to be about stabbing and battles, it never felt, when you were actually reading it, that anything was happening.

I did okay in Junior High and toward the end got straight A's a few times because I decided to make it a project, but I never got the feeling back I had in fifth grade with Mr. Click, the feeling that nobody could come up with the kind of things I could. I think Mr. Click thought I was kind of amazing, and that got me in a really good mood. I doubt that anybody thought I was amazing in Junior High. I know I didn't.

When I think back, the main thing I did in Junior High was try not to feel too bad. I didn't want to get into that nervous, black feeling I could get into in my bed at night where I'd think about some terrible thing about my body or that somebody had said to me, then circle back to it again and again until it connected to something that was even worse, so it felt like I was caught in a spiral of awfulness that was taking me down and down into a complete darkness that, if I went down into it all the way, was going to be the worst thing there was.

Sometimes I thought I could stay out of the spiral if I just kept doing things, even stupid little things, anything that would keep me up on the surface. For instance, I got really good at writing with my right hand, and with my left hand I learned how to do about six absolutely different kinds of handwriting, so I always had something to do in class that looked like I was working. I started buying baseball cards and trading them with other kids and building up my collection. It wasn't too interesting, but it was just interesting enough to keep me doing it. I liked knowing the players' names—Ted Kluzewski, Dee Fondi, Minny Minoso, Robin Roberts, Jesus McFarland, Nelly Foxx—just by the look of their big meaty faces. I liked the colors of their hats and the idea that their whole lives could be boxed into the little paragraph about them on the back of the card, along with their batting averages and pitching records. There was also something a little sad about baseball cards, because after you had a bunch of them, you realized that most of the players weren't that good and were never going to become famous stars. Most of them had batting averages of around .230 and had been in the Minors and were probably going to be in the Minors again. After a while I had a whole shoe box full of baseball cards, and it gave me the feeling that I actually had all those guys captured in there, their lives shrunk down to cards.

I also started collecting comic books, which gave me the same kind of feeling the baseball cards did. Comics seemed to have a kind of thin life of their own. The people, like Archie and Veronica and Little Lulu and Superman, were just drawn outlines filled in with colored ink, but you could still go into their little worlds right away and stay there for a while. Sometimes I would go over to a kid's house who had a whole stack of comics I had never seen, and I would just sit down somewhere and read all of them, without even having to talk or to think. It wasn't like seeing a movie, because you never felt much about anything in the comics; comics just held you there in that thin world. I remember whole mornings and whole afternoons just lying around reading comics and then feeling that the only good thing was that time had passed.

By then we had a TV and just about everybody else had a TV, but I didn't like to watch it too much. First of all, I can't stand anything that keeps repeating, and the commercials, with the same people saying the same obvious things and the same pictures coming up in the same order, always made me want to go out of the room. Also, just about all the shows were terrible. You knew what was going to happen right away, and then it happened. I don't know who thought up there having to be laughter after just about anything anybody said, but it never sounded right and made me picture a terrible kind of world where people really did laugh at things like that. The whole effect was to make me hope that I would never know people like Lucy and Mr. Peepers and Our Miss Brooks or live in the kinds of places they lived.

Maybe it was my fault, but everything about life then, whether it was TV or comics or Junior High, seemed designed to bring you up to a busy but annoying surface where you had to pretend things were important that you knew you could never care about. I can't remember any miracles in Junior High or ever feeling like I was close to the other world. I didn't know how to get into that mood. All I could think about was figuring out something to keep me interested enough, something like working on a new handwriting or inventing my own language, to keep from getting caught in the spiral of terrible thoughts.

The spiral would usually start when I saw some kids at school who were pretty tall and looked good in their clothes and were obviously having a good time shooting baskets on the outdoor courts or goofing around the student council candy table. I would start to compare myself to them in the worst way, picturing myself as even smaller and skinnier than I was. I would see a kid's crew cut that looked dry and clean with perfect square edges, and then I'd go into the boys' lavatory and look at my crew cut and it would look all smashed down and ratty, probably because my father gave me the haircut with the new shears he bought. He said he knew all about giving crew cuts, that they were the easiest haircuts to give, but mine never looked anything like the dry, square-edged ones the kids had who got to go to the barber's. When I was in that kind of mood, I looked really terrible in the mirror. Besides my mashed down, shiny hair, my head looked way too big for my neck, and if I looked long enough, my nose, and especially my nostrils, started to look huge. I would go away picturing my face like some kind of monster skull with horrible dark nostril holes. That could really get the spiral going, or catching a glimpse of the tops of my skinny arms coming out of a short-sleeved shirt, or just seeing some kid's nice-sized arms, or really anything.

The thing I felt the most terrible about was Patsy Prentiss. I couldn't do anything to make those feelings go away. I wasn't her friend anymore. I didn't even feel like I was the same kind of kid as she was. She had gotten pretty tall and had a figure now. She always looked comfortable in her clothes, and she was always wearing something, like a bright yellow sweater or a pleated plaid skirt or new saddle shoes, that made you want to keep looking at how she was dressed. Kids wanted to be around her, and the seventh and eighth graders let her into their group, and whenever I saw her standing around somewhere, she was with tall kids from the student council and the teams. She seemed to belong naturally around a bigger kind of kid than I was, which I couldn't blame her for, but I couldn't stand it.

I kept picturing her brown cheeks and pretty teeth and the croaky way she talked and laughed. I could feel being skull to skull with her and how she felt leaning into me in the dark at the end of one of the fifth-grade Shock Theater parties. I don't think I forgot anything we ever did, but I hated knowing it was over, that something had carried her up to a higher level where I wasn't included, which must have been because I was so small.

I also knew there was something not right about my clothes, but I couldn't figure out what. All I know is that it felt really terrible to have the love feeling for Patsy all by myself. It made me cry. It made me think that the only reason I got the love feeling in the first place was so that I would know how terrible I could feel. That is what the spiral was like. You got the feeling there was a big plan to hurt you and surprise you and disappoint you in more and more terrible ways. It made you wish you were never born and that it would be better to be dead than to go down the spiral all the way.

SEX AND MUSIC

I don't know if it happened naturally or because I heard so many thousands of sex jokes and stories from kids like Warren Keener and other kids in Junior High, but starting about then I linked my sex feeling to the jokes and the stories. Almost all the girls now had boobs you could at least see. They started out like little buds, not much bigger than mine, but sticking out a little in their sweaters. After a while they got to be about the size of eggs and started to look really nice, and people got bras. Some of the fat girls' boobs were as big and full and droopy as women's, even in sixth grade, and the kids who talked about sex all the time in Gym and at lunch talked about the fat girls' boobs as if they were the sexiest thing. Those kids also used the word "tits" for boobs, which made them sound dirty. They would say things like, "How'd you like to get your hands on Barb Frolich's tits," and you were supposed to act like that would be really amazing, even though no one even wanted to sit next to Barb Frolich on the bus or talk to her at lunch. I never for a second wanted to get my hands on Barb Frolich's boobs, but I was aware that my sex feeling was starting to be connected to that kind of talk and those kinds of pictures.

    I started to get interested in pictures of women in magazine advertisements. Mostly they were just pictures of big, smiling women holding a box of detergent or walking down a city street in shiny stockings and high-heeled shoes, but I was starting to see something sexy in them, and that would get the little tickle of the sex feeling going. About twice a year we'd get Sears Roebuck and Montgomery Ward catalogs in the mail, and if I was by myself, I would look at the brassieres section, which went on for about twenty pages, showing hundreds of little boxes of women's necks and shoulders and breasts with brassieres on. It would only take me about two pages to get the sex feeling, and I would have to close the catalog.

My sister Annabel was a freshman in the high school, and even though she was just starting to get a figure herself, she never talked about it, or about her body or boys or anything like that. The summer I went to camp, I got the idea that something terrible had happened to her, because when I got home Mother took me into the living room by myself and told me that Annabel had had her period. I had no idea what that was, and when my mother told be it was about Annabel's female eggs coming into their place and getting washed out in blood through her thing for a few days every month, I really wanted her to stop talking about it. Mother said it was completely natural and healthy and that every girl had periods, but it sounded serious and disgusting to me. Maybe every girl does get periods, but I don't think Annabel thought that hers were completely natural and healthy. I tried to ask her about it in a nice way, but she gave me a sad, scared look, and I could tell she never wanted me to know things like that about her. I think Annabel hated having periods, and even though we never talked about it, I'm sure she would have hated the sex feeling. It's too bad that certain people like Annabel have to go through sex, which only scares them and hurts their feelings. I think now that if Annabel didn't have to go through sex, she would have been able to have a regular life, quiet maybe, but doing really nice things for people, because that is the way she was. But as it turned out, having her period and having to go through sex was worse for Annabel than knowing what happened to Anne Frank.

I loved Annabel and never would have tried to hurt her feelings by talking about sex, but I did get the sex feeling sometimes when she had certain friends over to the house. Annabel was actually really pretty herself. Natalie Wood was her favorite movie star, and she had a way of making herself look like Natalie Wood, a look that made you feel like taking care of her. The friends in her grade, though, looked a lot older and bigger. I remember the house seeming to fill up with a lively, exciting feeling when they would come over and start giggling and shrieking in Annabel's room, trying on clothes and putting Rock and Roll records on Annabel's little portable record player. Annabel's friends had complete figures, like thin women, and they gave off a feeling that they could barely hold all their energy in, so that it came bubbling out in extra fast talking and giggling. They all said I was "cute," but that was not what gave me the sex feeling. I got it because I could just tell that these girls were glad about their periods and going through sex, and that made me kind of glad too.

Because of alphabetical order, I sat next to Barb Frolich in a lot of my classes. By seventh grade, any time anybody started talking about boobs, they'd get onto Barb Frolich's. One of my friends, Gary Wade, called them "jugs," and at least that sort of described them. "Tits" made me picture little, flitty things, like paper airplanes or swallows, and something about calling somebody's boobs "tits" seemed a little mean.

Barb Frolich was actually nice enough. She was pretty fat, though, and she had puffy little pouches under her eyes, which made her look like she had been crying or was really tired. Maybe she was. I know it really hurt her feelings to have everybody teasing her about her big boobs. People had been doing it for almost two years, and you can really get to hate that kind of thing. I was pretty nice to her, but we didn't have any of the same friends or talk much. I think she thought I was in with the group that was always talking about her boobs, but I wasn't the one who would ever bring them up. Actually her boobs, which were right there next to me, about three inches away when we were in classes that sat around tables, made me kind of sad. She used to wear sweaters made out of a slinky looking cloth called Banlon. You could tell what everything looked like under the Banlon, so I could see the extra pouch of fat she had between her shoulder and her armpit, and I could see the straps and stitches of her bra. Barb Frolich used to cross her arms under her boobs, which probably helped hold them up. She also carried her books under them to make a kind of shelf when she was going somewhere. We had so many classes together that I ended up looking at her boobs a lot without meaning to. They never gave me the sex feeling, because something about the sad, heavy way Barb Frolich sat in her chair made any kind of sex feeling impossible, although I did wonder sometimes what it would be like to have big heavy boobs like that growing out of your chest and what it would feel like to run or jump.

Barb Frolich wore a big silver heart on a chain around her neck. Sometimes it would be tucked under the Banlon, and sometimes it would be on the outside hanging down in the ridge where her boobs came together. Gary Wade got the idea that it would be really funny for me to try to touch her boobs. He told me I should pretend I wanted to look at her silver heart, and while I was grabbing for it with my hand, give her boobs a feel. He thought the idea of doing something like that in class was extra funny. I didn't want to at all, even though I was sure I'd probably get away with it. Every chance he could, Gary Wade, who was a really goofy looking kid, would be looking over at me from his side of the room, doing fake coughing and gesturing, trying to get my attention, so I would go for Barb Frolich's necklace. It got annoying, but I also saw that I could fool Gary Wade. So after almost a whole class where he was mouthing things to me, like *"Do it,"* I nodded to him and then leaned in close to Barb Frolich and pretended I was writing something in her notebook, which she bent over to see. Then I turned back to look at Gary Wade, who was so excited he was standing up at his place. He was mouthing, *"Did you?"* and I nodded that I did. He made a high shriek, which he probably couldn't help, and said out loud, "Oh, *man!*" which got him sent out of class. After that all Gary Wade could do was go on and on about how "Force got a piece of Frolich's jugs." I didn't care what he said, but I hoped that Barb Frolich wouldn't hear about it, because she certainly didn't need to feel any worse.

It was really pretty strange, going all through Junior High with the sex feeling. If it wasn't down there in my thing, it was hovering all around me like I was wrapped in a huge bubble of it. It mainly felt like one of those permanent diseases like asthma or diabetes, which you always have but only rise up every now and then. But walking around in that new bubble could make certain times unbearable. For instance, any time I even caught a glimpse of Patsy Prentiss, I would get so excited and confused it almost made me sick. By seventh grade, she hardly even remembered me, and if I hadn't known her so well and loved her so much in fifth grade, I would probably not even have recognized her. She got really tall and had a complete figure. She wore lipstick, and her hair was in an actual hair-do that flared out in a great way. She was one of the popular kids, but not with the kids in our grade. Practically all her friends were in the older grades, and she always had a boyfriend who was really popular and on the teams. By the time we were all in eighth grade, her friends and boyfriends were in high school, and she was going to dances and out on dates in cars, with kids driving.

It is hard to describe the effect Patsy Prentiss had on me. The thing that made me sad and almost sick was that my original love feeling, the skull-to-skull feeling in fifth grade, had not gone away. I still had it and felt it, and it ached. It seemed completely wrong and unfair that anything like that could be taken away. But at the same time, I could see her now, with her height and her figure and her hair-do, and know that she had grown out of me into something else. But she was still beautiful to me. I could still see her old face in her new face, and because of that her new face seemed even more beautiful. When I was by myself, I pictured it every second I could, but I couldn't make a picture of her with me in it. Picturing her kind of gave me a sexual feeling, and it kind of didn't. It was a little vague. I remember thinking that when it came time to have actual sex, like feeling bare boobs, then feeling inside their pants, and then sticking it inside to have intercourse, I wanted it to be with Patsy Prentiss, but when I actually saw her, I never felt like doing any of that. I couldn't picture it at all.

Looking back on it, going through sex and going through Junior High mainly made me duller and stupider than I really was. I did all those surface things to keep busy, but there were long stretches where I can't remember caring much about anything. When I'm in that kind of mood, that's when I usually get sick, and for practically the whole winter all through sixth and seventh and eighth grade, I was either getting the scratchy burning feeling in my chest that told me bronchitis was coming, or I had it with all the fevers and crud in my chest, or I was getting over it, back in school, but still hacking away and trying to keep my nose from running. We had a lot of photographs around the house, which are now arranged in albums, but there are almost none of me when I was in Junior High, and I'm glad, because when I look at

The Other World

an old picture of me then, all I see is a too-big head with dark eyes, a big nose and, if the body is showing, everything too skinny.

* * *

Thank God for music. Music was the one thing I could do while I was in Junior High that was completely good. Nana and Papa had a Baldwin grand piano in their living room, and from the time Annabel and I were old enough to stay overnight at their house by ourselves, we would take turns playing it. We couldn't really play anything when we were little, just little trick songs where you rolled your knuckles over the three black keys that were in a row, then plunked the next one up. It made a little tune, but it wasn't very interesting. We also learned to play chopsticks, which was even less interesting, except when Papa sat down with me and played low, beautiful chords that made it sound like a great song. It started to irritate me that I couldn't play anything that I really wanted to hear. I tried a lot of experiments, but it didn't sound all that great. One thing I could do was pick out notes one at a time that would play the melody of a song I liked, and after I repeated it a few times, it would sound just like the song. Papa said that I had "a good ear" and told Mother that I should take piano lessons, but I never did, because we didn't have a piano at home to practice on. But I kept fooling around on Nana and Papa's piano, trying to work out a system, and then in Junior High, I got it.

In Junior High I was allowed to stay over at Nana and Papa's practically every weekend, sometimes for both nights, so there was a lot of time to work on the piano, especially when my chest was full of bronchitis and I couldn't go out. Two things happened that made me able to start making real music on the piano. The first was learning how to play "Heart and Soul," and the second was watching Liberace on TV. There was an old upright piano at the back of the lunchroom at school, and a bunch of kids knew how to play "Heart and Soul." Usually two kids would play it as a duet, with one kid playing the melody notes up high and the other kid making chords down low. Even though the kids playing were usually not musical at all, if they knew the pattern of the chords and the simple melody line, they could make it sound pretty good, even though they were just banging on the keys. I had a kid show me how to do the chords, and it was easy. Then at Nana and Papa's I showed Annabel how to play the melody, and we got to be really good at "Heart and Soul." Sometimes Papa would lean over me and play extra chords below mine, and that really sounded good. For a long time I couldn't get "Heart and Soul" to stop repeating in my head.

One Sunday afternoon at Nana and Papa's when I was playing the piano by myself, it hit me that the "Heart and Soul" chords went with a lot of other songs, and I started trying that idea out, and it worked perfectly. I couldn't believe it. Pretty soon I was playing "Blue Moon," "The Way You Look Tonight," and about sixty Rock and Roll songs, just using the "Heart and Soul" chords. That night when my parents showed up at Nana and Papa's for dinner, I showed them all the songs I could play, and they seemed pretty impressed, but after a while they wanted to eat. I had to eat, too, which was frustrating because all I wanted to do was keep figuring things out on the piano. After supper on Sunday nights everybody always watched The Ed Sullivan Show and Fred Waring on Nana and Papa's TV, which I usually liked, except the TV was in the living room, which meant I couldn't play the piano. I could hardly stand to look at the screen. All I could do was imagine my fingers forming chords and silently pressing down the keys.

Every now and then I got to go over to Nana and Papa's on a weekday after school and play the piano, but usually I had to wait till Saturday or Sunday. Playing the piano kept getting better and better because Papa started showing me things, including a lot of chords that were not in "Heart and Soul" and a bunch of minor chords which had a feel of their own. He also showed me all the different keys you could play in. Everybody played "Heart and Soul" on the white keys, which is the key of C, but you can play it in lots of other keys just by shifting it up or down and learning which black keys you have to use instead of white ones. This actually took a few days to figure out, but I loved working on it. Nana would come into the living room every now and then and say, "You *can't* still be playing the piano!" but I always was. I went into the living room right after breakfast and worked on it until Nana called me for lunch. After lunch I would go right back and work on things until the room got dark and we would have to eat again.

I started to realize that I could play anything, which gave me the chills. When I heard a song on the radio or on a record, I could always keep it in my head, and after I started playing the piano for a while, I could play the melody of the song right away with my right hand. Getting good chords with my left hand was a lot harder. Sometimes I had to try a lot of chords or change around one of the ones I knew to get it to sound right, and this could take a long time if the song was complicated, like "Smoke Gets in Your Eyes" or "Some Enchanted Evening." Sometimes I had to wait until Papa was around to help me figure out a chord, but he didn't always know. If I got too frustrated, I'd play something like "Mack the Knife" or Rock and Roll songs, which were so easy they just went automatically and my mind could rest.

In seventh grade, on Christmas Eve, we got our own piano, a black upright. I wasn't expecting it, and it took a while to believe that we really had it, that I was going to be able to play the piano as much as I wanted, any day of the week. I liked our piano, especially the easy way the keys went down. Our piano sounded clinkier and brighter than Nana and Papa's Baldwin, but once I learned a new song I really liked, I couldn't wait to play it on the Baldwin, because it made everything sound fuller and deeper and more important.

I started to get a little conceited about how well I could play the piano, and this was partly because Annabel liked it so much. She would sit down next to me on the piano bench just watching my hands and not saying anything. When she had a new favorite song, she would ask me if I would learn it, and as soon as I did, she would sit next to me and listen to it over and over. She was always really nice about telling me how good I was, and after I played a song she liked, she would say, "I wish I could play the piano." I taught her how to play a few songs, which she learned pretty well, but she didn't know how to store things up in her head.

I could tell my mother and father thought my piano playing was kind of amazing by the way they talked about it to their friends. When I started to get good, my father would take out his trumpet and play along with me. He knew just about every song there was by heart, and he would play harmonies to the melody line and also sneak in little extra notes between the ones I was playing in a way that almost made me laugh. One thing I didn't like, though, was when he would ask me to play something I didn't really like that much when certain friends came over. That was just about the only time playing the piano wasn't any fun. It felt like I was being ordered around, and a few times I could feel myself not playing very well almost on purpose, and I could tell that made my father mad.

Once when I was fooling around by myself, I tried playing a song in the key of F, which is all white keys except for one, with my right hand while my left hand was playing in the key of F-sharp, which is mostly black keys. It was a little confusing to do at first, but then I got the hang of it. I couldn't believe how completely terrible it sounded, and I knew it would be a great joke if I could figure out how to use it.

I don't know how I ever got the nerve to try it out when we had company, some of my father's friends from work. Something bothered me about the way he asked me to play for them. It was like he had a special trick he wanted to show them, and I was the trick. That's not explaining it very well. Something about the way my father asked me to play for people made it seem like whatever I did was all because of him. Anyway, the smart part of myself just shut off, and I started playing the song my father asked me to play, "Melody of Love," in F with my right hand and F-sharp with my left hand. I tried to look extra formal and serious to make it funny, but it didn't work. I heard my mother saying, "What on earth—" and then my father said, *"That's enough!"* I would have been willing to play it the right way, but I could tell he just wanted me to get out of there. I went out to the kitchen feeling pretty nervous, and in a minute my father came in, shut the door, and gave me a tremendous crack in the head.

The other great thing that happened to my piano playing was watching Liberace on television. I'd never seen a show like that on

TV. It was on Monday nights, and it was a half-hour long, but it always seemed to me like it barely lasted a minute. Liberace was the first amazing piano player I ever heard, and he was a very unusual person. He had kind of a plump woman's face, but really friendly. His hair went way up in front and then was slicked back around the sides like Elvis Presley's. He always wore a tuxedo with long tails, which he flicked out behind him just before he sat down at the piano bench. He had a great-sounding piano, and the chords he played made me see crystal formations behind my eyes. It was also a great-looking piano, and the panel at the back of the keyboard was shiny as a mirror, so you could see his hands working the keys in the reflection. I couldn't take my eyes off his hands while he was playing. He played some tremendous classical songs by Chopin and Liszt and Tchaikovsky, which I seemed to know already, but there was something about the way Liberace played them that told you this was exactly the way they should sound. He also played a lot of popular songs, which were just as good. In fact, he could make an ordinary song on the radio, like "Unchained Melody," sound like Chopin wrote it. He could play anything, including boogie-woogie and the fastest, hardest songs I ever heard, songs like "Bumble Boogie," Tiger Rag," and "Dizzy Fingers." A lot of times his fingers were going so fast up and down the keyboard they were just a blur, but you could hear every little note, and he never made a mistake. Liberace had a way of making his face look like a cat, and when he got to an especially hard and fast part of a song, he'd get a little secret smile on his face. The room he played in on TV was really nice, too, with flowers all around and a big candelabra on the piano. His brother George, who looked pretty regular, played the violin, and sometimes Liberace played a duet with him. He was always really nice to his brother George on the show, but I always wanted to get right back to Liberace.

 Liberace really changed the way I played. Every now and then my parents weren't home on Monday night, and I got to watch Liberace all by myself. On those nights, as soon as the show was over, I'd turn off the TV and go right over to the piano and start playing. There was usually a song or part of a song I had stored up during the show, and I would try to play it while it was still fresh in my mind. One night when I was playing a song, "Night and Day," that Liberace had just played on TV, I realized there was something about my playing I didn't like any more. Just playing the melody and the chords of the song, even though I was playing them right, sounded completely uninteresting compared to Liberace. I finally got mad at myself and smashed my fist down on the keys, mainly because I couldn't figure out what he did to make his songs so jumpy and lively and complicated-sounding.

The next Monday night when I was by myself, I watched the whole Liberace show, just concentrating on one thing: how he got his complicated sound. He had a theme song, "I'll Be Seeing You," which he played and sang at the end of each show, and since I knew how to play it, I tried to see what he did that I wasn't doing. It turned out to be pretty simple. He wasn't really playing the melody at all. Even though you could hear the melody and it sounded great, the actual notes of the melody where wedged in between hundreds of other notes. The notes of the melody just happened to be on the way to where Liberace was going in a zigzagging chain of notes. Realizing this also helped me to see how Liberace could sometimes seem to be playing really fast while the song came out slow. The trick was all the extra notes holding the melody in place. So there were two things I had to learn—how to play the zigzagging chains and how to work it out so the melody note you needed came up at exactly the right time.

This might sound easy, but it practically drove me crazy. Once when I was trying some Liberace zigzags on the old upright piano at the back of the lunchroom, Mr. Larson, the band teacher, came up behind me and listened for a while. "I see you are practicing arpeggios and glissandos," he said. I couldn't understand what he was saying. He showed me that you made a glissando by turning the back of your thumbnail or fingernail against the side edge of a key, and then sliding it up or down the keyboard as far as you wanted it to go.

Most people thought Mr. Larson was really dorky because he had dark hairs growing out of his nose, and he wore his pants really high, but I thought the glissando sounded amazing. It plays every single key along the line in a second, but so fast you can't hear any particular note, just all of them together in a really exciting *zshiiiiiiiiiiiiiing!* Then he showed me an arpeggio, which turned out to be a little pattern of three or four notes you played together really fast then skipped up or down to the next group of the same notes and kept going. This was a big relief to me, because I thought Liberace was using all kinds of different notes in his zigzags, but there were only three or four played over and over all up and down the piano. Mr. Larson showed me three different kinds of arpeggios, which sounded great when he played them and definitely had the Liberace sound. I couldn't play them right on the spot, but once I figured out the fingerings at home and practiced them about thirty thousand times, they started sounding amazing. The trick is getting the fingering so automatic you don't even think about what your fingers are doing. Your mind just says something like "arpeggio—now *go*" and suddenly your hands are making blurry little loops up and down the keyboard like Liberace.

It ended up taking quite a while to work all the arpeggios and glissandos I needed into my songs, but it felt wonderful to work on it, even when I had to slow way down and repeat certain passages for a whole afternoon. One great thing about being able to play songs that sounded like Liberace is that once you could do it, you could also stop doing it at certain places in the song, so all of a sudden the melody would be really simple and stand out in a beautiful way. Papa told me he liked the way I would go back into my simple style. For some reason, he didn't like Liberace at all. He said Liberace was "all schmaltz."

I wasn't in Stage Band, because I couldn't stand the kind of songs they played, and also their concerts sounded really sour and terrible, but whenever there was a school concert, Mr. Larson would ask me if I wanted to play a solo. My first thought was a big no, because I didn't want people to think I was like anybody in Stage Band, but after I thought about it, I started to like the idea of playing something pretty great in front of the whole school.

The first time I did it, I was so nervous just before it was my turn that my mouth went completely dry, and I had to keep sucking on my tongue to get any juice back. I decided I would play my Liberace version of "Twelfth Street Rag" because it was really fast and had some great tricky sections that you wouldn't think a kid would be able to play. For a minute or two while I was backstage, I couldn't picture the first notes I was supposed to play, but after a minute of feeling terrible, I got into a little trance and walked out there and played "Twelfth Street Rag" as fast as I could. It was completely automatic. When I was almost done, I knew the only way I could wreck it was by starting to think about what I was doing. Then I played the final chord and made a glissando from the bottom note of the piano all the way to the top. The kids made a huge roar and kept on clapping. When I stood up to look out into the audience, I could only see a milky blur. The rhythm of the clapping seemed to be shaking up the air in the room. I was still pretty much in my trance, but I liked the feeling of that applause.

Kids in Junior High thinking you're an amazing piano player is okay, but it's not like being a star on the teams or an officer of Student Council. I actually played quite a lot of concert solos by the time I finished Junior High, but I never got as excited again as I did when the kids were roaring after "Twelfth Street Rag." Even when teachers and kids said how great it was after I played something, I would start to get that irritated feeling I got when my father made me play for guests at home. I loved to play the piano, and I loved to figure new things out, but there was something I couldn't stand about being thought of as "the kid who can play the piano." People who said things like that probably thought they knew the kind of kid I really was, but they didn't know anything—and I didn't want them to.

I like playing the piano the most when I'm by myself somewhere, and the very best times are when it's late in the afternoon, and as I'm playing, the room keeps getting darker and darker, and I just let it. When I'm by myself I can play the piano for five hours straight, and it will feel like about ten minutes. My mind goes completely blank except for crazy little imaginary scenes where there's a meeting of world leaders like Stalin and Churchill and Roosevelt, and they set up a system that says if somebody in some country around the world is picked at random and can come up to the stage and play "Stairway to the Stars" perfectly, some big war will end. They pick me, thinking I'm just a regular person, and I play it perfectly, and as I am picturing this, I am actually playing the song in our living room in the dark.

Another scene I liked to imagine was playing in a big required-attendance school concert, and Patsy Prentiss is sitting somewhere in the middle of the audience with her friends, but I can't see her. I finish playing a tremendous song, like "Dizzy Fingers," and she thinks it's so amazing she can't believe it. She just sits there in her chair after everybody leaves the auditorium. She is remembering me, and she is figuring out a way to get to know me again.

LOSING ANNABEL

There's no way I could describe what happened to me in High School. It wasn't just that it was such a huge jumble; it was more that I stopped being able to picture things the way I used to. Even in Junior High, no matter what kinds of things were going on around me and no matter how crummy any of it was, I still thought of myself as being in a secret story that was going to come out in some amazing way. But in High School everything seemed so huge and set up in advance, the only thing you could do was get into the stream of things and see what happened.

It actually was like being in a stream, a stream you could never get out of. If there's one single thing I remember about Palatine Township High School, it's moving through the corridors. The red brick building was enormous, dark and heavy looking from the outside. It was the biggest building in town, and something about the way the stone blocks were set around the main entrances and along the roofline made it look like a fort. You never really had to do it, but it would take at least ten or fifteen minutes to walk from one end of it all the way to the gym at the other end. Your freshman-year classes would be in one part of the second floor, and when you got to be a sophomore with classes on the first floor somewhere else in the building, it was like you were in a completely new place. Moving from class to class or to Gym or to lunch made me feel like I was in one of those newsreel scenes of someplace like Singapore or New Delhi, places where there was barely room on the streets for all the people. The rule at Palatine was that you had to stay to the right side of the corridor in the direction you were going, so you wouldn't smash into the people coming the other way. You were wedged in so close to the other people and all their books that you could feel them against your arms and shoulders and bumping into your back while you were walking. If you ever forgot something and had to go back the other way, you almost couldn't do it.

The Other World

In High School I completely forgot the other world. If somebody had tried to tell me about it, I would not have known what they were talking about. I still thought about myself and pictured myself all the time, but in a different way. It was as if the kind of kid I was before, being able to come up with things nobody else could come up with, being able to do certain things in sports, being able to play the piano like Liberace, was all erased, and the only thing I was at the High School was what I looked like and the clothes I had on. That's the way I thought about myself. When I got home from school and started thinking about the next day, all I could picture was what I'd wear and what I'd probably look like.

I can't remember one really funny thing about High School, but a few things were a little funny, like Morning Announcements. At the beginning of first period every day, the teacher would turn on the public-address speakers that were hung over the blackboard at the front of every room. Morning Announcements were only supposed to take two or three minutes, but the farther you were into the year, the longer they got. The funny part was that somebody like Mr. Gladhead, the Dean of Behavior, would say something that was supposed to be really strict and serious about vandalism or stealing and then the next voice would be some giggling girl trying to get kids to go to the Diaper Dance that weekend.

Morning Announcements had the effect of making the whole school seem confused and kind of crazy. I used to have to dig my thumbnail into my palm as hard as I could to keep from laughing out loud at certain times, like when the faculty advisor of Student Council would read the thank-you letters from We Pin, our Indonesian foster child. Maybe there was something wrong with me, because her letters weren't all that funny, but there was just something funny about sitting there listening to a kind of radio show with nothing but people like Mr. Gladhead warning us not to write obscene words on people's lockers, followed by a girl with a high screamy voice telling people about cheerleader tryouts, followed by a tired-sounding teacher telling you how to sign up for the field trip to the stock yards. But it was especially funny when out of the blue you'd get the letter from We Pin, thanking us for her new underwear, socks, stationery, and Kleenex.

Maybe it wasn't that funny. Maybe it was just a little relief before the rush of classes and everything else you had to do. On the first day we were handed out cards with our class schedules on them for the year. You taped them onto your notebook, but after a few days you knew where to go automatically, you knew who sat around you, what the particular smell and look of each room was, the different ways the teachers dressed and how they talked. The classes in High School were forty-six minutes long, but I remember feeling in the middle of the morning and the last period in the afternoon that time had somehow stalled completely. You got a lot of little grades for homework and daily quizzes, and about every two weeks you got a big grade on a test or a composition you had written at home. The kids talked about how much there was to do and how hard it was in High School, but it didn't seem to me harder than Junior High. There was just more of everything, and it all counted. There were Mid-Semester Report Cards, Semester Report Cards, and Year Report Cards, and your report card grade average qualified you for the Honor Roll. It took mostly A's and B's to make the Honor Roll, which wasn't that hard if you were in Accelerated or Fast classes, because those teachers were supposed to give A's and B's.

I always did fine, except for math, which got away from me completely when I got to advanced algebra and trigonometry. Mother always said I could do better than I did. She said I was relying on my natural ability and that I was slapdash and that I did my big assignments and projects at the last minute. She was right. I tried to change my system a few times, but I couldn't stick to it. I always got back to the feeling that if I could just clear out as much time as possible before I had to start working on some school thing, I might get some relief.

One really stupid thing I remember doing when I was getting used to High School was making charts to keep track of my grades and averages. I actually spent a lot of time doing this at home in my room and during study hall at school. I'd use a ruler to make a rectangle with all my classes listed inside on the left with a line of little boxes going off to the right. Each little box had a diagonal line cutting it in half, and on the left side of the diagonal line I'd write in my most recent grade, and on the right side I would put down what my new average was in that subject. I spent a lot of time on these charts. I would do them first very lightly in pencil, and when I had it right, I'd go over the lines in dark ink. It took a while to figure out all the new averages every day, and I'm sure my mother thought I was working on my actual schoolwork. Later that year when we started working on graphs in algebra, I made up a little graph to go along with each of my classes. Even though I always knew exactly how I was doing without the charts, it still gave me a great feeling to see the complicated-looking tables of neatly written entries and the peaks and dips of the graphs.

I remember one time going into such a slide in algebra I was actually starting to worry about it. We were supposed to be solving equations with two unknowns, and I couldn't even follow the really easy sample problem that was in the orange box on the front page of the chapter. Our teacher was Miss Stein, a bony little woman with red runny eyes. She didn't like the boys in our section, because she thought we were always fooling around. There was a little fooling around, but some of the kids she thought were doing it were actually just complaining because they couldn't figure out the problems. She'd go up to the board and do them, and she'd even do some of them two or three times, but she couldn't explain how she went from one step to the next. She'd just do the problem, and it would come out right. Even when I copied every step she put on the board, I couldn't figure out how things were getting factored out and how the letters got down to just one equaling the right answer. I decided I might be able to come up with my own system, which had sometimes worked for me in the past. I factored and reduced and cross multiplied things the way I thought you were supposed to, but my solutions would go on and on down the page, and the second unknown would keep being a letter I couldn't get rid of. I started to get some really terrible math grades, but I didn't feel too bad about it as long as I could enter them and my new average and the new extension of the graph line in my notebook. I probably should have been getting worried, but instead I felt extra calm, as if I were studying myself like a scientist.

Richard Hawley

Stepping back like that and not even being inside myself for most of the day was the only way I could stand being in High School. I still did everything, and I even tried out for new things like Cross Country and Chorus and Winter Play, but freshmen and sophomores barely made it into anything and when you did, you just followed along doing what they said until somebody noticed you were any good.

The main effect of trying out for everything and being in activities and on teams was that nothing felt like after school anymore. All the way through Junior High I used to love after-school. After-school gave me a great feeling every single day. It even made me kind of like school, because I knew that as the day went along, no matter how terrible anything was, I was getting closer to after-school. It's like liking the days before Christmas because Christmas is coming. But in High School there was only about ten minutes between the last class and having to go down to Boys' Lockers to change into my gym suit and sweat suit, rub tangy analgesic grease into my legs, then go out and run quarter mile laps, walk a lap, then run again until my lungs hurt and my leg muscles were burning in a sickening way. By the time I took a shower and changed back into my clothes and got all my books together, it would be starting to get dark.

* * *

A big part of the reason I felt I was starting to disappear that first year of high school was that Annabel really did disappear. I know if I had been smarter then and way nicer, I would have seen that something was wrong, but I didn't see anything. To me Annabel almost wasn't like a separate person. When I was just born and still in my crib, one of the first things I figured out was that Annabel was always around, like a shadowy extra self. Even after I was allowed to get out of the house and to start doing things, when I came back inside, it was like coming back into my Annabel self. Annabel is the only person I ever knew who completely liked me, no matter what, even though I did some rotten things to her every now and then, like taking some of her stuff or scaring her on purpose by mentioning things, like poisonous spiders and dogs getting hit by cars, things she absolutely couldn't stand.

Most of the time I was pretty nice to Annabel, because how could you not be. She was so quiet and careful, and she never bothered anybody. Nobody knew it, because she was so shy and got put in the Vocational Ed track, but she was really good at a lot of things. She was an amazingly good artist and could draw the heads of wild animals and good-looking dogs like collies as well as people did in magazines and books. She could also draw the faces and bodies of movie stars, and the ones she liked best, like Natalie Wood and Audrey Hepburn, she could draw without even looking at their pictures. She was also a great singer, but she would only sing when I played the piano or when just my mother and father and Nana and Papa were around. Mother told her she had a beautiful voice and should try out for Chorus at school, but Annabel just looked at her and didn't say anything, and I knew what she meant. Actually, Annabel was tremendous, but everything about her seemed a little bit off, a little bit too delicate for the regular world, especially High School.

Maybe it was just because she was my sister, but I really thought she was beautiful. She was beautiful in that almost too-perfect way the movie stars looked in Annabel's *Hollywood Glamour* and *Teen Screen* magazines. She was also really small, even smaller than me. She weighted ninety-five pounds, which was perfect for her and not skinny at all, but nobody could ever believe she was a junior in high school. She had dark shiny hair that was kind of long, down to about her shoulders and curled under in a style she called a pageboy. She spent a lot of time getting her hair like that, and she went to bed with curlers on and a kind of bag over the whole thing so she could set up her pageboy in the morning. She wore lipstick now and a dark little line around the rims of her eyes. I used to like to watch her sitting in front of her mirror, very slowly and carefully drawing that bluish black line, without blinking or changing her expression. Everything she did was extremely careful like that. Her room was always perfectly neat and cleaned up, and her china animal statues and special souvenirs were set up in order on her shelves. Her jewelry box and mirrors and colored bottles of perfumes and creams were arranged on the top of her dresser in a design. It was actually really nice in her room, her own little world.

In Junior High and at the beginning of High School Annabel seemed to have regular friends. She would sometimes go over to other girls' houses or girls would come over to our house after school or sometimes for a sleepover. They seemed really nice and lively, and I always thought Annabel was having a pretty good time. But by sophomore year nobody would come over, and Annabel said she didn't care. She just wanted to stay in her room and draw and listen to her records. A few boys would call on the telephone, and my father would call them her "boyfriends," which was a mistake because I could tell it made Annabel feel ashamed. I actually saw who some of them were at school, and I was really glad Annabel didn't like them, because you could tell right away there was something wrong with them, something you could never get used to, like big flakes of dandruff coming out of the part in their hair or having practically no chin or being maybe not really fat, but having the kind of body that if you took your shirt off, it would be really terrible.

I'm sure it was because I was only thinking about myself, but I didn't know Annabel was getting mentally ill. I say "mentally ill," because that's what Mother said and what she told me to say when somebody asked me about it—that, or just "sick." To me mentally ill meant people going nuts and thinking they were other people and shrieking and flailing around for no reason. That's not what happened to Annabel. She just got quieter and quieter. She was so quiet anyway, I didn't even notice.

One night at supper Mother asked her something, and she didn't answer. Mother kept asking her, and Annabel didn't even look at her or change her expression. That got Mother really scared. She got up from the table and walked Annabel upstairs to her room and stayed up with her until it was late. When she finally came out, I met her in the hall and asked what was wrong. She told me it was nothing, Annabel would be fine, but I could see Mother looked really tense, which made me start to get really tense. I tried to get her to tell me more, but she said she had to

The Other World

talk to my father. I asked her if I could go in and talk to Annabel, but she said no, Annabel needed to rest, and I should go to bed.

The second I woke up in the morning, I knew something really bad was happening. My parents were already up. Mother was on the telephone, and her voice sounded sharp and scared. When I got downstairs, Annabel was in the car with my father, and Mother had her coat on and was about to go out. There was no breakfast or anything on the table. Mother was flying around the kitchen looking for her purse, stopping to write things down. She looked at me as if she was surprised I was there. She slapped some money down on the kitchen counter, and told me it was for lunch and if I needed anything when I got home from school and they weren't there. She said Annabel was sick, and they were worried about her. Then she went out to the car, and they drove away.

I didn't know what to do. I knew I should do something, like go upstairs and get my books ready for school or go over to the kitchen table and sit down, but I couldn't make myself move. School was going to be starting in a few minutes, and it didn't seem to matter, but after a while I went anyway, because it was the only thing I could think of. I didn't pay attention to anything in any of my classes, and if somebody called on me, I said I didn't know. I didn't care if I got in trouble. I remember thinking that if anybody gave me a bad time or tried to make me do anything I didn't feel like doing, I was going to stop talking completely. It felt like that was a way I could hate them, and it made me feel like Annabel.

Annabel never came back home, at least not to live. For a while she stayed in a psychiatric hospital in Chicago, where I visited her two times, but then Mother told me she was having bad reactions and had to be put on a special ward where she couldn't have visitors. Mother said that would only be temporary, but it lasted for a long time, all the way through freshman year. I know I asked Mother what was wrong with Annabel, and she must have told me, but something inside me just shut off and cancelled out whatever she said. Mother visited Annabel every day she was allowed to, and when she wasn't allowed to, she went to see the doctors or talked to people on the phone. If I listened to things my mother told people over the phone I could take it in, but whenever she tried to sit down with me by myself and tell me something about Annabel, I would freeze.

The first thing Mother told her friends was that Annabel had a major depression. Later, when Annabel was on the special ward and couldn't have visitors, Mother told people she was catatonic. That summer when Annabel was moved to the Residential Center in Elgin, Mother would tell people things the psychiatrists said. One time I heard her tell somebody that the psychiatrist told her Annabel was "very angry." I tried to picture Annabel being angry, but I couldn't do it. I also didn't believe it, and I'm pretty sure I'm right. First of all, I'd like to see what they call angry. If anything, Annabel was too nice and too gentle. I couldn't picture her angry with anybody or anything. She just felt too small and left out. It made me want to go back to when we were little and start being really nice to her and doing a lot more things with her instead of with my friends. The truth is, I was the one who was angry. It made me feel like finding anyone who hurt her feelings and belting them.

* * *

At the end of that summer, Annabel came home for two weeks, and she did that every few months for as long as I was home. I would always get really excited to see her, but after a day or so I could tell that it wasn't going to be anything special. She didn't talk at all except sometimes to make an *mmm* sound in the back of her throat, which meant yes. The skin on her face was a bad color. Mother said it was because of her illness and the medicines she had to take, but I think it was because she never went outside and did anything. She hardly had any energy when she was home, but she sat in the same room with us when we ate. At first I talked to her a lot. I don't think she wanted me to, but she didn't mind me being around her. She wouldn't look directly at me, but every once in a while I would catch her eye and get the feeling that she still knew we knew each other better than anyone else.

As soon as I realized that Annabel was never really going to come back and live with us, our house started to feel different.

The Other World

When I was on my way home from somewhere and knew that nobody was going to be in the house, I got almost afraid of it, of being in the rooms by myself, even though nothing bad ever happened. We still had our meals and certain routines like TV shows everybody would watch, but it felt like we were just staying there, not living there. Mother had to be away a lot to see Annabel, and I couldn't blame her, but it made me kind of sad to be in the empty house so much. My father must have been home at the regular time at night, but I can't even remember him being around. It even made me sad to know that I could sneak out and do just about anything I wanted on a school night and no one would catch me, but I didn't feel like it. The only thing to do was school, and the only way I could think of to make it interesting at all was to picture myself being tremendously popular and a huge success.

I know I sound really conceited saying it, but by the time I was a senior at Palatine, I actually was tremendously popular and a huge success. You could look at the yearbook. All I had to do was give up my own story and my own pictures and keep joining things.

The summer between my freshman and sophomore year I started playing American Legion League baseball with a lot of good players from the high school and even from the next town over, Barrington. For some reason this made me feel completely like a man, because there were hardly any practices, and the coaches just showed up at the park about when we did. They were usually college kids or old guys from town who still liked baseball, and all they would do is make up our line-ups, coach third base, and sit there and watch. They didn't talk to us like we were kids or treat us like kids. We were just supposed to show up and play. It seemed like we had a game just about every night, and I got to like that. I also got to like the other guys a lot, because I didn't know them except as players, and they didn't know me or about Annabel or anything about my life.

I was pretty good too, not great all the time, but I pitched some good innings and got some hits. When I was in the outfield, I had a lot of fun fooling around with the kid who was in the field next to me. We'd have ridiculous contests to see who could say

Richard Hawley

some horrible word the loudest without people really hearing it. It would start out in almost a whisper, but loud enough so the other guy could hear it, and then the next guy would have to say it louder, and so on. Sometimes it used to get me laughing so hard I thought I would choke. One of the best ways to do it was to start it out with a cough or a fake sneeze and finish up with the word. That way if somebody heard you, they'd think you just coughed or something. The other way was to barely say the first letter and shout the rest, so when people heard it, it would mainly sound like …UCK or …OCKUCKER. Maybe nobody even heard us. We didn't care. We weren't trying to offend anybody, we just wanted to be as crazy as possible in the outfield when there was nothing else to do on those warm summer nights.

    That summer I also had an indoor job during the day at the bank. My job was to run mail through the postage machine in the basement, clump bunches of it together in rubber bands, and stuff the clumps in big mail sacks which I'd drag over to the post office before I went home in the afternoon. I also had some upstairs jobs like entering numbers from the travelers-check stubs in a ledger and getting the tellers coffee and rolls across the street at June's. I got forty dollars a week, which was actually more like thirty-two when they took everything out. My father said his salary was forty dollars a week when he married Mother. I think he said that to make me think I was making a lot of money, but I knew that in his day everything was really cheap. The only thing frustrating about the bank job was that you had to mail all the cancelled checks with the statements, and if somebody wrote a ton of checks, I could barely seal the envelope, and the fattest envelopes sometimes got smashed up inside the postage machine and made it stop. When that happened, one of the tellers or the manager, Mr. Hardert, had to come down and open up the machine and fish everything out, which got them a little mad at me, but they never told me a way to stop it from happening.

    But mostly I liked that job, or at least the idea of it. I had to wear nice pants and a white shirt and a tie, and it actually felt good stepping outside in the morning all clean from the shower and kind of dressed up walking along the sidewalks downtown with the other people who were going to work. None of my friends had indoor jobs with paychecks. They maybe cut people's lawns or caddied at Barrington Hills. Something about being at the bank all day and then going home to eat, changing into my uniform, and heading over to the ball park made it easier to give up. It didn't even feel all that bad. I wasn't figuring things out in my room and then doing them anymore. I was just letting the job and the games and everything else pull me up into them, the way people from earth get taken up into alien space ships in a science fiction movie.

I don't think anybody who knew me or spent any time looking at me would have thought there was anything wrong with me, and maybe there wasn't. For most of my time in high school I had the feeling I was crying. Not crying out—I never cried anymore—but crying in.

ONE OF THE POPULAR KIDS

About halfway through high school I started to get popular. By the end of freshman year I barely got a C in algebra, but I had a bunch of A's in other classes, and they cancelled out the C, so I still made the Honor Roll. Sophomore math was geometry, which I was really good at, so after that, thanks to being able to talk my way into a special section of junior-year advanced algebra that was supposed to be for kids who didn't get it but were still smart, I got great grades for the rest of High School.

The English teachers thought I had an excellent imagination because of the way I went at my composition assignments. Whatever they asked me to write about, like whether Santiago had succeeded or failed at the end of *The Old Man and the Sea*, I'd come up with something I was sure nobody else would think of, saying things like there's no such thing as success or failure, there's only fishing.

If there was any way to turn the assignment into something funny, I'd try to do it, and teachers usually got a kick out of that, because by then I had figured out how to get off a certain kind of good one in writing. By junior and senior year, I got A's in just about everything, and Mother said she was really proud of me when they would get my report card, but this embarrassed me a little, because one big reason for my A's was that I signed up for classes like Journalism and Advanced Journalism, Modern Drama, Music History, and Current Topics, when the really smart kids were taking things like Chemistry, Physics, and Calculus. But I didn't mind getting all A's or the English teachers signing me up for special state contests, like Mightier Than The Sword.

Once I gave up, everything I did started to work out like that. By junior year I finally got an athletic letter in Cross Country, and that made me an automatic member of the Athletic Council, and I got to wear my letter sweater on Fridays, which were usually the days of the biggest games and, if they were home games, there would be a Coke Dance afterwards in the

The Other World

gym. Wearing your letter sweater on Fridays automatically put you in a group with the athletes, because at Palatine there were so many kids, almost nobody could get on a varsity team like Football, Basketball, or Baseball. Even if you got on one of the teams nobody really cared about and they didn't cut anybody, like Cross Country or Wrestling, it was almost impossible to get enough Win points to earn a letter. I only barely got mine. In Cross Country you got Win points if you finished in the top five places on your team. I was never in the top five and only barely in the top ten, but you also got a Win point if you finished ahead of the fifth runner on the other team, and Palatine was pretty good. We had meets against some really pitiful teams from little towns out in the country and against old beat-up schools in Chicago where even the best kids were terrible, so I got in ahead of their fifth runner quite a bit and got my letter. If anyone stopped and analyzed it, they'd say that a letter in Cross Country was probably the crummiest letter you could get, but on Fridays when you were horsing around in the main foyer before school in your letter sweater or moving through the corridors with everybody else, you were up there with the athletes, and I got a secret kick out of that.

Because the Journalism classes were completely easy and mostly just fun, I got to be one of the main writers for The Palatine Tribune and on the Editorial Board when I was a senior. I started out doing news and sports stories, which other kids actually worked on, but I could always knock off in about three minutes. I really liked working on feature stories that I could make funny, and when I was a senior, I got to write just about all the editorials, which were usually pretty lame because they had to be about a topic the advisor suggested, like should we revise the honor code or what we could do to improve school spirit. But no matter how lame they turned out, I liked seeing the way my articles looked when they were actually printed in the paper. It's pretty strange, because no matter what they said and how well I already knew it, I would read my articles over and over the day the paper came out, and after that I couldn't stand them.

Richard Hawley

It wasn't like I was trying to do it or had some kind of plan, but kids would tell me, "Jonathan, you do *everything*." I suppose that's the way it looked, and I didn't mind if kids said it, especially girls.

In the winter I was in the plays, and starting my sophomore year I got pretty good parts. The first good part I got was a character named Patrice in a play called *Ring Round the Moon* by Jean Anouilh. I actually didn't get this play too well, but it all took place in a big mansion in France that had drawing rooms and billiard rooms and indoor gardens. It was a comedy about couples who were in love with the wrong people at first but then it works out. My character was really goofy, too goofy to be one of the real lovers, but he would go along with things to help the other characters out. When the director, Mr. Canaletti, explained the character to me, he said to picture someone so preoccupied and so innocent and sissy-ish that you can't even imagine him getting along in a real place, like Chicago. Almost right away I came up with something pretty good. It helped a lot that Patrice's lines were actually pretty funny. He never had a clue what was going on or what anybody meant when they said something. I started imagining a guy who barely knew how to get dressed in the morning and was surprised by what he had on. I imagined a really weak, babyish man who thought every room he walked into was a strange new place. I also came up with a high hooty voice that sounded like everything was going wrong and I was about to cry.

Mr. Canaletti was crazy about my scenes. When we got into dress rehearsals under the lights and were wearing our real costumes, I could hear Mr. Canaletti cackling away in the dark, even though he had heard me do the scene a hundred times. I actually loved getting him to laugh like that. I pretended I didn't hear it and just went on being really dense in my part, which would get him laughing so hard the kids backstage and up in the booth would start laughing too, and that told me exactly what to keep doing. After rehearsal when we sat down for director's notes, Mr. Canaletti would give me a lot of compliments. One time he said that there was no formula for comic timing. It was something you just had to feel. He told the other kids to watch how I came on stage. He told them to watch me before I even said anything. I don't know what I actually did, but I know the feeling he was talking about. Because as much as I liked it when Mr. Canaletti cracked up during rehearsal, it was nothing compared to the way the actual audience exploded the second I stepped onto the stage.

Drama was a big deal at Palatine, and *Ring Round the Moon* ran for three weekends in a row. Everyone who came told me they thought it was great and that they especially liked Patrice. There might actually have been something great about it, something not even connected to the rest of High School. Only one bad thing happened while I was in the play. After the performance my mother and father went to, they came backstage to see me. I was still in my makeup and rented tuxedo tails, and I was barely back in the regular world. Mother was saying nice things, telling me I did a good job. I could tell she really liked the play and was surprised by what I came up with for Patrice. Then my father stepped up next to her and said I was really something. Then he said, "You were a real fruit cake up there." He was smiling in a nice way, and I think he was trying to give me a compliment, but something about saying I had been a fruit cake made me start to feel terrible, terrible about even being in the play. I don't know if I said anything back to him. After they left, I couldn't get back in a good mood. I just got madder and madder and wished my father hadn't even come.

* * *

There were a lot of big dances at Palatine, theme dances like the Diaper Dance, Lady's Choice, and Spring Fever, plus formal dances like Homecoming and the Prom, but the real socializing took place at the Coke Dances. There was a Coke Dance every Friday night that there was a home football game or basketball game. They were pretty basic. You'd just walk down to the Girls Gym, pay a quarter, take off your shoes, and hang around, maybe dancing a little with someone toward the end. They were called Coke Dances because you could also buy little paper cups of Coke out in the hall. They cut the lights way down, so it was pretty dark inside, and the music was just records played over the P.A. system, which I actually liked much better than the regular dances where they had dance orchestras come in. The men in the dance orchestras dressed in tuxedos, and everybody would have the same music stands with swirly letters on them saying things like The Stardusters or The Mood Makers. I could tell from listening to the dance orchestras my father played in that they were good musicians, but there was something about the sections of saxophone players and trumpet players that didn't go with the kids in High School and the kind of dancing they liked to do. The orchestras mainly played songs like "Sentimental Journey" and "Blue Moon," and they thought kids really liked their fast ones, like "In the Mood" and "The A Train," but all anybody really wanted was something like Elvis Presley or Dion and the Belmonts, which is what you got at the Coke Dances.

 I liked Coke Dances, because they were completely relaxing. The music was so loud you had to really exaggerate to get anyone to hear what you said, and you didn't have to say anything if you didn't feel like it. If kids had girlfriends, they'd meet up right away and dance only with them. You mostly stayed around your friends, but if you were interested in somebody, like a girl in one of your classes you barely knew, a Coke Dance was the perfect chance to meet her. You could just cruise around to where she and her friends were standing and, if you felt like it, ask her to dance. Because of the loud music you didn't have to talk much once you were dancing, maybe just say a few things that you had time to plan, things you'd shout in an exaggerated way, like "great game" or "I love this song." If you liked the person and had any money, you could go out in the hall and get a cup of Coke.

 One Coke Dance in the winter of my sophomore year changed the rest of my life. When the game ended, I looked out the windows of the gymnasium foyer and saw that there was a big blizzard outside. Heavy-looking sheets of snow were slanting down over the street lights, and you could hear the scream of people's tires spinning in place as they tried to get out of their parking places. It felt really good not having to go out, knowing that I only had to walk down the warm hallway to the Coke Dance. I had kind of a plan that night, or at least some kids had a plan for me.

The Other World

As huge as Palatine Township High School was, it seemed like nobody ever left and nobody new ever came, so when somebody did, especially if it was a boy who was any good at sports or a girl who was decent looking, it was a big deal. A girl named Elizabeth Meeker had moved into Palatine at the start of the semester, and there was a lot of talk about her, especially by the girls. They were saying that Elizabeth Meeker was "absolutely brilliant" and "so gorgeous," which was kind of overdoing it, but it was the way they talked when they wanted to be nice. Elizabeth Meeker actually turned out to be really smart. She was in all Accelerated classes, including my English section, and in math she got put in an Accelerated section of Juniors. She was from Houston.

I kind of had my eye on Elizabeth Meeker from her first day in English, and I might have gotten to know her even if the girls hadn't made a big deal out of "fixing me up" with her at the Coke Dance. But that was the plan, or at least they thought it was, as we all headed down the hall toward the Girls Gym.

I had actually noticed quite a bit about Elizabeth since she came into our English class. My system of liking girls' looks is kind of complicated. It starts off with a very strong impression I don't even think about. It just hits me. Either a girl is basically okay or basically not okay. If she's basically not okay, I can still be as nice as possible and maybe even friends, if she happens to be friends with other people I already like. But there would be no way I was going to be able to honestly enjoy looking at someone who was not basically okay. Basically okay didn't mean she had to be tremendously pretty. There just had to be that little something that made me feel I could keep looking at her. It was in the way all their parts, especially the parts of their faces, went together and how their faces went with their bodies. I found that if a girl looked basically okay, I sometimes got a better and better impression of her the more I got to know her and the longer I looked at her. A few girls I knew who I thought were only basically okay turned out to be really beautiful. It's like hearing certain new music. It can be barely okay when you first hear it, with maybe something vague and a little irritating about it, but then after you hear it twenty times, you see the whole design, and you can't believe you ever didn't like it sooner.

My first impression of Elizabeth Meeker was strongly okay. She was a little shorter than I was and had dark hair like Annabel's but shorter and fluffed up around her face in a pretty way. She was slender but not skinny, and something about her bones was extremely delicate. She had a sharp, cute little nose, her ankle bones stood out like blades, and her wrists were tiny. She was extremely clean and neat. Most of the girls I liked were clean and neat and cared a lot about their clothes, but Elizabeth was extra clean and neat. She seemed almost shiny. Nothing she wore ever looked wrinkled or like it was the second day.

When she got called on in English, she knew exactly what to say and was obviously very smart. Some of the girls got to know her right away, but until the Coke Dance, I hadn't even met her. I remember walking into the dark gym and thinking maybe I'd ask her to dance, and maybe I wouldn't, but right away a tall funny girl in our group named Sally Peters came up to me with a goofy look and told me she had someone she wanted me to meet. I kind of knew she was going to do that, and I knew it was going to be Elizabeth Meeker. I went over to Sally's friends where Elizabeth was, and Sally introduced me.

Elizabeth didn't look as if she was shy about meeting me at all. She actually stared at me pretty hard, and I got the feeling that there was something about me she already didn't like. If I had known her then as well as I did later, I would have realized there would be plenty of things about me she didn't like, like my clothes and my posture and my manners. One thing about Elizabeth, she was very critical. But she was also really cute, way better looking than I thought. I remember deciding right away that I was going to make her like me. It would be a perfect project. I didn't have a girlfriend, and everybody was starting to get them. Elizabeth was new, from Houston, and that made her stand out from everybody familiar. I liked the idea of people thinking of me having a girlfriend like Elizabeth Meeker.

Later when we were really close, I found out that when she first met me at the Coke Dance, she wasn't exactly thrilled. She told me she had the idea I was a smart aleck from the some of the things I said in English class. That bothered me. I thought back and tried to remember what I might have said that sounded smart alecky, but I couldn't think of anything. I was actually in a fairly calm period. It made me think that maybe there was something about my face that just looked smart alecky, like my nose. She also told me that I was wearing a terrible sweater that night. She said "dreadful sweater." That also bothered me, because it was a sweater I kind of liked, a sweater a lot of kids had. It was a crew neck, extra thick for winter, with dark orange and black stripes going up. When she made the remark about my sweater, I tried to be cheerful about it, like I really didn't care. I said something like, *really?* I wanted her to tell me what was wrong with it, but she just gave me an exaggerated look saying how could I not know what a terrible sweater it was. She said it made me look like the Cheshire Cat.

But the night of the Coke Dance I had no idea Elizabeth thought and said things like that. I just assumed she would be shy like a girl, and maybe especially shy because she was new and I was fairly popular. I asked her to dance, and she said yes. Without staring at her, I tried to figure out if she was glad she was dancing with me, but it was impossible to tell. The first few songs were fast ones, and we were jitterbugging, and she had a way of concentrating on what she was doing that seemed to close her off from me. A lot of girls do that, dance with somebody in a way that makes it seem like they're dancing by themselves. She wasn't completely unfriendly, though. She kept dancing with me.

We went out into the hall by ourselves, and I bought her a cup of Coke, and she said thank you very nicely. She seemed to be relaxing a little. I asked her everything I could think of about what it was like in Houston and how she liked Palatine and what kind of family she had. She was very nice telling me all that stuff, and it was starting to feel easier to be with her, but it was taking effort. She told me she lived in one of the new developments, one of the nice ones they put up in the fields where I used to play. She had an older sister in college in Wisconsin and a little brother who wasn't even in school yet. She called him The Mistake, which later I found out was one of the Meekers' family jokes, but I didn't get it when she first told me. I thought she hated him.

We went back into the gym and danced some more. I felt a little confused. I liked looking at Elizabeth, and I liked the idea that she was only dancing with me, which meant that now we really knew each other and could talk between classes and do anything we wanted, but it still felt like a lot of effort, and I had a feeling that at any second I could completely lose my confidence.

Maybe that bad feeling had to do with Elizabeth Meeker, but maybe it was a secret reaction to what happened next. All of a sudden there was a commotion down at the far doorway to the gym where they took tickets. There were some loud voices and then a lot of kids huddling into little groups and whispering. Almost nobody else was dancing, and I knew we were missing something. I asked Elizabeth if she wanted to see what was happening, and she came with me as I followed the other kids toward the far door. Even before I got there and could see anything, I could hear people saying "Patsy Prentiss." Maybe they were saying it, or maybe I was reading their minds, because I still had the aching, awful feeling of missing her so much after we stopped knowing each other in junior high.

I don't know how I got there, because there we so many kids crowded around the doorway, but all of a sudden I was right there by the ticket table, about ten feet from where Dean Gladhead and two policemen were standing, one of them holding Patsy against the wall by her shoulders. Her camel-colored coat was practically falling down off her arms, and she was half crying and half shrieking at the policeman, saying, "You *jerk!* Take your big filthy hands off me—I'm calling my parents—*why can't I call my parents—*"

It was awful. Even though she was screaming and not making any sense, she also looked incredibly tired and old. For a minute I felt like I was not in the regular world, or that I was and Patsy had somehow crashed in from the other world in a terrible way. The kids around me were saying, "She's *drunk.*" "Prentiss is drunk." I couldn't take it in, except as a kind of message that wherever Patsy went off to in Junior High, it was some kind of hell, and for some reason I was supposed to see it now. I looked up from Patsy and saw that farther down the hall some other policemen

The Other World

were holding two men against the lockers. They might have been older kids, kids who graduated from Palatine. They had on long overcoats like my dad's.

I remembered I was with Elizabeth and went to look for her. They started playing music again, and as I made my way across the gym to where I could see Elizabeth and the other girls in her group, it seemed that every voice I heard was talking about Patsy, saying that she was such a lush, that she was a mess, that she was a slut.

I tried to pick up my conversation with Elizabeth but I couldn't concentrate. I don't even know what I said. The Coke Dance was practically over. They were playing slow songs, which they did toward the end to calm everything down. Most kids only bothered to dance the slow ones if they had a girlfriend, because you could dance close. I was just standing there about two feet from Elizabeth, so we danced. I didn't have anything else to say, and neither did she. I just started into the fox trot, holding her hand out as lightly as you could hold hands. I could feel her side and her hip just touching mine, and her hair was brushing against my cheek. You can't really look at someone when you're doing a slow dance, and I remember feeling that even though it was the new girl, Elizabeth Meeker, I was barely holding onto and that just a little earlier I was starting to get interested in her, she almost wasn't there. I was only holding onto the outer edges and tips of a person, with nothing inside the shape. What wasn't inside the shape was Patsy Prentiss, who seemed to have been taken away from me again in a new way, but this time it was as if she moved away or died. It made me too sad to talk or even think. I just wanted to get out of there and out into the blizzard.

* * *

Elizabeth Meeker was my girlfriend for the rest of high school. I gave her a ring, but we were way beyond going steady. It pretty much started at the Coke Dance, because after we danced together like that, the girls in our group started saying that I liked Elizabeth now. I didn't mind, and after about two more Coke Dances,

I was dancing close with her and walking her home, and we were a couple. I felt like I was being completely carried away, which I knew happened to certain kids with girls, so I just gave up and let myself go.

Going with Elizabeth felt right in certain ways, but it was not always great for my confidence. At Palatine, at least in our group, other kids like it when you pair off and become a couple. It kind of makes everything in the group feel more permanent, and everybody knows what to expect. It definitely makes you more popular, but that wasn't my main reason. Once you work out the routine about what you're supposed to do with your girlfriend, you can start to feel relaxed and organized and safe. It's like being in a club of other people who have girlfriends.

With Elizabeth there was a lot of going back and forth between feeling pretty excited and feeling really terrible. She was not a relaxed girl, and she had really strong opinions, which I've found goes with being incredibly intelligent. If you just saw her from the outside, you'd think that because of her neat clothes and hair and the intelligent way she talked that she was completely confident. She didn't mind being even a little mean sometimes. But it didn't take me long to find out that in some departments she wasn't confident at all.

Being a couple at Palatine meant that whatever event was coming up, like Homecoming or Prom, you automatically went with your girlfriend. You didn't even ask her or talk about it. The first big dance that came up after Elizabeth and I were a couple was Spring Fever. Spring Fever was semi-formal, which meant I had to wear a coat and tie, but not a suit all one color, and I had to buy a corsage. I liked everything about the idea. I liked not having to think up who I would ask and what kind of a time I'd probably have, but what actually felt best was knowing I would be allowed to use the car. I'd had my license for a few months, and driving gave me one of the best feelings I've ever had, but I didn't get to use the car much, except for errands like shopping for my mother or picking up my father at the station when it was raining. Rarely, very rarely, I got to take the car over to a friend's house, but I could tell my father was suspicious. He said he thought I would be out "tearing around and burning rubber," which I had no interest in doing, but I did want to drive around a lot more than I was allowed to. I especially wanted to drive around more by myself. I wanted to be able to get out in the car and just explore. I couldn't see that happening, but I knew I would probably get the car to take Elizabeth and Gary Wade and Karen Shiels to Spring Fever.

The other great thing, which made me play little games with myself to keep me from thinking about it too much, was that, besides dancing close, Elizabeth and I had started kissing. I had hardly kissed anybody, actually only one person, in a serious way before Elizabeth, and I really, really liked it. After the dance I knew we would go out to eat and I would drop off Gary and Karen at their houses, and then my idea was that maybe I would kiss Elizabeth for a while in the car before she went in. In the car seemed to me way better than on her front porch, where there would only be one hug and kiss, maybe two, if you broke it up by saying something. My thoughts about kissing Elizabeth in the car were pretty vague, but the whole idea of driving and kissing and being out by ourselves made me look forward to Spring Fever.

Spring Fever was our first big date as a couple, and it started off pretty well. I didn't know about corsages, and it turned out Mother didn't either, but Elizabeth knew exactly, and I got her probably the best corsage at the dance. She knew the exact name of the different flowers and the different ways they could be set up to go around your wrist, and since I could tell she really cared about it, I got just what she told me, which ended up costing seven fifty, which to me was unbelievable. The whole dance only cost five dollars. My father had already given me ten dollars for the dance and afterwards, and I knew I couldn't tell him about a seven fifty corsage, so I took an extra ten out of my savings account which had hundreds of dollars in it from my summer jobs, but it was supposed to be for college.

The dance itself was fine. I was starting to realize that as a junior and a kid who had a varsity letter and was in the plays and on the paper and got straight A's and now had a regular girlfriend, I was turning into the kind of kid I never thought I would be in High School, one of the popular kids, one of the kids everybody knew. I could feel it. When I let Elizabeth and Gary and Karen out at the door of the gym and drove over to the lot to park, there were a lot of little freshmen and sophomores on the walk getting dropped off by their parents, and I could feel them looking at me, driving along in my own car. They probably knew who I was from something they saw me in at school. They probably knew I was in the popular group and looked at me the way I used to look at juniors and seniors who had letter sweaters and steady girlfriends and their own cars. When I was little I would make pictures of myself I really liked. I would be building a fort you could actually live in or having my own rifle and hunting all day in the north woods. In High School, starting when I gave up, I never made my own pictures anymore. In High School the pictures seemed to be already there, like the picture of a popular guy with a letter sweater and a girlfriend, and you just made yourself into that picture.

Spring Fever didn't get ruined until we went out afterwards to Howard Johnson's. We had a pretty good time at the dance. Elizabeth had on a new black dress with a skirt that flared way out, and with her dark hair and lipstick and makeup she looked really different. The dress made her hair and eyes and lips seem even darker, and something she had around her eyes made them look moist and sparkly in the blue light they used for dances. The dress made a straight line over the top of her breasts, and just above the cloth you could see the beginning of the little line that went down between them. I thought she looked great, and I was starting to get in a really good mood.

There wasn't a Howard Johnson's in Palatine, but there was one two towns over, in Fox River Grove. Howard Johnson's was the right kind of place to go after a major dance, because it was bigger and fancier than a regular hamburger place, but it wasn't ridiculously fancy with everything costing at least ten dollars. On the way we listened to Top Forty on the radio, and Gary got off a lot of wise cracks from the back seat, and I got off a few good ones myself. I was still in a pretty good mood when Gary and Karen got out of the car and I got out my side and headed into the restaurant. The three of us were standing just inside the door seeing if there was a table when I realized Elizabeth wasn't with us. I thought maybe she had gone down the hall to the Ladies, so I waited for a while. After a few minutes I went outside and looked around. I walked over to the car and saw that Elizabeth was still sitting in the passenger seat. Her arms were folded in front of her, and she was crying. I opened her door and asked her what was the matter. She couldn't talk for a minute. Her chin was wobbling, and when she tried to talk, she had to stop. I felt terrible. I kept asking her what was wrong, if she was sick or if I had said something.

She stopped crying and gave me a really mean look. "Let me tell you something, *Jonathan*," she said. "In case you don't know, a *gentleman* opens the door for his date when he gets out of the car." I was stunned by how bad she felt. It took me a minute to make sense of what she said. I asked her if she meant opening the car door or some other door. She told me the car door. I'm pretty sure I said I was sorry and didn't mean to hurt her feelings, because I really didn't, but my head was spinning. She was still sitting in the car, and she didn't look like she was about to get out. I didn't know if it would make it better or worse to say that no one ever told me that if you wanted your date to get out of a car, you had to walk around to her side and open the door. For a while I stood there with the door open and her just sitting there, and I think we both felt terrible. Finally I asked her in a nice way if she wanted to go in and get something to eat. She said she didn't and that all she wanted to do was go home, but then she got out.

Gary was still in a loud, goofy mood when we found him and Karen at the table. He tried to make a joke about our ditching him, but when he saw how miserable Elizabeth was, he quieted down. Normally I'm really hungry and like a burger with fries or a big sandwich when it's late after a dance, but seeing Elizabeth cry like that did something to me. I felt a weird combination of being sad and being mad. When the waiter came to get our orders, I ordered a Club Sandwich Special, which was the first thing I saw on the menu. Elizabeth ordered a cup of soup. She was sitting across from me, but she wouldn't look into my eyes. When someone gets in a mood like that, you can't ignore it. Pretty soon none of us had anything to say, and we just sat there waiting for the food, and I started going down the spiral into my worst feelings.

The Club Sandwich Special when it came was ridiculous. It was at least a triple-decker, and each triangle stood up so high I couldn't hold it all together between my fingertips and my thumb, and it kind of collapsed in a mess over the plate. I took the toothpick out and scraped away the toast and top layer and thought maybe I could convert it into a regular sandwich, but even the part left over was almost too big to close my teeth on, and I wasn't going to look like even more of an idiot by stretching my mouth open as far as possible to get my teeth over the thing, so I just left it all in a big mess on the plate. Elizabeth had about two sips of soup from her spoon and then just sat there. By that time I was just mad, although I couldn't have said what I was mad at. I just wanted to get out of there, and so did everybody else.

Needless to say, there was no kissing in the car in front of Elizabeth's house. Who wanted to. I pulled up into Elizabeth's driveway, shifted into Park, and practically ran over to the passenger side door where I felt myself doing a kind of bow as I opened the door for her. I walked her to her front porch, and we stood there for a minute while she looked for her key. Just before she went in she turned to me and said thank you for taking her to the dance and for the corsage, and in the same voice said, "I had a very nice time." For a second I didn't get it. She couldn't possibly have had a nice time, but by the time I was back in the car, I understood that it was the kind of thing she had learned to say, that it was just her manners.

* * *

It took me a while to get used to having Elizabeth as my girlfriend. There were things I was just never going to know about until they happened, like opening the car door for her. There was also the business of seeing her in curlers, which got her just as upset as she got at Howard Johnson's. Once I was doing an errand and had the car to myself on a really nice Saturday afternoon in the spring, and I decided to drop over and say hi to her. We were going out somewhere that night, and I knew I would be seeing her later, but I was in a good mood, so I thought I'd just knock on the door. Her older sister, Tricks, was home for the weekend, and she gave me a funny look and told me Elizabeth was in the back yard, and I should just go around and find her. When I got back there, Elizabeth was leaning back in a lawn chair, sunning herself. I said hi, which kind of woke her up, and she looked at me in a horrible way. Her hair was full of fat curlers, like Annabel's, and it was all held together in a kind of kerchief. She turned her back to me and said, "Go away." I didn't get it. I asked her if something was wrong. She told me to go away again. She said *"please"* in a really desperate voice. I asked her what I did wrong, and she said she didn't see people when she was in curlers. I tried to be really nice about it and say I didn't care, but she wouldn't turn back to look at me, so I went home.

About every two or three weeks there would be something like that, and I never saw it coming. The worst one was the time I came to pick her up to take her out for her birthday. The plan was to drive all the way into Evanston to a little restaurant I found out about and then see a foreign movie at the Arts Cinema. It was the middle of July and really nice out, and I decided to try to make it a special occasion. Nobody got very dressed up for dates in the summer, but Elizabeth really liked to dress up, so, since it was her birthday we decided to make it pretty fancy. At the time I had a sports jacket I liked a lot. It was mainly white with little flecks in it. I thought it looked pretty good in the summer, because I used to get really tan, but since I had worn that jacket a bunch of times with Elizabeth, I decided to get a new one for the birthday date. There was a new fashion that year, and some kids started getting Madras jackets, which had patches of all different colors and patterns on them. I actually thought it was kind of confusing to look at a Madras jacket, but they were lightweight and comfortable, and kids who had really nice clothes started wearing them.

My big mistake was trying to buy one cheap. There was a men's clothing store downtown called Parnell's which always had exactly the kind of button-down shirts and wool sweaters and khaki pants you'd want to wear, but usually only men bought stuff there because everything cost twenty dollars or thirty-five dollars, amounts nobody our age ever had. You might get something from Parnell's as a present or save up for maybe one thing, like a sweater, but everybody went to Zimmerman's instead, or ordered from Sears. That summer on the highway just outside of town, a huge new discount store, the first one I ever heard of, called Topps, opened up, and everybody started going there, even Mother sometimes. I thought it was pretty amazing. You could get pants and shirts and sweaters for three or four dollars. A lot of them were pretty terrible, and things from Topps looked definitely worse when you got home than they did in the store, but sometimes you'd find pairs of pants or shorts that you couldn't tell from normal, and they hardly cost anything. One night after a game, some of us were looking through stuff at Topps before it closed, and I saw a whole long rack of Madras jackets. They were all twelve dollars. I had never bought a sports jacket for myself before, but I didn't think twelve dollars was too much, especially for something like a Madras jacket, which was the kind of thing I thought you could only get at Parnell's for probably more than a hundred. It seemed perfect to get a jacket like that just before Elizabeth's birthday, so I got one.

I probably shouldn't have been in such a big hurry, and I should have asked somebody to help me figure out the size. The one I chose seemed pretty big, with the sleeves coming down over part of my hands and the front coming out a little bit extra, but I was in a tee shirt and shorts, and I thought that being dressed up in a shirt and tie would kind of fill everything in. What I really needed was somebody who knew something about Madras jackets. It wasn't until afterward that I realized the jacket I got wasn't much of a Madras. It was made up of a lot of different colored squares, but they were small and dark, I think dark green, red, and purple. Some of the squares had little black streaks going through them. When I tried it on at home, it looked pretty dark, mostly purple and shiny, not summery light blue and pink like the ones at Parnell's. It was also pretty big on me, but I figured that since summer was supposed to be more casual, it didn't have to fit like a regular jacket.

The Other World

    I didn't think about it much the week before my birthday date with Elizabeth, except that I was really looking forward to going out to Evanston. I took twenty dollars out of my savings, and my father gave me a little extra, so I was pretty loaded, and that always felt good. That Saturday was really hot, and I was outside all day, cutting lawns in the morning, and we had a legion baseball game in the afternoon. When I got out of the shower and got dressed to go pick up Elizabeth, my face felt like it was glowing from all the sun. As I was leaving the house, my father looked at me and asked what kind of jacket I was wearing. I told him it was a Madras, but I knew he wouldn't know anything about them, so I didn't think about it.
    I rang Elizabeth's bell and when she came to the door, she looked at me and didn't say anything. Finally she said, "You're not going to wear that, are you?" She wasn't kidding. She looked completely miserable, and it gave me the same rotten feeling. I asked her what was wrong with it, but by then it didn't matter what she said, I knew there was no way we were going out or having anything like a decent time if she was in that mood, which meant that I had to drive home and take off the Madras jacket and put on my white one with the flecks.
    Elizabeth is just one of those people you have to be really careful with. Sometimes the littlest thing you said could make her mad or hurt her feelings. It was probably good for me that she was like that, because otherwise I might have gotten too relaxed and gone on thinking I was a lot smarter than I was. And it's not that there weren't any good things about going with her. By the end of High School we were boyfriend and girlfriend for so long we got included in everything, every party, every hayride, every tobogganing trip. Altogether we spent a lot of time with each other. In the spring I would walk her home from school, stopping to get a soda or something on the way. She probably lived a mile or a mile and a half from the school, but the routes we would go, and with stopping in stores or sitting down somewhere in a park, it might take three hours, and that was just to her house. Every Friday or Saturday night that we didn't go out somewhere, I would go over to her house, and we'd play Scrabble or cards until her

parents went to bed, and then we'd watch the Late Night Movie in her den.

We actually never watched the movie. We would just turn it on, and after about three minutes, get comfortable on the corduroy cushions on the floor in front of the TV and start kissing. It felt wonderful to know that it was completely all right and she expected it. Kissing like that, just on and on, put me in another world. When the movie and the last commercial were over, a trumpet would play "The Star Spangled Banner," and then the screen would buzz, and all you'd see is gray flecks and a design in the middle of the screen. This would happen at twelve-thirty or one, and I'd have to go home. Whether it was nice out and I walked or whether I drove, I was always in the same kind of trance after the kissing. When I woke up the next morning I could never remember a thing about getting home, brushing my teeth, getting undressed and going to bed.

It was actually more than just kissing. I would pull Elizabeth over into me so that we were front to front all along our bodies, and then we'd just let ourselves get more and more tangled up while we kissed. I would rub her back and her neck while we were kissing, and she would sometimes squeeze the back of my neck with her palm, which didn't really feel like anything, but I liked the idea of her wanting to do it. Maybe a year after we started kissing, I decided to try to feel her breasts. I had a hunch she wouldn't like it, but I had been thinking about it for a long time. I tested it out by rubbing her shoulder for a while and then dragging my hand slowly down her front, not even stopping on her breast, just passing over it on the way down. I think it scared her. She sat up straight and stared at the TV. She told me we shouldn't do that, but she didn't seem mad or miserable and we got back to just kissing. Sometime not too long after that, she started letting me, and we never said anything about it, and it got to be a nice part of those kissing nights.

I never told Elizabeth this, because she wouldn't have liked it and I was only half aware of it myself, but one of the reasons I liked kissing her so much and felt like I could keep kissing forever was that it took me right back to the first time I kissed somebody for the feel of it. I had only kissed one girl before I started kissing Elizabeth.

It was Sue Ellen Lester, and it's amazing that it even happened.

* * *

Sue Ellen Lester wasn't even close to being a girlfriend. She was just a really tall, lively girl in some of my classes in sixth grade. She was the best singer in our grade, and we once sang a duet together in a concert. I forget the song except that it was about Switzerland, and my solo part went

Land of William Tell

A story we know well

Of apple, boy, and old cross bow

And how Tell conquered every foe, so—

Dear old Switzerland…something, something.

One thing I liked about Sue Ellen Lester is that she had a lot of nerve. She'd do anything a boy would do on the playground. One time Jim Mahler said she butted into the lunch line ahead of him, and she said she didn't, that her friend was saving her place, and Jim Mahler said oh right, oh sure and called her a stupid beanpole. Sue Ellen stepped right up in front of him and said, "What did you say?" He said stupid beanpole again, and Sue Ellen slapped him right across the face. Jim Mahler was about as big as she was, but he didn't do anything back. In fact, he started to cry.

I really didn't know her that well, but there was something about Sue Ellen I always liked. The summer I kissed her I was playing on a Pony League baseball team, and our games were on the good diamond under the lights. After a game the kids who played would meet up with kids getting out of the pool, and we'd hang around the park for a while, until they'd turn the lights out and people would walk or ride their bikes home. Sue Ellen was usually one of the kids hanging around, because she lived pretty close to the park, in a new house one street in from the fields. Her mother and father both had jobs, and she told kids they could come over to her house any time they wanted during the day. Some kids who knew her said she sometimes had boys over during the day and they played games like strip poker.

The night that I kissed her, Sue Ellen and I were fooling around with a bunch of kids by the candy machines outside the pool. The lights were going off, so people started going home. Sue Ellen was walking, and I was going in the same direction, so we started walking along together. We were having a nice time. When you got close to Sue Ellen's house there were two ways you could go. You could go down the main sidewalk to the front of her yard, or you could take a path through the trees at the edge of the fields and go through her back yard. Because it was night, I thought we'd keep going on the sidewalk under the streetlights, but Sue Ellen said why not take the path. She said it was more fun, and it was. There was plenty of light in the sky from the town, and it made the grass and the leaves and the bark of the trees silvery. It was one of those soft nights where the ground feels like a cushion under your feet as you walk, and it felt like Sue Ellen and I were going along our own secret lane. Just before we got to where her yard started, she stopped and leaned back against a tree. She asked me if I had started kissing yet. It didn't feel embarrassing at all or too personal. She just wanted to know. I told her not really. She asked me if I wanted to try it, which was kind of a surprise. I didn't hate the idea, and the longer we stayed there talking in soft voices by the tree, the more I wanted to. Maybe I was thinking about the strip poker, but it was starting to feel pretty exciting. I think I would have been even more excited if Sue Ellen weren't so tall. She was really tall, one of the tallest girls in our class. She was the kind of tall girl I didn't even feel bad about being smaller than, because everybody was. That also took her out of the even possible girlfriend category. But I couldn't think about that when I was back there with her in the trees. I said sure, and waited to

The Other World

see what she would do. She took a step toward me and leaned over so that her face was down in front of mine, and she put her arms around my back and pulled me in closer. I put my arms around her back too. Her nose was touching against my nose, and then she got it out of the way, and then we pressed our lips together. My eyes closed automatically, and I just felt it. In my mind everything disappeared except the soft, full feeling of Sue Ellen's lips and a picture of her big happy face just an inch in front of mine in the dark. I could tell Sue Ellen wanted to keep it going for a minute. She moved her lips around a little, so you could keep feeling it. Then we were done, and I opened my eyes, and Sue Ellen had a big smile on her face. We talked for a few more minutes, and then she ran off into her yard. I wished I could have figured out how to walk all the way home on that path through the trees. I was saying to myself: *I kissed a girl.* I kept thinking that and feeling Sue Ellen's warm, dry lips all night and for a long time after that. It didn't matter how tall she was. There was absolutely nothing bad about it.

*   *   *

One other thing about kissing Elizabeth. You had to keep it dry. One of the first times we watched the Late Night Movie in her den, she sat up all of a sudden and told me, "I don't like French kissing." I didn't know what it was, and she told me it was with your tongue in the other person's mouth. I told her I didn't like it either, so we never did. When I got to know her better she said she turned against French kissing when a boy she knew in Houston tried it on her. She told me he was a pig and that all of his friends were pigs too. Elizabeth said that besides trying to French kiss her, he used to clear his throat and spit gobs of stuff out onto the sidewalk in front of them when they were walking somewhere. I knew Elizabeth could be really fussy, but I saw what she meant about a person who would do that. She really hated Texas, and he was a big reason.

The best way to get along with Elizabeth was to get to know her really well and keep track of the things she really liked and the things she couldn't stand. It didn't take me long to figure out she couldn't stand surprises, which meant a lot of my jokes were out, such as putting something ridiculous, like some guy's sweaty gym stuff, in her locker or writing her a crazy note that was supposed to be from somebody whose handwriting I knew how to imitate.

I think the thing Elizabeth cared about most was her family and the special way they did things at her house. She really enjoyed talking about her mother and father and sister and the particular way they did things like buy a new couch or rake leaves or all take a walk together in the forest preserve before they had Thanksgiving dinner. She also really cared about the stuff in her room and in their house, and she knew things about furniture and fabric and dishes that you wouldn't expect someone our age to know. I thought her house was pretty nice and very clean, but a little bit empty looking. They didn't have carpeting in any of the rooms, just bare, shiny wood floors with little rugs in front of something like the couch or under the table. Their house actually looked slightly like it was from another period in history. Elizabeth knew the names for different kinds of furniture and that they were antiques. She would call an old wooden cabinet a "hutch" or a "commode" and tell me the town or the store where they bought it. Their stuff did have kind of a look to it, but some of it just seemed beat up, with nicks and old burn marks on the wood and veins of cracks running through the china. I know you were supposed to like antiques because they were old and valuable, but I couldn't see having stuff that you couldn't really use, no matter how antique it was. For instance, the Meekers had a couple of little antique rocking chairs, very beat up, on each side of the fireplace, and next to one of them there was an old-fashioned wooden crib on rockers with a pile of kindling wood in it. Some white birch logs were set up in the fireplace, but the bricks underneath were perfectly clean, because the Meekers never used the fireplace, and nobody ever touched the arrangement of kindling wood, and no one was allowed to sit in the rocking chairs, because they would break. I tried to be as nice and as interested as I could when Elizabeth told me about some hutch or candlestick or embroidered saying on the wall, but it didn't all come together to make a great-feeling house like Nana and Papa's. Those things were really important to Elizabeth, though, and I had to learn that.

The way Elizabeth talked about her family and their routines and their stuff had the effect on me of making me wish there were special things like that going on at our house. Since Annabel went away, our house felt pretty quiet and basically kind of dead. We had our meals, and the jobs got done, and we still went over to Nana's and Papa's for Sunday dinner and TV, but I couldn't imagine my mother and father making plans and saving up for a special trip up to Wisconsin so they could buy an old wooden box. I was starting to think that maybe it didn't matter if things like antiques were good looking or valuable or not or if the special way the people in your family opened their presents on Christmas was better than any other way. It was just really nice that people thought so. It kept people like the Meekers together and made them like each other.

I'm not sure the Meekers liked me all that much. It might have just been that I wasn't in their family, but maybe they noticed things about me they thought were terrible, like my expressions or my clothes, and never said anything about it. They weren't actually that bad when I was over there. You just had to get into their ways of doing things. You had to remember that for them certain things that happened in their family, like Mrs. Meeker forgetting to take the rolls out of the oven or The Mistake peeing in his pants whenever they went to the movies, were going to be funny forever.

Every family has its own little world, but the Meekers really had one. They had special names for everybody. They called Mrs. Meeker "Mamie." Elizabeth actually referred to her as "my Mamie" and would say things like, "We better be going home, or my Mamie will be very cross." It was supposed to be kind of a joke, but it was mainly a Meeker joke. She called her father "Fahrver," and her sister Letitia was "Tricks." The Mistake's real name was Philip, and they called him the whole thing, never Phil, when he was there, but when he wasn't around, he was The Mistake. The effect of the whole thing made me realize how different and separate her kind of family was from mine. Elizabeth would tell me things like, "We all went to the movies to see 'Fantasia,' and, *once again,* The Mistake wet his pants almost immediately. Fahrver tried to get him to sit on his newspaper until the movie was over, but precious baby kept whining out loud, 'I'm *wet.* I'm *cold,*' until my poor Mamie was beside herself and told Fahrver we had to leave at once. Wretched Mistake. I can't wait to tell Tricks." It made Elizabeth happy telling me things like that about her family, but I couldn't picture being in on any of it.

One thing that held Elizabeth and me together was presents. I liked presents, and I'm sure everybody does, but presents meant something completely different to Elizabeth, and that was something I had to learn fast. The first winter when she was starting to be my girlfriend, I got her a bad present. I didn't mean to. I just didn't give it enough thought. I was in Zimmerman's getting stuff for my mother and father, Nana and Papa, and Uncle Desmond, and I saw a stack of angora hat and mitten combinations in the Women's section. I liked the bright colors and the soft look of the angora, so I got a red set for Elizabeth and, at the moment, actually had a good feeling about it. Until I realized the way Elizabeth felt about presents, I didn't give them that much thought. To me getting someone a present was pretty basic. So long as it wasn't ridiculously crummy, it would be fine. But in the Meeker family people gave presents a lot of thought. It kind of went with having antiques and stories that went with all their stuff.

On the afternoon of Christmas Eve before we all went over to Nana and Papa's for supper, I got to use the car to drive over to Elizabeth's to give her my present. Her parents left us alone in the den, and she gave me my present first. I could tell by the box it was going to be clothes, and it turned out to be a dark blue crew neck sweater. I saw that it came from Parnell's, and it was really nice. She had figured out my size, which was 40, and she told me it was a blend of lamb's wool and cashmere. I didn't know what kind of actual cloth went into sweaters, but I could see that this one looked really good. I took off the one I had on and put on the new one and looked in their mirror. It was amazing that a sweater could look so good. I thanked her a lot, and I really meant it, but I was already starting to feel bad about my present, because a crewneck sweater from Parnell's was such a bigger deal. She took off the wrapping paper very carefully and opened the box, which was a box we had at home, not one that came with the hat-mitten set. She held them up in front of her and said, "A hat and mittens." She said it in a nice way, but I could tell she was holding back, and I was already feeling terrible. I told her they were angora. She said thank you very much in a nice way and put them back in the box. We talked for a little while, but neither one of us could get in a good mood, so I got up and went into their kitchen to say Merry Christmas to the Meekers and drove home. After that something clicked in me, and I decided that when it came time to buy Elizabeth a present again, I was going to empty my bank account if I had to and get her something no one would believe. I didn't care if it was a diamond necklace or a car. I was never going to feel that rotten, cheapskate feeling again.

Of course the sweater she got me turned out to be the best one I had, the only one I would wear if I wanted to look decent. It also taught me the kind of thing I would have to buy if I wanted to look good all the time. Before that, going back to junior high when I first started noticing how kids were dressed, I always thought there was something about certain kids that automatically looked good. I usually linked it up with being tall or, after I got to know Patsy Prentiss, being rich. I thought that a kid who had a certain look just looked good in clothes, but the sweater Elizabeth bought me and the stuff I started getting after that made me realize that it's the actual clothes that made you look like that. But you had to get good stuff.

Elizabeth really liked shopping. It was one of her favorite things to do, and when a shopping trip was coming up with her mother or with Tricks, she would be in a good mood all week. She liked to go to the big Chicago department stores on Michigan Avenue or to the new ritzy malls they were building in Evanston and the other rich suburbs. By the time I was a junior, I could get the car every now and then on a Saturday, and Elizabeth and I would go on a shopping trip by ourselves. At first I did it because I thought she would really like it, and she did. We would usually go to a big mall with stores in it like Saks Fifth Avenue and Marshall Fields and Lord and Taylor. Elizabeth knew all about every store and which floor and section would have what she wanted. She always had a plan, and sometimes the whole purpose for a trip would be for her to get one tiny bottle of Chanel No. 5 perfume. Most of the time she wanted us to split up and for me to go off and get my own stuff while she got hers. She said I made her nervous just hanging around her, and I actually couldn't stand it either. The first few times we went shopping together, I realized there was practically nothing I could afford to buy. Normally if I had five or ten dollars in my wallet, or even fifteen, I would think I was in pretty good shape, but in those stores one shirt might cost fifteen dollars, and we would also have to eat something while we were there, and maybe I would have to get some gas. But by this time I had a lot of money, over a thousand dollars, in my savings account for college, so I started taking a lot of extra money with me, thirty or forty dollars, plus what I already had.

I usually didn't know where to go when I was walking around the mall by myself. I would find myself in the men's section of a place like Marshall Fields, and there would be pants for fifty dollars and sports jackets for a hundred fifty dollars and ties for ten dollars, and I would keep telling the salesmen no thanks, I was just looking and maybe every now and then think about getting one thing, like a belt, even though it was way too expensive. One time Elizabeth and I were at a mall in the summer, and it was a lot lighter than usual in the atrium where the sun came through the glass, and somehow everything seemed friendlier. There were a lot of big sales, and as I was wandering around by myself, I went past a little store that sold only Italian shoes. The regular ones cost ninety dollars or a hundred and ten dollars, but some of the ones on sale only cost twenty, which meant I could buy a pair. The ones on sale were pretty different, but I actually liked them. They came to a sharp point at the end, and the sole underneath was really narrow, so it looked like your foot was wrapped all the way around in leather. They looked a little like the shoes people wore in the pirate days. I was in a pretty goofy mood, so I bought a pair.

Later when Elizabeth and I were having lunch, she asked me what I bought, and I showed her the shoes. She didn't hold back. She said, "Jonathan, you go right back there and take those back." She made a face at me and said, "What's *wrong* with you?" I should have known better, but I tried to joke around with her a little and say I thought they were pretty cool, but she was serious. I didn't want to let her know it, but that kind of thing still made me feel bad. I knew she knew all about clothes, but I didn't see what was so bad about being a little goofy every now and then. I went back to the store to get my money back, but the guy said that because they were on sale, I could only exchange them for something else. The only other cheap ones were the kind I knew Elizabeth would hate, so I decided I'd just get a million pairs of socks, even though all they had was thin black socks I knew I'd never wear. As it turned out, you only got about three pairs for twenty dollars anyway.

But one thing I learned from all that shopping with Elizabeth, and that was to buy her really good presents. Most of the time she let me know what she really wanted. It was always something very particular, like a camel-colored cashmere scarf that she could wear with a certain coat or a pair of really soft leather gloves that went way up her arm. I got used to the fact that those kinds of things cost fifty or sixty dollars, and once I knew it, it stopped making me feel so nervous. The best thing, though, was being able to surprise Elizabeth by getting her even more stuff and better stuff than she expected. In order to do this, I would call up her mother or Tricks and ask them some of the things Elizabeth wanted. They always knew, and they were always right. Elizabeth would practically fall over after she would open what she thought was her main present from me, which was something really good, and then I'd pull out of the bag something else, or maybe two things, that were even better. I loved doing that. It's great to give people way more than they ever expect. That saying from the Bible is true.

Maybe the best thing about having Elizabeth for my girlfriend for so long was that it made my life feel so safe and organized. Gary Wade used to tease me about having a wife, and he would call Elizabeth "the little woman." He was mainly fooling around, but I knew what he meant. The longer you have the same girlfriend and keep doing things with her, the more of an official couple you are, and after a while you can't even picture yourself not being in the couple. But at the same time, I had a weird feeling that any second Elizabeth would break up with me for some reason, and it would be all over. I don't think it was just because she was so high strung and got mad at me every now and then. She never talked about breaking up. I was the one who thought about it. I even had dreams about it, dreams where I would do something horrible to her, something I would never actually do, like call her names and slap her and then start yelling at her whole family. Obviously, I kept things like that to myself.

* * *

By the end of the summer before senior year, my situation started getting a little crazy, and not just in my dreams. It was like I had a mental illness, schizophrenia, where you have two complete lives at the same time, and whenever you're in one of the lives, that's all there is and it's fine, but the two lives don't have anything to do with each other. That's the way I felt about being a senior. One life I was going to have was to be in sports and plays and talent shows and get all A's and have Elizabeth as my girlfriend. It was going to be exactly like junior year, except I was going to be even more important, maybe even in the Homecoming Court, but the main thing about it was that everything was going to be familiar, and nothing was ever going to change. The other life was completely opposite. I was going to have to figure out a place to go to college, move out of our house, move away from Palatine, break up with Elizabeth, and start doing all new things with new people. I knew that both of those lives were coming up, and the effect it had on me was to make me think that no matter what I did, it was going to get cancelled out. It was like I had a main self that went through the days, but also a kind of zombie anti-self that was going to wreck everything the first self did.

The real craziness might have started the night Elizabeth and I were supposed to go on a double date to see *Flower Drum Song* at the Drive-In with Gary Wade and Karen Shiels. That would have been a fairly normal night for us, because we did a lot of things with Gary and Karen. Elizabeth thought Gary was a big-mouth, because he was kind of a goof-off in school, but she liked Karen Shiels, so we usually had a pretty good time together. Gary and Karen were also at about the same level of kissing as Elizabeth and me, so nobody had to worry about anything. But a few days before our double date, Gary and Karen broke up, and Gary decided to ask Lou Scanlon to go with us to *Flower Drum Song*. If he had told me in advance, we probably would not have gone. There was no way Elizabeth was going to get along with Lou Scanlon. Lou Scanlon wasn't in our group, and although she wasn't in Vocational Ed, she was definitely not in College Preparatory. I didn't mind her, but I didn't know her very well. She had a reputation, and the girls in our group said she was "cheap." She had dark hair and dark skin and wore a lot of make-up. I thought it was too much make-up, because it made her face look kind of oily when she was actually not bad looking. Whether she really was cheap or not, the guys she went out with talked about her a lot afterward, saying you could do anything you wanted. Lou Scanlon and her friends had a look. Their skirts were tight around their hips and bottom, and their sweaters were really tight. They also smoked.

When Gary picked me up at my house, Lou Scanlon was sitting next to him in the front seat, and I was already starting to feel nervous about picking up Elizabeth. At first it was better than I thought. The worst thing Elizabeth did when she was upset was to look off in some direction and not talk at all, but she was fairly friendly on the way to the Drive-In. In fact the whole double date might not have been too bad if we had only gone to a regular movie where you had to sit up in your chair with a lot of other people around.

When we got to the Drive-In, it was still light out, so we got a bunch of food and popcorn and listened to the car radio. Gary actually seemed to know Lou pretty well, so it wasn't as awkward as I thought being in the car together. By the time it got dark and the movie started, I was starting to relax. *Flower Drum Song* didn't turn out to be much of a movie. It was a musical, and I don't know what it is about movies of musicals, but they always seem a little ridiculous, even if the music itself was pretty good. The problem is that movies are too realistic, and it doesn't work if someone up on the screen is walking down a real street in a real city and then starts singing something like, "I enjoy being a girl" as other people keep walking by. My main memory of watching *Flower Drum Song*, though, is sitting back with my arm around Elizabeth and watching the screen fill up with a swirl of Chinese people singing "A Hundred Million Miracles." They can't have been singing that for the whole movie, but that's what it seemed like, probably because once Gary and Lou Scanlon slid down out of sight I couldn't think straight.

If it had been Karen, Gary would have had his arm around her and they would have been kissing, which Elizabeth and I would have been able to tell by the way their heads went together. That would have been fine and nobody would have minded, because we would have been doing the same thing. But when Gary and Lou Scanlon slid down and disappeared, I got the feeling that anything could happen down there and that Elizabeth would have one of her fits. It probably would have been all right if they had just held still and not made any noise, but it was as bad as you could imagine. Gary was a big kid, and we could feel the back of the seat bulging out against our knees and hear the sound of their bodies rubbing against the upholstery. I wanted to turn up the volume on the speaker in the window, but to do that I'd have to lean over and see what was going on in the front seat, and I didn't want to do that. It kept getting worse. They were breathing really loud, and Gary was grunting and Lou Scanlon was making *"mmm mmm"* sounds, and you could hear the swishy sound of cloth moving around and all kinds of snapping and zipping. Knowing Gary, I knew there was no way he would remember Elizabeth and I were back there and pull himself together. He was out of his mind. There was absolutely nothing Elizabeth and I could do but listen and picture things. The only thing that ever seemed to be on the screen was the swirls of people in Chinese costumes singing "A Hundred Million Miracles," and the idea of Elizabeth and me kissing or doing anything ourselves was way out of the question. I couldn't even turn my head to look at her.

There would be a regular pattern of creaking and movement in the front seat, then it would stop for a while, then it would start up again harder than ever. I didn't think they would ever be finished. I only heard them say one thing. There was a quiet spell, then a little more creaking and swishing. It was impossible to figure out exactly what they were doing to each other. Then Lou Scanlon said, "lower." Gary said, "What?" And she said, "*lower.*"

After that night I remember wishing I had never heard that. Nothing, no dirty words, no actual description of the most sexual thing could have hit me the way "lower" did when Lou Scanlon said it. I couldn't get it out of my head. It had the effect of making me feel that no matter what kind of sex I could picture, there would always be something worse, something lower, and no matter how hard I tried to stop it, I was headed there. After that night with Gary and Lou Scanlon at the Drive-In, I just wanted to get back in the Meekers' den and watch the Late Night Movie with Elizabeth, but only kissing. I also made sure we had some dates in between where we didn't even kiss. But no matter what I did to stop it, as soon as I was alone in my room at night, the word "lower" would flash into my mind, and all kinds of new sex thoughts and pictures would start coming up.

It was probably good that senior year was as busy as it was. Just as I thought, Elizabeth and I got elected to the Homecoming Court, which was the biggest honor in the school, because the whole senior class could nominate people, and every kid in school voted. It helped a lot that Elizabeth and I were a couple, because kids usually thought of the Homecoming King and Queen as a couple. The top five boys and the top five girls formed the Homecoming Court, and they got to march through a special archway into the gym and walk along a red carpet to a little stage set up with two thrones on it. The whole school was sitting in the bleachers, and all the lights were out except for a spotlight that followed you up to the thrones when it was your turn to walk under the arch with your partner.

You couldn't imagine a bigger deal. The King candidates all had rented tuxes with white jackets, and the Queen candidates wore formal gowns and held bouquets of roses in front of them as they walked. As soon as the first couple was under the arch and the spotlight picked them up, The Palatones, who were the twelve best singers in Girls Chorus, would sing "When You Wish Upon A Star," and as soon as they started, all you could hear was the sound of girls squealing and sniffling in the dark. When all the candidates were lined up around the thrones, Dean Gladhead would announce the King and Queen, drawing it out as long as possible to increase the tension. As soon as he announced King and Queen, there would be a tremendous shriek, and the girls who didn't get it would run over and hug the Queen, and the boys would shake hands with the King. Then the lights would go out again, and a spotlight would follow the King and Queen as they walked all the way around the gym, waving to kids they couldn't really see in the dark while the Palatones sang "If."

If they made me a king

I'd be but a slave for you

If I had everything

I'd still be a slave for you

If the world to me bowed

Yet humbly I'd plead to you

If my friends were a crowd

I'd turn in my need to you

If I ruled the earth

What would life be worth

If I hadn't the right to you?

The Other World

    You had to cry. When I was a freshman and a sophomore, I did everything I could think of to try to get people around me to laugh, but the feeling just came over you when you heard the singing start and saw the couples moving across the gym under the spotlight. I remember being glad it was dark when the girls around me were crying and squealing, because nobody could see you if you happened to get choked up yourself.

    Being an actual candidate, I mainly felt numb. Even though I kind of knew I would be nominated because of all the stuff I did and we were such a major couple, it felt good when it really happened, and they read the names over Morning Announcements. Elizabeth and I weren't going to win, and everybody knew that, so there was nothing to feel tense about. The King was usually either the President of Student Council or a terrific athlete, provided he was also a fairly nice guy. The President of Student Council our year was Dan Retsik, and he was absolutely perfect for King, and so was his girlfriend, Polly Imarino, who was also on the Student Council and on a lot of other committees. I can't remember feeling bad for a minute about not being King, and I don't think Elizabeth minded not being chosen either. By the time you were a senior at Palatine, you pretty much knew where you were.

    But as much as the year started up exactly the way I predicted it would, my anti-self was making things miserable, making me feel like I was standing back and didn't care, even about major things like Homecoming Court. It was like a voice talking to me, trying to cancel out any little thing that might get me excited for a minute. Even walking across the gym in the spotlight, with Elizabeth's hand on my elbow, listening to the squealing and sniffling and trying to feel how amazing it was right at that moment, terrible things started popping up in my mind. I remembered "lower" all of a sudden and then started seeing sex pictures and imagining a bunch of kids, kids I didn't know, laughing at me out in the dark bleachers.

ALL THE PRIZES

Nearly everything to do with college could get me in the downward spiral.

What I really wanted was for the guidance counselors or the government or somebody just to assign me to someplace and have that be the end of it. My mother and father didn't go to college, so they didn't know much about what you had to do, like what achievement tests to take and how to get the applications and what to write in the blanks for the essays. Mother had been really smart in her high school in Chicago and would have gone to college, but her father practically had no money during the Depression, so she couldn't go and got a job as a secretary instead. My father's family didn't have any money period, and he told me he wasn't the college type back then. All he really liked was sports and playing the trumpet, and he actually earned decent money, for those times, playing in dance bands.

After he got out of the army my Uncle Desmond graduated from Northern Illinois University in DeKalb, where he studied library science. He told Mother I might like it there, but he wasn't sure. He was always extremely nice to me, and I think he thought I was a lot smarter than I was, because he thought I should apply for scholarships at major places like University of Illinois or University of Iowa, places he said he wished he had gone. On three Saturdays in a row, he drove me in his car to DeKalb to see Northern Illinois University, to Carbondale to see Southern Illinois University, and to Champagne-Urbana to see University of Illinois. I kind of enjoyed driving up and down the state with Uncle Desmond, but honestly, what I liked best was stopping in some new town and getting something to eat in a restaurant.

Kids at school said all kinds of things about different colleges. Southern Illinois was supposed to be a "party school," with lots of dances and beer and everybody stuffing themselves into cars and driving down to Ft. Lauderdale in the spring where about thirty people stayed in one hotel room. Northern Illinois was supposed to be friendly, but a little dorkier, depending on who you talked to. University of Illinois was supposed to be pretty great but really huge. The best thing about it was supposed to be certain fraternities like Sigma Chi and Sigma Nu where, if you got rushed and you got in, you automatically had a great time and you would be best friends with your brothers for the rest of your life.

By the time Uncle Desmond and I got to the campuses, it was usually afternoon, and we would go to the admissions office and pick up some handouts and maps and go on a tour of maybe the library, the stadium and some dorms. It may have been that my anti-self was putting me in a fog, but I didn't get much of an impression of any of the universities, except they all seemed huge, like little cities of their own. There were nice-looking major buildings in each place, but I couldn't really see any big difference between them. The main picture I got was of kids streaming along the walkways. That was probably because when we got to Northern Illinois, a football game was about to start, and every street and every sidewalk was full of college kids heading toward the stadium. You could hear the drums of a band up over the trees in the distance, and it seemed like thousands and thousands of people were heading up to where thousands more were already huddled up together. It had the effect of making you want to get out of there.

By Christmas I ended up applying to a bunch of places, including University of Illinois, University of Iowa, and University of Wisconsin. I also sent in applications to Southern Illinois and Northern Illinois, which were a lot cheaper and everybody got in. When we talked about college at home, Mother would always want to look at the catalogs and try to figure out all the different things you could study and what the special programs and major fields were. She thought the catalogs were pretty confusing, and so did I, but I wasn't worried about any of that stuff. I was sure that once you got there, they had official people to tell you what you had to take, and you could always figure it out from what everybody else did. My father didn't seem too interested. He was even a little mad about the whole thing. I think it was a combination of being worried about how much it would cost and also the fact that he didn't go to college and thought I had it way too easy. I didn't blame him at all. It was a big deal for our family to get a new car, which in our case was always a used car, but a pretty good one, only a couple of years old. My father took me with him when we got our last two cars, both Ford Fairlanes, which he said were the most reliable. I remember the last one, the '59, cost $1800, but my father got them down to $1500. College was going to cost at least that much—each year. He would look at Mother when we were talking about the different colleges and say things like, "And where's the money going to come from?" She'd give him a look and tell him it would all work out. There must have been some savings or something, because my father let me go ahead with all the applications, even though he complained about the fifteen-dollar fee you had to send in with each one.

It was nice to have all of that over with, but I didn't like picturing actually being at any of those places, so I tried not to think about it. My girlfriend Elizabeth was really excited about college. Her sister went to the University of Wisconsin at Madison and had told Elizabeth a lot about it. She was in a sorority and seemed to be having a really good time. She taught Elizabeth a slightly dirty song from her sorority, and one night Elizabeth sang it for me.

Never trust a Sigma Nu

An Inch above the knee

I trusted one the other night

To see how it would be

He told me that he loved me

He said he would be true

But the son of a bitch he left me

With a son of a Sigma Nu

The Other World

If it hadn't come from someone in her family, Elizabeth would never have sung me a song like that.

Elizabeth applied to a bunch of small colleges, but also to the University of Michigan where they had a special honors program for a hundred kids a year who were really smart and got complete scholarships. I figured she would get that easily, which she did, because she was about the smartest student at Palatine High School. She had an 800 on the math S.A.T., which is a perfect score, and something way up there on the verbal. She said she hoped I got into Wisconsin, so she could come visit me and her sister at the same time. I told her I thought that would be great, but I hadn't even seen Wisconsin and didn't want to think about being up there with thousands of people like her sister.

Mainly, I tried to keep my mind on other things. I probably set a record for activities my senior year at Palatine. I kept up with my sports, and I was one of the editors on the paper, and I was in Boys Chorus, plus Mixed Chorus and Ensemble, which was eighteen of the best singers who got to sing harder music at the concerts. I also got picked to be one of twelve kids in Madrigal Singers, a new group that got formed to compete in a state madrigal competition. I had never heard a madrigal before, and I thought they were really weird and very hard to sing, especially at first. I was one of the tenors and had to work on what the director called my "half voice," which made me open my throat and relax so I could sing notes way higher than I could in my regular voice.

Madrigals have a strange effect on you. There's never any regular harmony where you just sing the same line a few notes above or below somebody else. Instead your part just comes up all of a sudden in the middle of everyone else's. I could only see my part in a madrigal by picturing a piece of string that would twist in and out of the other pieces of string to form a knot. Learning a madrigal took us a long time, and you couldn't imagine it was ever going to sound any good, but once you learned it, it kind of got to you. I don't think I've ever had a harder time getting a tune out of my head than a madrigal. When we were driving somewhere in the car together, Mother would ask me what on earth I was singing, because if you're only singing your part to a madrigal, it sounds very weird, because of all the sudden starts and stops. Also, practically all of them are in Italian, which nobody understands, so Mother would just be hearing things like *Quest'e quell dolce tempo,* over and over.

Madrigal Singers turned out to be worth it, because we won the District and Sectional championships and first place at State. We got gold medals for each level, and they were the same kind of medals you got in sports if your team advanced in the post-season. I pinned them on my letter sweater, the way our state champion diver and the state champion doubles team in tennis did, and nobody said anything.

But if I wasn't driving off on some Saturday morning to sing madrigals, I was doing something else. I started writing some of my own songs for the variety shows, and I still think some of them were pretty good, even though what kids mainly wanted to hear was my Jerry Lee Lewis imitation. I also started writing a lot of poetry. One of my classes was Creative Writing, and some of the assignments got my ideas going, but then I just kept it up, even in my other classes when I was supposed to be doing something else, and at home at night. Besides writing the poems, I liked looking at them when they were typed out on a clean sheet of paper. Maybe it's the shape of the indented lines going down the page broken up neatly by the stanza breaks, but to me poems are really good looking. They also take only a few minutes to write, so as soon as you get the thought, there it practically is. My poems felt really personal, so I didn't like showing them to Mother, but for some reason I didn't mind showing them to my Creative Writing teacher and my English Teacher, who were really nice about it, even though after a while I was giving them so many that they started taking really long to give them back to me.

Palatine's literary journal was called *The Quill,* and it came out three times a year. In the winter and spring of senior year, practically everything in *The Quill* was by me. Once I got in the habit, the poems would come really fast. Practically anything could set one off. I remember sitting in the main floor study hall one morning, just listening to the radiators hissing and banging. I was still cold from walking to school so I wrote the word COLD on the

The Other World

top of a page in my notebook and then just wrote a poem straight through without stopping.

When it got so cold the whole world froze

You could not feel your nose or toes

You could not feel your feet or face

You could not feel your feeling place

When it got so cold the air was ice

Your head was held in a steel-cold vise

There was a white veil over everything

And the only sound was a singing ring

When it got so cold and got so white

The hawks that had attempted flight

Were held like statues where they were

Above still mice with frosted fur

When it got so cold I was all alone

Just inches from the telephone

If only I had gotten through

If only I had talked to you

You might have loved me still, who knows

But it got so cold the whole world froze

When I was in a certain mood, there was nothing I didn't think I could write a poem about.

* * *

The winter play that year was "Little Foxes" by Lillian Hellman, and I got the part of Ben. The director, Mr. Canaletti, said I was a strange choice for Ben, because in the play he's described as a big fat guy with indigestion, but he had a hunch I could do it. The play is all about a family in the south who wreck everybody's lives by trying to get the family money for themselves. I had only played funny parts before, and I thought I knew exactly what to do if my character was funny, but there was nothing funny about Ben. In one scene he slaps his wife in the face, and in another scene he beats up his son. He's one of the meanest people in the play. I had a slightly bad feeling about playing Ben, because the kid who got the part of my son was way taller than I was, and I couldn't imagine the scene where I beat him up would be very believable. Mr. Canaletti said that would not be a problem and that a lot of fathers dominated sons that grew up bigger than they were. I just had to work on developing a character that could do that, so I started getting into it. We had to learn southern accents for the play, and Mr. Canaletti brought in a friend of his from the south who coached us on how to say certain things. He said the point was not to come up with some big, obvious southern accent, but just to suggest it a little, so we learned to say things like *fahn* instead of fine, *dinnuh* instead of dinner, *hud* instead of heard. After a while, you didn't even think about it, and we all started sounding pretty southern.

It took me a few rehearsals to figure out how to play Ben, but then I really got it. At first I tried leaning backwards a little when I walked and holding my hands on my gut, as if I had a big one, but that felt pretty lame. Mr. Canaletti asked me to think about things people had done to me (meaning Ben) when I was a boy, things I still really hated and never got over. I pictured getting cracked in the head by my dad, the worst cracks in the head I could think of, from somebody who actually wouldn't have minded killing me. I would think about that as my lines were coming up, and I could feel it tighten up my face and tense up my shoulders and my stomach, and when it came time to say my line, it came out in a completely new voice, kind of quiet but really mean. Mr. Canaletti liked it right away. During notes after one of the rehearsals he told people I had a genius for character. I don't know if I did or not, only that when I played Ben, I pictured myself as a scowling rat, and kids who saw the play told me afterward that I completely reminded them of a rat.

At the cast party for "Little Foxes" Mr. Canaletti asked me where I was going to college. I told him where I applied, and he asked me if I was sure I wanted to go to colleges like that. He could tell that I was pretty vague about it and asked me if I had ever thought of a place like Yale. I told him no, because I hadn't. I had heard of Yale and Harvard from people's conversations or from things I read in books about important people who went there. I knew from the Sunday sports section of the paper that Yale's football team was in the Ivy League, but I didn't know anybody who went there, and I don't think anybody at Palatine ever did. Mr. Canaletti said he had gone to the Yale Drama School after he graduated from his regular college, and he had an amazing time. He said it was "magic," and he was being really nice, not fooling around. He said I should consider applying to Yale.

I asked him how much it cost, and he said he didn't know, but I was sure it was more than Illinois or Iowa and way more than Northern Illinois and Southern Illinois. But after that I started thinking about Yale. The pictures in the Yale section of the main college catalog in the guidance office looked really nice with old stone archways into the buildings. Everything looked settled and old, like the pictures of England in my grandmother Nana's *Lovely Britain* book. Sometime around then *Life Magazine* had a story about Yale students getting in some kind of trouble in New Haven and being chased by the police inside the college walls

Richard Hawley

where they all ran into the chapel and the police didn't go in after them because of some tradition. The article was mainly photographs, and whatever the students did wasn't too big a deal, but I couldn't stop looking at the pictures of the Yale students running under the archway or peeking out the chapel door at the policemen. They looked like kids from another time. They were pretty dressed up, wearing tweed jackets and raincoats with the collars turned up. Their hair was long on top, and nobody had a crew cut. It was hard to describe, but they looked like a completely different kind of people in a completely different world than the crowds of kids heading up to the football stadium in DeKalb.

But thinking about Yale and trying to picture it didn't make it seem real. The way I thought about things at the time, the roads that led out of Palatine through Illinois and into Indiana did not actually connect up with the roads that went to Connecticut and places like Yale. But Mr. Canaletti kept talking to me about it, and he was serious. He talked to some of my other teachers, too, and to my guidance counselor. He told me he was a member of the Yale Alumni Association of Chicago, and he wanted to talk to them about me. He told me it was a long shot and that the admissions deadline was practically over, but he would talk to the Yale people if I wanted him to. I said okay, which meant I had to tell my parents.

It turned out I was right about how much Yale cost, which was about $4000, if you included everything. My father said that was completely ridiculous and what were we talking about, but Mother said we should at least consider it because it was a once in a lifetime opportunity. I told Mr. Canaletti Yale was going to cost too much for us, and he said that I should apply anyway, because he thought they had scholarships for people who couldn't afford it. I told that to my father who still seemed pretty sour about the idea, but later I heard him telling Mother that someone at the bank told him Yale was about as hotshot a college as you could get. He never said that to me, but he gave me the fifteen-dollar check that went with the application.

I hated the feeling that I was trying to get some special favor out of my father and mother so that I could maybe get into Yale, because honestly, I wasn't dying to go there. I still didn't know anything about it, except it was supposed to be great and famous and the kids I knew thought no one like us ever went to a college like that. Even my teachers, when I asked them if they would send in one of the recommendation forms, said things like, "My goodness, *Yale.*" Elizabeth said, "It would be just like you to end up somewhere like Yale," which might have been some kind of insult, but I didn't feel like figuring it out. All I knew was that it was starting to become a really big deal. Mr. Canaletti called Mother and came over to the house one night to talk about what Yale was like, and a guy from Chicago who went to Yale came to Palatine and met with me and my guidance counselor and talked to Mr. Canaletti and some of my other teachers. The idea was that I was supposed to knock myself out to make a good impression and what a terrific thing it would be if an underdog kid from Palatine made it into Yale, but there wasn't a single person I could tell that I didn't really want to go there at all, and that maybe I didn't want to go anywhere.

Once I sent the application in, I was pretty much able to put it out of my mind. All I wanted to do was keep doing school things so I wouldn't have to think. Sometime in March, I started hearing back from the colleges. When I got home from rehearsal, Mother would have put the envelope on my dinner plate. I got into all the Illinois places, and I remember getting the Northern Illinois and Southern Illinois envelopes on the same day. A little while after that I got into Iowa and Wisconsin. I had about four weeks to choose, and there were a lot of forms for my parents and me to fill out that went to the place I decided to go. Mother was very nice about each letter and told me I was an awfully lucky boy and that she was proud of me. I knew she meant it, but it mainly made me start feeling sad again that she never got to go to college and that she had actually wanted to. I also couldn't stand the idea of filling out all the forms.

Then one night, way into April, there was an envelope on my plate from Yale. I don't know if it was the tension I felt from Mother or my own, but it practically made me sick to my stomach to see it there on the plate. Something in me already knew this was it. I opened it and, sure enough, I got in. Mother said it was wonderful. My father said, "My son, the Yale man." He was being nice about it. Mother started calling people up, and we never really ate. I remember feeling, okay, it's over, and I couldn't wait to get into my room so I could be by myself.

The rest of the year was just ceremonies and prizes. The effect of all the college business was to make me feel like some big force had come up behind me and shot me forward to someplace way ahead of where I expected. Just doing everyday school things made me feel like I was in a play where my part was to act normal. Unless you were failing something or a delinquent, they didn't make you do much at Palatine at the end of the senior year. There were no final exams, just senior traditions, like Skip Day and Beach Day where the seniors all wore shorts and sandals and goofy hats. I did all that stuff, but my heart wasn't really in it. What I mainly felt was sad. I wasn't sad about having to graduate from Palatine or the idea of missing people. In fact, I was having kind of a hard time even liking people, especially when everybody expected you to be in a goof-off mood because it was Beach Day.

Also, starting with Yale, I kept getting things, which for some reason made me even sadder. A kid who did all the things I did at Palatine should have gotten a few things, like maybe the Drama Prize or the Literature Prize or something for school spirit, but they practically gave me everything. I knew I was getting something at Senior Awards Assembly because they called Mother and invited her to come. But what I got was ridiculous. I got the English Prize and then another English prize I didn't know about for Creative Imagination. I got the *Quill* prize for Most Promising Writer. I got the Journalism Prize for Best Contribution to the Tribune. I got the Choral Music Prize, and while I was standing up on stage as the director read the citation, he announced that they were also giving me a special Music Department Award for all the piano playing I had done at concerts and variety shows. By this time I knew the other kids were thinking the school was overdoing it, but on and on it went. I got a Special Citation from the Illinois branch of Mightier than the Sword for something I wrote in a

The Other World

writing contest I had completely forgotten about. I got the Drama Prize. After that I went into as deep a fog as I could get, but they kept calling me up on stage for awards named after Palatine kids who died in accidents but had tremendous spirit or character. It got almost silly, and even Mother had to tell her friends on the phone later that the school should have spread things out a little. It was a long assembly, and I was so deep in my fog by the end, I almost didn't get up for the last award, Spirit of Palatine, which is the absolute top prize. I never once for one minute thought about getting Spirit of Palatine. I'm sure like everybody else, I thought Dan Retsik would get it because of the kind of Student Council President he was and a lot of other good qualities. Dan Retsik was a kid you really liked and never felt jealous of because, even when he was a freshman, all he ever cared about was being nice and being fair. By the time he was a senior, I thought Dan Retsik was more like a grown man than most of the teachers. I really wish they had given him The Spirit of Palatine, because he completely deserved it, and I was not that kind of person.

It was very awkward being around the other seniors after Awards Assembly. Nice kids I barely knew said congratulations, but my friends didn't really know what to say to me, and it almost seemed like they wanted to avoid me for a while, and I didn't blame them. Elizabeth, who got the Math Prize, came up to me and bumped me with her hip. All she said was, "Well, well, well." I knew my goofy friend Gary Wade would say something, and of course he had to come running over and bow down and start saying things like, "Your Excellency, can I touch you? Can I touch your awards?" Actually, that kind of helped. But then it got worse.

After the assembly all the seniors were supposed to go down to the main floor study hall and get their yearbooks, *Memories*, and then we had the rest of the morning free to walk around school and sign each other's books. That should have been relaxing and kind of nice, but the Senior Poll wrecked it. I almost couldn't look at it. Under each heading, like Nicest or Best Hair, there would be four boys and four girls, ranked first to fourth. I looked at the page, and all I saw was my name, *Jonathan Force*. I was Most Talented, Funniest, Most Creative, Most Musical, First to be Famous,

First to Wed (with Elizabeth), Most Involved, Marches to Different Drummer, Best Handwriting, Eats Most, Weighs Least. The last heading at the bottom was Most Likely to Succeed. It would have been sickening to get that instead of Dan Retsik, but he got it. I was second.

* * *

I got through my final days at Palatine by keeping vague and making a project out of getting rid of Elizabeth. There was no way to explain it, so I didn't even try. There was no reason, anyway, just a tremendously strong feeling that I had to get as far away as possible from her and her whole family. The timing was pretty terrible, because the day I decided to get rid of her was about three days before the Prom. The prom was a huge deal for Elizabeth because of her dress and all the thought she put into things like that, but I didn't care. There could actually have been something wrong with me, because I didn't feel bad at all about calling her up and saying I couldn't take her to the prom. She didn't understand what I was saying at first, but when she got it, she was quiet for a while. Then she said, "Why? Why are you doing this to me?" I told her I didn't know and that I was sorry about the short notice. I actually wasn't sorry. I was glad, glad I wasn't going to the prom, glad that I was the one deciding, and glad nobody could understand what I was doing. Too many things had been happening to me that I felt I had no control over, but I could control this, and it felt really good.

Not that breaking off with her like that made Elizabeth disappear from my mind. For most of the summer, I thought of my days and weekends as not-Elizabeth times. If I thought about what I was going to do on Saturday night, I would think of it as Not Watching the Late Night Movie at Elizabeth's. Each not-Elizabeth thing I did made me feel livelier and stronger and more like myself. It also made me a little mean, but I hoped that would only be temporary. For instance when she would write me a long letter asking me why I suddenly changed and what she had done to deserve being dropped like that, I wouldn't write back. She called a few times, and I only said things like, "I can't explain" and "that's just the way I feel." When her girl friends called to tell me how miserable Elizabeth was and that all she did was cry, I said, "Sorry to hear that." They said they didn't get me, and I didn't say anything, because the only thing I could have said was that not getting me was the point.

* * *

I got through all the graduation business by getting into a not-Palatine frame of mind, which was a lot like not-Elizabeth. I don't think I was rude to anybody, but I said as little as possible to the people saying congratulations, I didn't hang around after any of the ceremonies, and I didn't go to any of the parties. It felt great. It also helped that I had a new job for the summer. Part of the Journalism Prize I got was to be a paid intern at Palatine Press, the town paper that came out twice a week. Not having to go back to the bank and see all those people felt like part of the clean break I was making with everything else. Also there was something about the Press I already liked. My journalism teacher set me up as a sports stringer for the Press when I was a junior, which meant I got two dollars for every Palatine box score I phoned in after varsity football and basketball games. It was not much of a job, because all I had to do was get the facts right, but for some reason I got a kick out of calling Bob Laski, one of the sports writers at the Press, on the pay phone outside the gym and reading him the statistics. He always sounded like he was incredibly tired, and he made everything I said into a joke to keep from being bored. He called me "Chief" or "Ace," and I liked picturing everybody at the press being like Bob Laski. I was looking forward to working at a place like that for a change.

As it turned out, everybody at the Press wasn't like Bob Laski, but some people were. I didn't have to be in the editorial office until ten in the morning, which is the best starting time for a job I've ever had, and I got off at five, or whenever I got all my work done. The Press was an amazing place to work for someone my age because, almost from the first day, they gave me real things to do, things that actually had to go into the paper, like rewriting press releases for community events, or formatting the county's list of driver's license revocations, or writing headlines for news and feature articles. I liked the fact that they assumed I already knew how to do things like count column inches and count headline spaces, because I did. I also knew news style and feature style, and after they saw my first rewrites of press releases for things like a Kiwanis Club picnic or the Palatine Players' next play, they just piled copy onto the tray on my desk with a little scribbled note saying what they wanted me to do. Every single person was really nice to me and told me I was a "natural" and a "born writer" and how glad they were that there was an intern who didn't need a babysitter. Bob Laski was on the night staff with most of the other reporters who did sports and municipal beats like City Council, Zoning, School Board, Park District, or Municipal Court, so I only saw him when I stayed late to work on something.

    The night-staff writers were like a kind of club all to themselves. They started showing up in the editorial office around five in the afternoon. They sat around smoking and reading over their articles in that day's paper, then went out to cover their beats. They'd come back after their meetings at about nine and start typing up their stories. The whole time they were working they would be ragging on each other, insulting each other in incredible ways in order to crack the other guy up or at least surprise him. Except for my father, nobody in my family swore much, and nobody ever used sexual words. The night-staff writers only talked to each other in foul language. After a while it didn't really bother me, because people were never serious or mad. A guy would come into the office, sit down at his desk and say to Bob Laski, "You know, Bob, you've always had a very fat ass, but I think that it's gotten a lot fatter this week." Bob Laski would make a point of not looking up from his typewriter, and then he'd say, "You know, Phil, I think you might be right. I'm working on getting it fat enough to cover your whole face." They'd go on and on like that, back and forth, trying to keep the other guy from concentrating on his article. They would say the worst things you can say to a person. They would say, "Listen, you gaping asshole, I've got to get this piece of shit to the shop by midnight." They would say things like, "Laski, why don't you eat shit and die?" No matter what they were saying, you could tell that they were having a good time, that it was their way of liking each other.

They were never too hard on me when I was around. They might kid me about being skinny, saying things like, "Force, please don't turn sideways like that, because I can't see you." Once Bob Laski asked me if I was in the Homecoming Court at Palatine, and I said yes. He asked me if I was King, and I said no. He said, "Probably a good thing. It would have been a shame if the guy had to put the crown on your head and then—clunk—it's down around your shoulders and—clunk—it's down around your hips and—kuh*lunk*—it's down on the floor." He would go on like that, saying the stupidest things, but things you couldn't help picturing.

The hardest thing for me to get used to was that they would also talk that way around Ceci Long, the Managing Editor. Ceci's job was to assign and edit all the news and feature copy. She came in after lunch and left at about ten at night, so she overlapped the shifts of the day and night staffs. Everybody liked Ceci Long and everybody respected her. She was in charge of training me and assigning me work, and there was something about the nice way she explained everything and the way she let you know how the whole paper worked, from the advertising staff to the print shop, that made you feel confident and relaxed. She was an excellent explainer if I didn't get something, and she was great about leaving me alone.

But it made me uncomfortable when I worked on into the night shift and heard how the night staff writers talked to Ceci. I actually think most of them were crazy about her. She was a very unusual person, not like anyone else I had met before. Her age was hard to figure out. She was definitely out of college but not really settled into looking like a woman yet. I'm guessing she might have been thirty, although I didn't really know anybody in that age group. She had her own look. She was pretty tall, maybe five-eight or nine and very slender. She was so slender that when I first got to know her I wondered if she had some kind of illness.

But then I got used to the way she looked and actually got to like it. She was not really pretty, but there was something about her face that made you want to keep looking at her. She had a long slender neck, which I liked, and kind of a small head for her long body, with a sharp little nose and a pointed chin. She wore her hair really short, like a boy's, but it all came forward to form a kind of fringe around her face. That might have made her look little-girl cute, but she didn't act cute at all. She was actually pretty tough and very smart. She didn't seem to mind the night staff writers' foul-mouthed kidding around, and sometimes when I heard them ragging on her, I got the impression that she got a kick out of it. They said unbelievably dirty things to her, things like, "Ceci, you got any meat on those bones? I have a feeling you'd give me bruises in the sack." She wouldn't be offended at all. She'd just say something back like, "Bruises are the least of what you'd get from me in the sack" or "in your dreams, Phil." Just about all the kidding had something to do with having sex with Ceci, and her responses were all about there being too many things wrong with them, like their terrible breath or fat gut or tiny equipment, for it ever to happen.

Like their ragging with each other, there wasn't any real meanness in what they said, but you could feel a kind of special tension because they were talking about sex. They were all heavy smokers, including Ceci, and the ragging would usually start when somebody wanted to bum a cigarette from her. For some reason, I couldn't get Ceci out of my mind when I went home after work. A picture kept popping up of her tall, slender person's slouch and the way her loose clothes dropped away from her bony shoulders. I couldn't quite put together how friendly and well-spoken she was with me and the other day-staff people and her tough talk with the night shift. Bob Laski was the least foul-mouthed when he talked to her, probably because he really liked her, but he still kidded her a lot. He mainly said goofy things to her like how he met a Mexican guy who said he knew her, and when he asked the Mexican guy what kind of woman she was, the Mexican guy said, "Oh, Ceci, si, si" and on and on about seeing Ceci by the sea and Ceci being eecy to pleecy. When Ceci had had enough or needed to get back to work, she would say things like, "Bob, you are a complete tragedy" or "you are such a wit, or am I only half right?"

So far as I could tell, Ceci didn't have a boyfriend, which was maybe why she was willing to hang around the night-staff writers so much. I didn't know anything about her life outside of the editorial offices, but I had the feeling something terrible had happened to her, and that she was over it, but still really sad. I sensed it in the way she was so patient with people who didn't get things and the way nothing the night-staff writers said ever shocked her or made her mad.

In a way, Ceci was very unsexy. She liked to wear dresses that were cut like a man's shirt on top and continued down into a long skirt. You couldn't tell much about her shape in that kind of dress, except to see how thin she was at the waist. You couldn't tell for sure, because she hunched her shoulders and slouched, but she was probably pretty flat-chested because nothing seemed to push out the front of her dresses. It's hard to explain, but the way she was unsexy was also pretty sexy. For one thing, she seemed to know all about sex .She couldn't joke around with the night-staff guys like that and not know exactly what everybody was talking about. She never said anything immodest to me, but I just had the feeling that Ceci had had a lot of sex.

Or maybe it was that sex had some kind of grip on me that summer. I don't know if not having Elizabeth as my girlfriend anymore had anything to do with it, but it seemed like everything had a new sex-charged feel to it. Of course it was summer, and the way girls dress in the summer with their shorts and little tops showing off the sun tan on their legs and arms can't help giving you sexy feelings. Just walking through town on my way to the Press in the morning I'd feel myself zooming in like a camera on the way somebody looked. It could be the way their legs came out of their shorts or the way their ankles looked going into their shoes. I might glance at somebody in a convertible stopped at a traffic light, and I'd catch the way she was resting her arm over the door or the tilt of her neck or just that she was wearing pink lipstick, and I would hold that picture in my head all morning.

I decided not to play ball that summer, so I had a lot of time on my hands. I'd usually go home and eat dinner with my father and mother or, if I worked late, get a hot dog or something by myself at June's Grill, and after supper I'd just walk all around Palatine, circling it in a ring. I'd usually head for the park and maybe watch the end of a game, then, as it started to get dark, head off by myself. Something in me always wanted to get to what felt like the edge of town, the streets that used to be the last streets before the fields began. Walking along them then, you would never know there even were fields or that the town had an edge. There was just development after development on streets that didn't even seem all that new anymore, but the houses still looked new to me, the brick work a little too raw. The developments just kept going until they connected to developments in Schaumberg and Rolling Meadows, which didn't really seem like towns to me, just a name they gave to a bunch of developments. I'm sure the people who lived there thought they lived in real towns that were in the center of things for them, but to me all those clean cement streets and yards with skinny little trees seemed like big, lifeless add-ons that couldn't possibly last. One of the strange things about those walks was that even though I knew perfectly well where I would get to if I headed out into the developments, I had a deep feeling that the fields were still out there somewhere. It was a kind of craziness. I had driven around enough to know that when I drove into the developments, I would come to this or that new school or new park, and that pretty soon I'd get to a big intersection of the roads connecting Palatine and Arlington Heights or some other town. But even though my brain knew there was no more space in between the towns, it felt like the fields were still there somewhere. Sometimes I had a dream where I thought I could see where they were and how you could actually get there.

Even walking around town like that by myself in the dark seemed to be about sex. On summer nights there is something about the feel of soft air on your skin and how, if it's even a little bit damp, the fullness and smell of everything seems to seep out. As soon as I started walking, the sex pictures would start coming up and the old cycle of thoughts would keep repeating and repeating. It would usually start with remembering girls in my class like Lou Scanlon and her friends. In the picture they would be standing around smoking, or maybe just Lou Scanlon was, and they all really wanted to have sex. I didn't know about her friends, but I happened to know Lou Scanlon really did want to, at least according to my friend Gary Wade. I got the idea she wanted to as much as anybody, any boy or even any of the men on the night staff, and she wasn't ashamed of it and would bring it up herself and probably start things off and let you do everything and not stop you. She would not mind undressing in front of you, and she actually wanted you to look at her and to touch her. In my pictures she would walk right toward me in her underwear, and her eyes would be dark and wet with makeup and her lips red with lipstick. I wasn't saying or hearing or even seeing the word, but every step I took and everything I pictured seemed to be charged with sex, and if anybody would have happened to be watching, they would have seen that I was walking really fast.

 Even though it made me feel like a robot, I actually started going past Lou Scanlon's house on some of my walks. It was always dark, and I always walked right past, hardly looking in toward the windows of the house. It felt like some kind of requirement. I knew I could have called her up and made an actual date and that if I did, we would have gone somewhere and tried things, but I also knew I would never do it. I knew that if I did something like that with her, it wouldn't come even close to the feeling I had when I was walking toward her house in my trance. Not that I didn't think about actual sex with Lou Scanlon. In my pictures there was only one way it could happen. I would have to be just getting to her house, and she would have to be standing in her driveway for some reason, and she would have to stop me and say hi and start talking to me. She might be wearing only a bathing suit or a robe. She would tell me that her parents weren't home and that we could go inside. She would take me down to her recreation room in the basement, and we'd start to do everything without even talking. I didn't picture doing particular things, like touching her and stripping. It didn't seem possible to picture what we would actually do, and I didn't want to. I don't know how much I believed Lou Scanlon would ever actually meet me on her driveway, but the longer the summer went on, the more I wished something like that would happen, and in a way it did.

At the end of August I only had one more week at the Press, and then my father and mother were going to drive me to New Haven and drop me off at Yale. Even though I knew it was coming right up, I hardly ever thought about it, and when I did, I would just get a few pictures in my head of the way the old buildings and archways looked in the catalogs, and I didn't feel anything, good or bad. I'm not sure I believed I was really going.

Bob Laski surprised me by asking me if I wanted to come to a party at his house on Friday night, which would be after my last day at the paper and my last night in Palatine. I was surprised he asked me, because even though he and his friends on the night staff were always pretty nice to me, it was clear that I was just a kid to them and kind of a novelty to have around. I had a feeling those guys did things together every Friday night and the rest of the weekend too, because all of their ragging on Mondays would be about how loaded they got, and what crazy thing some drunk guy did, like back his car out of the garage without opening the door. I never imagined they would want to include me in any of that, and I thought it was really nice of Bob Laski to ask me. It was almost like telling me I had made an impression and they liked having me around. He said there would be pizza and stuff on the barbecue and booze. He said I could practice "getting shit-faced" for college. I hadn't done much drinking yet. The legal age in Illinois was twenty-one, and I was eighteen, but I probably looked more like sixteen. No one was going to mistake me for being older and serve me. My father had started letting me have a beer with him when we watched games on television, and on Thanksgiving and Christmas I always got a little glass of sticky sweet port with everyone else after dinner, but that was about it. I actually liked the idea of drinking booze with the night-staff guys and maybe a lot of other people at a grownup party, but I was a little worried I wouldn't be able to stand the taste.

On the Wednesday before the party, I did an impulsive thing. I hadn't been thinking about Yale at all, but Mother had been telling me all week that I had to decide what I was going to take with me and start packing. I didn't think it would be all that hard, but I was putting it off. I knew I'd take my typewriter, my clock radio, probably my baseball glove, even though I didn't know how good baseball was supposed to be at Yale, and a bunch of clothes. I must have had clothes on my mind, because on Wednesday afternoon it hit me that I should go out and get all new stuff, and everything was going to be better than anything I had before. It was completely clear. I didn't have anything to do that I couldn't do the next morning, so I left the office early while the bank was still open and took nine hundred dollars out of my savings account. My savings account was supposed to be for my spending money at college, but I had over $2,000 in it, and I knew that was way more than enough for a year. I don't know exactly why I decided on nine hundred dollars, except that it seemed like a lot, and I wanted to go to Parnell's Men's Store and get everything I could think of and not have to worry about it. Even at Parnell's it would be hard to spend nine hundred dollars, unless you were getting a bunch of men's suits, which I wasn't. If it turned out I had a lot of cash left over, that would be fine, because another thing I liked the idea of was having way more money in my wallet than anybody would imagine.

For some reason it seemed like I was in Parnell's for about three minutes, but I got a ton of stuff, the kind of stuff I used to look at, go home and think about, and beg Mother for extra money to buy. And if it was maybe a shirt and I got it, it would be the one nice button-down shirt in my closet with all the crummy old ones and never-wear ones certain people gave me for Christmas. It put me in kind of a trance to walk into Parnell's and not have to tell the salesman, for a change, that I was just looking. I went right over to the clothes and started picking out stuff I wanted without looking at what anything cost. The salesman said I should try on things like pants and the jackets, and he was right, but in a way I hated to have to do it, because it slowed me down. It's a good thing I did, because even though the khaki pants I tried on were the best-looking ones they had, they were actually too wide on me when I looked in the mirror. The cloth didn't even touch the skin on my legs, and all I could feel was a lot of air. The salesman told me they could taper the legs from a sixteen-inch to a fourteen-inch cuff, and since I was going off to college on Saturday, their tailor could make the alterations by the next day. He pinned in the pants to show me how they would look when they were fixed, and it made a huge difference. I bought eight pairs. I also bought some really nice corduroys, which I always liked when I saw other kids wearing them, and about ten button-down collar shirts, some light blue ones, some yellow ones, a pink one, and two with little checks that the salesmen said were tattersall. I didn't have to try them on because they were in my exact size. I got four or five crewneck sweaters, the kind Elizabeth used to give me for Christmas, dark green, dark grey, maroon, and black. I tried one on, and it looked perfect. I also got a camel-colored duffel coat that had a hood you could button onto the neck. I got a pair of shiny cordovan oxfords and a pair of red penny loafers which I had always wanted and which, it turned out when I got there, every guy at Yale wore. The last thing I got was two tweed jackets and a bunch of striped ties. The jackets looked great and the salesman said they were on sale for $99 each. There was a huge stack of my stuff on the glass counter when the guy was ringing up the total. While I was standing there, I looked across the store and saw a rack of leather belts and decided I wanted one, so I told the salesman to hold on for a second while I went over and picked one out. When I got back to the counter, he told me my total was eight hundred and something, and I held up the belt and told him I wanted that too. He gave me a big smile and said, "The belt's on the house." That was really nice.

 I couldn't even carry all of the stuff home with me, so I took an armful of boxes and bags and came back later with the car. The next day after I picked up the pants, I tried everything on in front of the long mirror in Mother's bedroom. I couldn't believe it. Everything fit, the creases were sharp, and everything hung down perfectly. I put on one of the new shirts and a pair of the tailored khakis. I put on the new leather belt with the round gold buckle. I put on the red loafers. The clothes looked even better than the ones on the people in the catalogs we got. I put on one of the

The Other World

tweed jackets, then I put on a new striped tie. Everything went together, and I couldn't stop looking in the mirror. I'm sure the feeling was in my skin, but it seemed like I was feeling the tingle of the cloth. I looked completely like someone else, like another kind of person.

On Friday afternoon, my last day, Ceci took me into Mr. Pearson's office for a special meeting. Mr. Pearson was an old, wrinkly man with completely white hair. He owned The Palatine Press, and he was the editor-in-chief. I met him on my first day, and I saw him come in and go out a few times, but he was hardly ever in the editorial rooms. He told me I had done an excellent job and that Ceci and the other staff said I was the best intern they could remember. He asked me if I was excited about Yale, and I said yes. He said, "I wish I had your prospects, young man," which I didn't really get, but I laughed a little, which I think was the right response. He told me that when I came home for vacations, I could have my job back, and if I came back next summer, I could get my own beat and work with the night staff. I couldn't really think about all that right on the spot, so I said thanks a lot. Then he got up, handed me a white envelope, and shook my hand. I didn't open the envelope until I was out on the street walking home. It was a check for fifty dollars. I had another check in my pocket for a hundred forty dollars, which was for my final two weeks at the paper. I still had about eighty dollars in my wallet left over from buying the clothes at Parnell's, and I realized that for the first time in my life I had all I wanted of everything.

* * *

On Friday when I was eating supper with my father and mother, I told them about Bob Laski's party and that I would probably be out late. I wondered if they would mind. They had been pretty relaxed with me since graduation, and they stopped telling me I had to be in by a certain time, not that it was ever a problem since I wasn't going out with Elizabeth anymore, and I hardly ever asked them for the car. My father asked me if I wanted a ride, and I told him no, because it was a nice night, and I knew roughly where Bob Laski lived, and it wasn't a bad walk. Mother said not to stay out too late because we were going to be leaving early in the morning.

In my room I had everything packed and ready to go, except for putting my new clothes in the big suitcase. I thought I'd leave them folded up on my bureau and hanging in the closet until the last minute, so they wouldn't have to be mushed together for any extra time. I also decided to wear some of the new stuff to the party. It wasn't too hot out, so I put on one of the new yellow button-down shirts and a pair of the khakis and the red penny loafers. I took a shower and got dressed and walked down the hall to see what I looked like in the long mirror. It was just like before. They could have just stood me up in one of Parnell's windows.

It turned out I actually did know where Bob Laski lived. It was at the edge of the old part of town just before you got to the forest preserve. The houses weren't too nice out there. Some of them used to be part of farms, and the area generally looked pretty beat up. The sidewalks stopped about a half mile from his house, and I wondered if I was going to scuff up my loafers on the gravel along the side of the road. As it turned out, I didn't have to worry about finding his house because it was the only one with cars parked all over the place. By the time I got there it was dark, and I could see people standing around in the back yard around the barbecue grill. There were a bunch of people from the day staff, and they were really friendly to me right away, so I didn't feel awkward at all. They told me Bob was in the kitchen and that's where the drinks were. They also said pizza was coming.

I opened the back door to the kitchen, and it was jam packed with people laughing and drinking. They were crowded around the kitchen table which had some open bags of chips, a big bowl of ice and a lot of liquor bottles. Bob Laski saw me come in. He raised his glass and said, "Hey, it's the boy wonder! Everybody, this is Jonathan Force, fearless cub reporter for the Palatine Press, on his way to Yale University to greater fame and fortune, *as we speak.*" He was being really loud, but friendly. He didn't have to introduce me, because I knew practically everyone there. It was mostly the night-staff writers and other Press people. There were some

The Other World

women I didn't know, probably people's wives or girlfriends. Ceci came into the kitchen from one of the other rooms, and for some reason that felt like a huge relief to me, because there was going to be someone for sure that would be easy to talk to.

Bob Laski told me to help myself to a drink. He said there was beer in the refrigerator if I wanted one. I said sure, found a beer and then stood around with the people listening to the night-staff guys telling funny stories and ragging on each other. Standing around like that put me in kind of a trance, so when my beer was finished I got another one out of the refrigerator and went back outside by the grill. Ceci was out there, and she came over to talk to me. She asked me if I got a nice bonus from Mr. Pearson, and I said yes, fifty bucks. She told me that was terrific. She said Mr. Pearson was not really a bad old guy, but he was really cheap, and giving me a bonus was a very big deal. That surprised me a little, because I didn't really know him at all and hardly saw him at the paper. I assumed the fifty dollars was Ceci's idea, and he was just the one who handed it over. She said no and that I had made a great impression and done such a good job. She was giving me really nice compliments, but it's the kind of thing you almost can't stand to listen to. I was saying things like "wow" and "really?" and "thanks," but there's not much you can say when people are saying things like that. I was glad, though, that Ceci was talking to me. One of the reasons she was so lively was probably that she'd had a few drinks. She had a tall glass of what looked like orange juice and ice, and I asked her what it was. She said it was a screwdriver, which was orange juice with vodka in it. She said it was "painless," and did I want to try one. I was almost through my second beer, and since I wasn't feeling any effects, I said sure.

We went back into the kitchen, and Ceci pushed her way through to the table where the liquor was. She said, "Jonathan is about to be initiated into true journalism. I'm making him his first screwdriver." One of the guys said "his first screw—*what?*" and everybody laughed, which made me laugh too. I was already in a good mood when Ceci and I went back out into the yard, and I was also starting to get really hungry. There were burger patties and hot dogs sizzling on the grill, and even though Ceci was talking up a storm, all I could picture was finding some rolls somewhere and wolfing something down.

The screwdriver was fine. It didn't taste like much of anything, just orange juice with a little extra gassy taste. After a few sips I hardly paid attention to what it tasted like, because somehow Ceci and I got into a long, serious conversation. I got up the nerve to ask her if she minded the way the night-staff guys teased her and if she minded all the foul-mouthed talk. I could tell that really made her think. She smiled and put her hand on my shoulder and said, "Oh, those guys. Jonathan, what I could tell you about those guys." She said me she shouldn't be telling me, but she told me some incredible things about them. She told me that Phil, who was married and had kids, had secret dates with a high school girl who babysat for him. I couldn't figure out a way to ask who the girl was, because I probably knew her, and I was trying to picture someone I knew, someone my age, going out with a person like Phil, with his oily hair and tired, wrinkly clothes and who never stopped smoking. She told me Bob Laski's first wife ran away with a guy who did odd jobs in the Press print shop, a guy Bob rented a room in his house to, just to help the guy out for a while. She told me some of the guys were in trouble with booze. She used the term "on the sauce," which made her laugh, and then she said, "I should talk."

Our glasses were empty, and she asked me if I wanted another screwdriver. I said sure. She looked at me hard and said, "You're okay, aren't you?" I told her I was fine. I was pretty sure I was. I was actually feeling pretty good, pretty relaxed, and I could even see getting a little bit goofy. We went back into the kitchen where the same people were still standing around, only now people were getting really loud, and the jokes seemed to be all about sex, and people were saying *fucking* this and *fucking* that. Ceci grabbed the big vodka bottle and went over to the refrigerator to get the orange juice. There were some open pizza boxes on the counter by the sink, and I suddenly remembered how hungry I was, but when I went over to get some, I saw that everything was practically gone, except a couple slices with the cheese and toppings mostly pulled off and sticking to the cardboard. I was so hungry I just piled all the stuff back on the crust with my hands, jammed the two pieces together and went out the back door past the grill to the dark cars where I could wolf down the pizza without people looking at me. When I walked back toward the house, Ceci was standing in the lawn holding the two screwdrivers looking around for me, and we started another serious talk.

The drinks were probably starting to have an effect, because even though the things Ceci was telling me seemed really important and personal, every now and then I would lose track of the main thing we were talking about, and I would be watching the two of us standing in the dark yard and hearing what we were saying as if I was watching us from above. I have a feeling we were talking for a pretty long time, because after a while everybody else in the yard had gone home or gone back into the kitchen. I remember just wanting to keep talking like that, no matter what we were saying. I was even pretending to be extra serious and interested in everything, because I wanted Ceci to keep going.

She was telling me college would be the most amazing thing that ever happened to me, and that it would be so good for me to get out of Palatine and into a new world. She told me she went to Northwestern, which was only about a half hour away, but her junior year she got to study in France where she lived with a family in Avignon, and while she was there she fell in love with a guy who was a cousin of the people she lived with, and he was the first guy she ever slept with and that he was the love of her life. She had to stop talking for a minute after she brought him up, because she was going to cry, and some tears actually came out. I had a really strong reaction to her telling me about being by herself in France and falling in love with the cousin. I felt like putting down my glass and putting my arms around her and pulling her in close to me. I kept picturing that as she was talking. I could almost feel the bones of her ribs against my chest and the bones of her back in my hands as I was hugging her. She told me she and the cousin wrote letters back and forth her whole senior year, and then she went back to France to visit him. They lived together for a while, but then it didn't work out. She kept not being able to get a job, and he kind of had another girlfriend. She put her hands on my shoulders and squeezed. "Jonathan," she said, "you can't even *know*." I said something stupid, like "I'm sorry," and then she went back to telling me I needed to get out of Palatine.

Our glasses were empty again, and Ceci said, "We can probably do one more." I told her I would wait for her in the yard while she got the screwdrivers, but what I actually wanted to do was find a dark place to pee, because I really had to go. When I got out of the part of Bob Laski's yard that was lit up by the light on his back porch, I realized I was way clumsier than usual and kind of stumbling around. I pictured myself like some drunken idiot in a movie, and it made me want to laugh. I wasn't that bad though. I peed and took some deep breaths, and by the time I walked back into the yard, I felt pretty normal. I also knew that something big was happening with Ceci. It was nothing that we were talking about, but I was feeling really connected to her. It felt like we were a couple, even though she was a woman and I was a kid. I had a feeling it would be okay to have sex with her, that she would let me and I would really like it. That feeling got stronger and stronger as we picked up our conversation and started drinking the screwdrivers. I can't even tell you what we talked about, except it was about big, vague things like relationships and books and getting out into the world and testing yourself. The whole time she was talking, I kept thinking that she was just opening herself up to me, wider and wider. I think she actually liked it that I was a kid.

I had to pee again, and since she was right there with me, I knew I would have to use the bathroom in the house. As soon as I started to move, I could tell I was pretty clumsy again, and I had to make a real effort to be sure my walk looked normal. I wasn't crazy about going in past all the people at the kitchen table, because I had a feeling that if somebody said something to me I wouldn't be able to talk right. I decided to plow right through the kitchen without stopping, as if I already knew where the bathroom was, but as soon as he saw me, Bob Laski shouted out, "Wait a minute, chief! I want to see if you're shit-faced yet. What do you think, folks, is young Jonathan shit-faced yet? Yes, I think he's there, or certainly getting there." I went right on through and found the bathroom. When I was finished peeing, I wished I could keep going. I had the idea that if I could just pee all the screwdrivers and everything else out of me, I'd feel clean and light and normal again.

I went out the front door of the house so I wouldn't have to go through the kitchen again. Bob Laski's front stoop was dark, and I stood there for a while and thought about going home. It would take me maybe a half hour to walk back, and by then maybe I would feel normal. I was definitely not feeling normal, but by the time I knew it for sure, it was too late, because I was starting to feel really terrible. I remembered that Ceci was probably waiting for me in the back yard, and as I made my way around the house in the dark, I tried to get back to the close, excited feeling I was starting to have before. When I got to the lighted yard at the rear of the house, Ceci was sitting on the back steps holding both of our glasses. She told me I was looking a little wobbly and asked if I was all right. I told her I was fine, but I actually wasn't. My forehead was all sweaty, and the cool night air made the sweat feel cold. If I closed my eyes, everything would start to swirl around in a sickening way, so I kept them open. It's hard to describe the feeling, except that it made me feel like I was inside some kind of thick padding, and the alive part of me inside could barely operate. There was also a gassy taste at the back of my throat, which, for me, is always a bad sign.

"No," Ceci said. "You're not looking so good, Jonathan." She said she would take me over to her house and get some coffee and maybe relax for a bit, and then when I was feeling better, she would drive me home. I don't think I said anything. I just looked at her like an idiot and followed her to her car, which was a Volkswagen, and got in on the passenger side. Ceci went back in the house to return the glasses and say good-bye to Bob Laski.

Volkswagens have a certain smell to them. It seems to come from the oil and metal parts in the engine, but it was definitely not agreeing with me as I was sitting in Ceci's car waiting for her to come back. Once we were moving, I didn't feel good at all, and I rolled down my window. Ceci said, "Oh, dear." I really did not want to throw up, but sometimes that's all you can think about.

But even though it felt like I was sitting inside a swirling, gassy cocoon, I was still excited to be alone in the car with Ceci, heading toward her house. I made myself sit up straight. I shook my head. I said, "I'm fine, I'm fine."

I wasn't sure at first where we were heading, because I wasn't paying attention, but when I sat up and started noticing, I saw that we were going through the new developments toward Rolling Meadows. Ceci's house was half of a new duplex, and when we got inside and she turned on the lights, everything looked brand new. There was hardly any furniture, and you could still smell the paint. Ceci asked me if I wanted some coffee, but I said no thanks, because I actually hated coffee, and the idea of the hot acidy taste of coffee in my mouth right then almost made me sick on the spot. I asked her if she had a Coke or a ginger ale or something, and she got me a Coke out of her refrigerator. She got a bottle of Jim Beam bourbon from out of a cupboard, and mixed herself a glass of bourbon and Coke. She said she thought it might be nicer out back, so we went out into her little yard where there were some lawn chairs on a brick patio. I was pretty thirsty, and the cold Coke tasted good, but almost right away things started swirling again. Ceci pointed up to all the stars and was saying how amazing they were, but I almost couldn't look up at them because they made the swirling worse. I lost track of what happened for a while, except Ceci said she wanted to go in and get a sweater or something, and then her phone rang, and I could hear her talking to someone for a pretty long time. When she came back outside, I had finished my Coke and didn't think I felt too bad, as long as I didn't move. Ceci had on a sweat shirt that zipped up the front, and I didn't think anything about it until she turned around a little, and the porch light caught the metal in the half zipped-up zipper, and I could see most of the white mound of one of her breasts. She didn't have anything on under the sweatshirt. As weird as I was feeling, I was also starting to get excited. Ceci kept talking to me in a normal way and didn't seem to mind that her front was practically unzipped. I really did not want to feel sick, and I did not want to sound thick-tongued when I talked, and I tried hard not to. I actually started talking about everything I could think of. I tried to get her going again on living in France and on seeing the world, but every now and then I'd start a sentence out in some direction, and it would just stop and hang there. At one point Ceci was leaning down in front of me, patting me on the head and saying I should probably be getting home. I was looking right into the bony space between her breasts. Whatever happened, I didn't want to go home yet. I started talking up a storm again. I asked her if I could have another Coke, and as she got up to get it, I asked her if I could try a little bourbon in it. She laughed and said, "Jonathan, I've ruined you."

Ceci could not have known how happy it made me to have her say that. When she came back with our drinks, she sat down at the foot of my chair, and we started talking again and having the best time. We talked about music and what each of us liked, and I got onto finding my uncle Desmond's Cab Calloway records and how great they were, and I was singing her my imitation of "Minnie the Moocher," which really made her laugh. We must have been getting a little loud, because she was shushing me every now and then and talking in an exaggerated whisper. We got onto certain people at the Press, and I was imitating some of them, and that cracked her up even more.

It had to be really late, past midnight. Ceci brought the bottle of bourbon out to the patio and every now and then she would add a little bit to our Cokes. I don't remember feeling especially bad. I just wanted everything to keep going. I wanted to keep coming up with things that would make her laugh, and every time I caught a glimpse of her breasts in the unzipped part of her sweat shirt, it was like something inside my own chest was opening up and wanting to shout. I really had to pee again, but when I tried to get up from the lawn chair, I almost couldn't do it. I said, "*Whoa*," and sat down again. Now my head was really spinning. Ceci looked at me and said, "Oh boy, Jonathan, you're wrecked, aren't you." She picked up our glasses and the bourbon and said she was going into the kitchen and make coffee.

* * *

Now something really serious was happening to me. All my thoughts were mixed up, but I knew I couldn't stand to have any coffee or even to look at coffee. Whatever happened, I had to be by myself. I stood up by my chair, and I almost fell over. It was worse than being just dizzy. I felt like I was being twirled around by some force, but the force was lopsided, and it wanted to throw me down on one side. *No good* was all I could think or picture. *No good no good no good.* I don't know if I was thinking it or saying it, but I knew I had to get out of there. I moved out into Ceci's dark yard, and I fell down to one side. I got up and tried to get farther away, and I fell down again on the same side. My balance was really screwed up. I got up and kept moving through the dark yards until I came to a big bank of bushes. I got down on my knees and started crawling through the space between them at the bottom. When I got through to the other side, I knew I was safe from Ceci and the coffee, but when I stood up, the lopsided swirling started and I threw up.

I don't throw up very often, and I really hate it when I do, but this was nothing like having the flu in my room at home. It came flying out of me, and it made a sound in my head like when you were standing under the elevated train tracks in Chicago and a train was going over you. I remember not knowing if something like that could kill you or not, but it didn't matter, because nothing was going to stop it.

I actually threw up a bunch of times, mostly the pizza, and some of it got on my shirt and my pants, but I didn't mind. I just wanted the gassy swirling to stop and for whatever was going to happen to me to happen. I heard Ceci calling my name from her yard. I could tell she didn't want to make it too loud, and I moved a few lawns farther away. I was pretty sure I knew where I was, but I needed to get out to the street so I could figure out the best way to walk home. I was moving along somebody's driveway in the dark when I saw a car's headlights coming from the left, and I slid down the side of the house on my butt. The car turned out to be Ceci in her Volkswagen. She was driving really slowly, and all her windows were open. I could tell she was looking around for me. I hunched down close to the house until she was gone.

When I got up and started going down the sidewalk, I thought I'd just keep walking along whatever street I was on until I saw something familiar. I tried to remember the way Ceci drove us through the developments to her house, and I figured I was a mile or two out into what used to be the fields beyond my grandparents' house. I actually don't know what I was thinking, I just had the idea that if I kept moving, I'd get to something, but I was also feeling terrible. I walked over to the curb where there was a sewer grate and threw up again. I decided to sit down on the curb, which felt a little better, but I saw another set of headlights coming up, and I didn't have the energy to get up.

I was sure it was going to be Ceci, but it wasn't. It was a man and a woman, and they stopped a few feet in front of me, rolled down their windows and asked me if I was all right. I told them I was fine. I told them I was just taking a rest. I don't know how normal I sounded. The guy backed up a little so that I was lit up in his headlights. He could probably see the mess down the front of my shirt. He asked if I was sure I was all right and did I want him to take me somewhere. I said no, I was fine. What I really needed to do was get up and start walking again, so that they could see that everything was okay and I was just a guy walking down the street, but I couldn't do it. They stayed where they were for a long time, with their headlights in my eyes. Finally the car clunked into gear and they drove away really slowly, but I could hear them talking in the car, and I heard "help" and "call the police." I knew I had to get out of there and get away from the street.

I tried hustling a little, but I was too clumsy to run, and even trying to made me feel like throwing up. This wasn't good. I might have gone a block or two, looking ahead and over my shoulder for headlights, when I saw the big arc lamps of one of the new schools shining over the tops of the houses. I knew where all the schools were, and once I got there I could figure out where I was and how to get back home. The lights turned out to be farther away than I thought, and I had to slip between houses and throw myself down on the ground a few times when I saw a car coming. The school turned out to be the new elementary school, which meant I was only about a mile from my grand parents if I could get the direction right. It didn't feel good walking past the school because the arc lamps were even brighter than the streetlights, and I knew I'd be easy to spot. So I crossed the playground and took a gravel path behind some service garages, where there were some scrubby vacant lots with high grass and skunk cabbage. I was far enough away from the lights so that it was mostly dark, and I could relax a for a minute. I sat down in the grass and tried to think. Crickets and peepers were screaming in my ears, and I got the strongest feeling that I was back in the fields, or at least where the fields used to be, and even though I was still pretty lost, something felt good. There were a few more empty lots in front of me, and it looked like they came to an end at the back yards of a row of new houses, but everything was pretty dark, and in the mixed up way I was picturing things, I thought that maybe if I kept going straight into the empty lots, they might open up to the fields the way they used to be. I don't know if I really believed it, but I wanted it to be like my dreams.

    I walked straight into the long dark grass, and I could feel it pulling at my shoes and the cuffs of my pants. It was so dark I couldn't really see where I was going, only the street lights in front of the houses up ahead. Then all of a sudden I stepped down into something, and I was on my hands and knees in cold muck. It was some kind of ditch with big puddle at the bottom, but it was more like a swamp, because when I stood up my loafers were completely under the muck, and when I tried to step out of there, one of them came off and was gone. By getting on my hands and knees I managed to crawl back up the bank of the ditch, but I couldn't keep going to the end of the lots without getting stuck in the swamp again. I stood there for a while looking around, and I could see that there was no opening to any fields. There were just back yard fences and, behind me, the elementary school.

    I stumbled back to the schoolyard, and in the light, tried to scrape some of the black muck out of the cuffs of my pants. I walked along the sidewalk for awhile with just one shoe, but it felt terrible, so I took off the other loafer and threw it into somebody's yard, somebody who was going to find a muddy shoe in the morning and wonder what was going on.

I knew if I kept walking down the street in front of the school I'd end up at an intersection I knew in the old part of town, and I'd be at the end of my grandparents' street, and I could be home in about five blocks. My socks were cold and soaking wet, and the bottoms of my feet were starting to feel pretty raw, but I thought it would be even worse if I took them off and went barefoot. I couldn't really think about it because something changed in my stomach, and I started feeling sick in a completely different way. My mouth and my throat were still sour and horrible tasting from all the throwing up, and I was burping up gas about every three steps, but now my stomach actually hurt, like somebody was holding onto it and squeezing it tight. Every now and then it hurt so much I had to stop and double over. It was like the cramps from diarrhea, but higher up in my stomach, and when it got to a certain point I had to throw up again, but after a few times almost nothing came up, except about a spoonful of the sourest, worst stuff I'd ever tasted. It looked dark to me, and I hoped there wasn't blood in it, and that I wasn't going to die.

I thought I was going to have to walk a mile or so along that street through the developments, but it seemed to go on forever, and when I looked ahead, trying to make out a traffic light or some sign that I was getting somewhere, all I saw was more of the same kind of street lights and more of the new brick houses and the lines of skinny new trees. It also slowed me down to keep turning around to see if any cars were coming from the other direction, because I didn't want to get picked up and taken home and have everybody start into me before I could even talk or think. There were a few cars, including one that had to be either a police car or a cab, and each time I spotted one, I had to duck up somebody's drive way into their back yard and lie down in the dark until it was gone. My feet were raw, my knees and hips hurt from walking, and I was getting the feeling that my stomach cramps were never going to stop. I couldn't really think. I couldn't make a plan or picture what might be going on at home or what was going to happen to me. Only one thing at a time would come into my mind, and it would be a single word or maybe just a phrase which I'm pretty sure I kept repeating out loud. Sometimes it was *shit-faced, shit-faced*, sometimes it was *half-wit, half-wit*, sometimes it was *Spirit of Palatine, Spirit of Palatine.* It could have been anything. The main thing I felt as I was walking along, probably because I hurt so much from so many different places, was that I was turned inside out, so that my guts and muscles and nerves were out there touching the air.

I'm sure if somebody had stopped me and tried to talk to me, I wouldn't have been able to answer them, or I would have said something completely stupid in my thick-tongued voice. But even though I knew that, some part of me was completely aware of everything, just the way I felt when I was looking down at myself talking to Ceci at Bob Laski's party, and the part of me that was watching wasn't sick or drunk, but perfectly calm. I'm pretty sure that part of me could have watched me die. Throwing up the dark, sour stuff made me think about dying a little, but not in a way that scared me, more like: oh great, and now along with everything else, you're going to die. As a matter of fact, I don't think I was afraid at all. The feeling was more like a huge sadness, a sadness I couldn't believe would ever end, a feeling of being too sad to cry, or maybe I was crying, but crying in, not crying out.

Something was wrong, because it didn't seem like the street I was walking down was ever going to end and I was going to be walking through the developments forever. When I finally did get to the old part of town, I wasn't anywhere near Nana and Papa's house. I was way across town in the ritzy neighborhoods where my old school friend Patsy Prentiss lived. I was glad I knew where I was, but I also knew I was about a mile and a half from my house. I didn't think I was even headed there, but all of a sudden I was standing in front of Patsy's house. They had a big front porch with white pillars, and even though I could see a light on in the front hall, I was sure there would be nobody home. They would be up on their island, if they still went there. After Patsy got in her big trouble at school, I heard her parents sent her away to a boarding school somewhere, and nobody ever saw her around after that. I hadn't thought about her for a long time, but standing in front of her house and looking at the way the lights around their swimming pool were making wavering blue shadows in the trees, I started picturing her and the way we used to play and how much I liked her. I pictured us lying skull to skull in the cold straw that afternoon when I got home so late. I pictured her smiling at me across the table at June's Grill, her white teeth and her suntanned cheeks and looking like all she wanted to do was have fun.

Something clicked in my brain, and I got a terrible feeling, a kind of jolt. I slapped my back pocket, and then I knew it. My wallet was gone. It must have fallen out in the ditch or one of the yards. I kept slapping my pockets, even though I knew it wasn't there. It had all that money in it, about three hundred dollars, which was ridiculous, and I started thinking that maybe the reason I loaded up like that was so that I'd lose it, as some kind of lesson. But the money didn't bother me as much as just losing the wallet. I started picturing what was in it, my driver's license, my social security card, and my old school I.D., and it felt like I had lost my name, who I even was. Then I remembered something worse. Behind my license and my cards were my two pictures of Patsy and my sister Annabel. They were just old school pictures, the smallest ones that came with your packet, from fifth grade. I only looked at them two or three times a year, but they were really important. They made me feel like I still had a little bit of Patsy and Annabel the way they were back then. Patsy's hair was kind of messy in the picture, and her front teeth looked slightly too big, but it was definitely the way she looked when we were in Mr. Click's fifth grade class before she grew up and changed. Now the picture was gone, and I knew I wasn't going to get that feeling back.

It was the same with Annabel's picture, which was so cute and so sad I could never stand to look at it for too long. She was in seventh grade, and I thought she looked really beautiful with her dark page boy and dark eyes and the expression like something bad was probably going to happen. That picture being lost made me feel like Annabel wasn't just away at the Special Care Facility, but that she was gone forever, just as if she were dead. It made me cry out loud, and I couldn't help it. I started walking toward our house, blubbering about my wallet, saying *my god damned wallet* over and over and not caring if anyone heard me.

As I got closer to our street, I knew I better start making a plan, but my thoughts were too mixed up to do it. I stopped throwing up, but the cramps still came along in waves. I knew I was a mess and that I was in tremendous trouble, but I couldn't focus on anything particular, like actually walking in the front door and having to say something to my father and mother. I never thought it out, but I guess I hoped they would be asleep and I'd get in the house somehow and get in my bed before they woke up. Then whatever happened could happen, but I didn't want to have anybody looking at me or saying things to me while I still felt so dizzy and sick, especially when I knew I couldn't talk right. The sky was lightening up a little to a kind of grayish green, and every now and then a car would back out of a driveway with its lights on and drive off, which probably meant that some people were going off to their jobs already. I thought it might not look too strange for a guy to be walking down the sidewalk now, but if anyone actually got a look at me, they'd see how filthy I was and that I was slogging along in my socks, so I decided to play it safe by going the last two blocks through people's back yards, which I knew by heart.

Besides hurting so much, I was also getting really tired. It seemed like a huge effort to climb over people's chain link fences, and one of them had sharp wires at the top, which I didn't realize until I tried to jump down, and it caught my pocket and sleeve and ripped everything. If a yard had fences, I started having to sit down for a while to rest. The birds were peeping and chirping now, and the sky was turning the bushes and trees a silvery color, which made everything look like a completely different world, but at least I could finally see where I was going. The house next to ours was the Thomases', and they had a pretty big spread in the back with fruit trees and a bunch of separate gardens, and it seemed like a good place for one final rest before I went home. They had an old hammock strung up between a tree and the back of their garage, and I lay down in it and rested until it stopped swinging back and forth. I could see the second floor of our house over the tops of their bushes, and when I saw that the lights were on, I felt terrible. No one was going to be asleep. All I wanted to do was lie still and rest, but I knew I had to start thinking, start making a plan. But I couldn't. The only thing I decided was to lie there until it got completely light out. I wanted whatever happened to take place on a new day.

I must have slept, and slept really hard, because when I woke up there was bright sunshine, and I was all cramped up in the hammock. It felt like my knees were never going to be able to bend, and the only way I could get out of the hammock was to fall out. As rotten as I felt, I realized right away that my mind was back, that I was thinking in my regular way. I sat there for a minute in the grass making my plan. I knew I had to get up in a minute because I didn't want the Thomases coming out and seeing me and wondering what was going on. I got up and stretched, and I saw a garden hose attached to a faucet coming out of the foundation at the back of the Thomas's house. I was tremendously thirsty, and I wanted a drink of cold water more than anything. Even if it woke up the Thomases, I had to get a drink. I turned on the faucet and picked up the nozzle of the hose just as the water came out, and it practically knocked my head off. My face and my shirt were soaked before I turned the pressure down, and then I drank what must have been quarts of cold water. It felt like I couldn't get enough of it into my sour throat and down into my stomach.

I wiped my mouth and stood up and then practically started laughing. I couldn't believe it. Something about all that water was giving me the swirly feeling again. I started picturing myself staggering home like a drunken idiot in the movies. It was completely clear. It wasn't going to be okay, and nothing was going to work out right. It was going to be worse than anything I could imagine when I got home. No one would know why I stayed out all night or what happened to me and why I looked this way, and I wasn't going to be able to explain, and when I did, it was going to be worse than they thought.

And then it hit me: I had no excuse. I had no explanation. I had done everything wrong you could. I got drunk, I got lost, I lost my shoes. I lost my wallet, I lost the fields, I lost Patsy and Annabel. I wrecked my clothes, I threw up all over myself, and

I had vomit and pizza and pond muck all over me. The clothes in my room weren't really mine. They were just a bunch of stuff from Parnell's I spent so much money on my father would scream if he knew. The clothes were just a cover up and couldn't change the way I was. Yale was just a bunch of pictures and didn't connect at all to anything about me, and the kid in all the activities who got all the prizes, The Spirit of Palatine, was the kid who just sprayed himself with a hose and was standing in the Thomas's driveway in his stretched out socks: me. Not only that, I didn't have anything to say. I stopped having anything to say when I couldn't get into the other world anymore, when school and all the things to do crowded the other world right out of my mind, the way the developments crowded out the fields. I didn't have anything to say since Patsy got so tall and my love feeling didn't have anywhere to go. Not only didn't I have anything to say, I didn't have anything, period. I actually *was* nothing, which, believe it or not, was a tremendous relief. Because now it felt just fine to walk down the Thomases' driveway and go home. I was nothing, so there was nothing to cover up.

When I turned onto our front walk, I saw that our car was parked in front of the house, and my father was carrying my suitcases and stuff out to the curb. It hadn't occurred to me that they would be getting ready to take off even if I wasn't home. Mother came down the front steps and they talked for a minute. I couldn't believe they hadn't seen me yet. I was standing right there on the sidewalk maybe twenty yards away from them. Then they did see me. Mother had a terrible, scared look as she walked over to me. She said, "*Jonathan!* Are you all right? *Where on earth have you been?*" I thought I was in better shape than I actually was. My head was still spinning a little from the water, and I couldn't make any words come out. The closer she got to me, the more scared she looked, and I really wanted her not to come any closer, because I looked and smelled terrible. She came right up to me and was going to put her hands on my shoulders but she pulled back. She said, "Jonathan? Jonathan, are you *drunk?*" I felt terrible for her, but I still couldn't say anything. "Frank," she said to my father, "he's *drunk.*"

If there was anything I could have done to make her feel better, I would have done it. I wished I could tell her that I had been drunk already and now I was better and it was just the water. I wished I could tell her how good it felt to know that I was just what I was, nothing. What I really wanted to tell her was that I loved her so much, and that I knew we were going to have to say good-bye. But all I could do was feel it. What I said to her, finally, was "I'm sorry, I'm very sorry."

She started telling me all the things that had happened overnight, all the calls and everything people had done to try to find me, but she lost track and turned back to my father and told him she had to go in and call people to say I was home.

My father had not come toward me. He was still standing at the open door of the car with his arms folded in front of his chest. He seemed different. I certainly felt different. For one thing, I wasn't afraid of him. I wondered what he would say to me, and I even wondered if he would hit me, but I wouldn't have minded, except that I knew it would make him feel bad. I still had the calm, sweet feeling of knowing I was nothing, and the relief of not having to pretend anything. I could feel him looking at me, but I didn't know what he was thinking. If he was angry, he was being angry in a new, quiet way. I wished he didn't have to see what a filthy mess I was, but I decided to go over to him anyway. I wanted to tell him I loved him too, and that we were going to have to say good-bye, but I knew I would probably only say, "I'm sorry."

When I was close enough to touch him, I stopped and looked into his eyes. He looked right back at me. He looked at me for quite a while, and then he said, "Jesus Christ."